Changeling Press LLC

ChangelingPress.com

Ace/Deuce Duet
A Riptide MC Romance
Anne Kane

Ace/Deuce Duet
A Riptide MC Romance
Anne Kane

ISBN: 978-1-60521-954-7

Publisher:
Changeling Press LLC
315 N. Centre St.
Martinsburg, WV 25404
ChangelingPress.com

Printed in the U.S.A.

Editor: Crystal Esau
Cover Artist: Marteeka Karland

The individual stories in this anthology have been previously released in E-Book format.

Table of Contents

Ace (Riptide MC 1)
A Riptide MC Romance
Anne Kane

Someone took a shot at my Emma -- and signed his own death warrant. No one hurts my woman and lives.

Emma:
After witnessing a cold-blooded murder, I run to the only person I can think of who can protect me. Ace is my high school fantasy turned big bad biker. Did I mention sizzling, sexy, and hot? His touch makes me melt and when his lips devour mine, I forget why I shouldn't let him near me. He makes me feel safe. Loved. Wanted. All the things I've never had -- and that's addictive as hell.

Ace:
I've always had a thing for Emma, but back in high school, she dated my little brother. So I Joined the Navy SEALs. When that last mission went south, I knew it was time to bail. Came home and patched into Riptide MC. Didn't think life could get any better. A knock on my door in the middle of the night changed everything. Emma fell into my arms, terrified and wounded. Some asshole shot my Emma. He may not know it yet, but he just signed his own death warrant. Once I've taken care of her, I'm going to convince Emma to stay with me. Forever.

Chapter One

Emma

It was midnight by the time I left work. My shitty excuse for a car had crapped out on me yesterday and transit didn't run this late, so I had to walk home. Short enough walk, but this wasn't the safest part of town for a woman alone to traverse after dark. I knew better than to take the shortcut through the park, especially at night. The bad guys came out when the sun went down, clinging to the shadows in the park as they went about their illegal activities. Drug deals, illicit arms sales and who knew what else. Still, that route would cut the length of my walk in half, and after slinging drinks at the bar all night, the temptation was too much to resist.

My aching feet won the argument with my common sense, and I risked it.

It was dark under the towering trees. The heavy branches blocked out the majority of the moonlight, making it feel eerily like the setting of a horror movie. More than half of the lights on the concrete path had been knocked out by kids throwing rocks. I stepped up my pace.

I was halfway through the park when the sound of a gunshot rang out loud in the still night air. I jumped, automatically turning toward the sounds.

In the clearing off to my left side stood a big guy holding a gun. He had it pointed at another guy who had a splash of red spreading from a hole in his chest. The shooter took two more shots, hitting the other guy right between the eyes. The victim crumpled to the ground as blood and brains splattered from the back of his head. His mouth opened, but no sound came out. A thin trickle of blood trailed from the corner of his lips and splashed the ground. In the light of the full moon, I could see the life fading from his eyes as he stared at the man holding the smoking gun.

I slapped my hand over my mouth, desperately trying to stifle a scream. I wasn't successful. I stood rooted to the spot, my mind trying to process the horror of what I'd just witnessed.

The murderer swiveled and looked straight at me. He was a huge monster of a man, with tattoos covering every available inch of skin on his heavily muscled arms. His chest was wide, and no doubt just as muscled beneath a skintight shirt.

His eyes were cold and hard as he brought the gun around and pointed the deadly weapon straight at me.

Survival instinct kicked in. I turned and ran.

Shots rang out behind me. *One. Two.* The bullets went wide, the shooter's aim hindered by the moving target.

Me.

I was the moving target. He was trying to kill me. The third shot scorched a fiery path across my side. When I brought my hand down to my ribs, I could feel sticky dampness oozing from a ragged hole in my jacket. A coppery smell filled the air. Blood.

No time to stop and assess the damage. That wasn't a warning shot -- it was meant to kill. Hopefully, that was a regulation gun, with a six-shot magazine like you see in the movies. Three shots to commit murder, and three fired at me. The asshole was going to have to reload before he could finish me off.

Enough time for me to escape? I had to hope so. One hand pressed to the throbbing wound on my side, I plunged into the heavy shrubs lining the pathways. I'd be an easier target if I stayed on the paths. Better to get a few scratches. At least it was too dark away from the path for the shooter to follow the trail of blood I was undoubtedly leaving behind.

The murderer didn't waste any time coming after me. His progress was marked by heavy thumps of his boots as he charged down the path. Hopefully he hadn't seen me dart into the bushes. "You can't escape, you little bitch," he snarled. "You're pissing me off, and that's going to make it worse when I catch up. Give up now and I'll take it easy on you."

I doubted that. Considering I'd just watched him kill someone in cold blood, he wasn't likely to pat me on the head and send me on my way. I paused and crouched down beside a flowering shrub. My heart beat so loud it was a miracle he couldn't hear it. Looking around, I tried to figure out the shortest way out of the park.

"Did you see which way she went?"

"No, but she didn't pass us, so she must be heading for the road."

Shit! There were two of them. I hadn't seen a second man, but then again, I hadn't stuck around long enough to take in details.

"Makes sense. We need to stop her." The sound of branches snapping filled the air.

"These damn bushes are thick." Even muttering to himself, the murderer sounded closer. And cold-blooded. As if he were discussing an annoying insect, not a human being. "You recognize the bitch?"

There was a long pause. "She did look familiar. Maybe works one of the bars in the brewery district? I think she might be a bartender. That shock of red hair should make her easy to find."

"Pity we didn't get a pic."

That remark was met with a derisive snort. "If

we had time to get a picture, we would have had time to end her and solve the problem."

"Do you think she can ID us?"

"I doubt it. It's dark enough out, even with the damn moon shining and she only saw us for a few seconds. I'm not even sure she saw both of us."

"Doesn't matter. The boss ain't going to be happy with a witness running loose. We need to find her and wrap up the loose ends."

I had no illusions about how they intended to wrap up the loose ends, meaning me. I needed to get out of here and call the cops.

I took a deep breath and forced myself to move. I veered to my left, away from the two thugs. Weaving my way as quietly as I could between the ornamental shrubbery, I stayed low to the ground. I didn't dare stand up and make myself an easy target. That damn full moon was not helping me now. The thought of being outlined against the sky terrified me, and the bullet wound on my side hurt like hell.

The distance between me and the assassination squad widened. They were following the path, but headed in the other direction, presumably directly out of the park. Which meant I needed to circle around and exit by a different route.

Thug number two raised his voice. "Come on out and discuss this, girl. It's not what you think. We can explain."

That would be interesting. How did he think he could explain shooting someone at point blank range? And the fact that he'd taken a few potshots at me didn't inspire much trust on my part. Not to mention their talk of ending the problem, with me being said problem.

I worked my way in the opposite direction,

lengthening the distance between me and them. It felt like forever before I reached the edge of the park, not too far from where I'd originally entered. Seemed I'd been walking in a circle.

I took a careful look around to make sure it was safe to emerge before scurrying across the road and into the sheltering darkness of an alley. I reached into my pocket for my cell phone to call for help. Not that I had a whole pile of friends who could come to my rescue, but the cops needed to know there was a dead body in the park. Maybe, if they were quick enough, they could catch the murderous twosome before they escaped the area.

Crap! The phone wasn't in my pocket. I knew I'd tucked it in there when I left work, which meant it had fallen out somewhere in the park.

An icy river of fear trickled its way down my spine. If the murderers found it, they'd know who I was. Sure, there was a password, but I wasn't naïve enough to think it couldn't be hacked, and guys who committed murder wouldn't balk at illegally hacking a phone. Even if they didn't manage to bypass the password, my home screen picture showed me grinning like an idiot while standing in front of the bar where I worked, the name of the bar clearly visible above my head. I thought it was cute when I tagged it as the home screen picture. It might as well say, *come and get me*!

Dumb. Dumb and Dumber.

Now what? I couldn't very well go home and wait for the bad guys to figure out where to find me, and I definitely couldn't go back to the bar.

The rustling of bushes in the distance made me jump. Sitting here stewing wasn't helping any. Sooner or later, those guys would double back to find me.

Where to go presented an issue. It wasn't like I had a loving family waiting to protect me. I only knew one person who might be able to help me. Then again, I'd dated his little brother in high school. I might have burnt that bridge behind me.

Justin Maclean and I had been close once upon a time. Friends close, not lovers close, although we had dated. It kept the other guys away. It was a tough neighborhood, and we'd had each other's backs. I'd had a crush on his older brother James though. Tall, dark and brooding. Just what every teenaged girl longs for.

Turned out the younger Maclean and I had very different dreams. I wanted to make something of myself. I enrolled in college and was on track to get a degree. I was determined to forge a life I could be proud of.

Justin hadn't been as optimistic. He'd gotten in trouble with the law and opted to join the Army instead of going to prison. As far as I knew, he was still there.

His older brother, James, joined the Navy right out of high school and became a SEAL. That just made him hotter. Nothing like a man in uniform to give a teenage girl wet dreams! I'd kept tabs on him. Just for fun, or so I told myself. I knew he mustered out after several tours. When he got back home, he patched into the Riptide Motorcycle Club. That was about as far from respectable as you could get. Still, I knew where he lived, where the Riptide's clubhouse was, and he had recently become president of the club.

Just the thought of his hands on me, touching me, stroking me could still make me melt, but I no longer fantasized about being his lover. I couldn't reconcile my dreams of respectability with the choices he'd made. The Navy SEAL thing -- sure. That was kind of hot, although waiting to see if he came home from missions in one piece would be nerve-racking.

A tattooed, leather clad member of a motorcycle club, however? Not a chance.

Now, though, his bad choices just might be my salvation.

* * *

Ace

Someone pounding at my door after midnight was never a good thing.

Flinging the blankets off, I grabbed a pair of sweatpants and a tee shirt and pulled them on. Swiping my phone off the night table beside the bed, I opened the security app and checked the surveillance camera.

Yeah, I had cameras covering every inch of my property. Came with the territory when you were the Prez of a motorcycle club.

Staring at my front door, panic written all over her face, was my kid brother's high school sweetheart, Emma. Odd to see her here, since they hadn't been an item for at least half a dozen years now.

She looked terrified. What the fuck?

Disengaging the locks, I threw the front door open and grabbed Emma's arm to pull her inside and behind me. I visually searched the area for whatever had put that look on her face, but the quick glance around revealed nothing. The darkness could conceal a multitude of sins, though, as I knew well from experience.

I slammed the door shut and made sure the deadbolts were in place before I pivoted to face her. Want and lust slammed into my gut as I stared into her terrified eyes.

Somewhere between high school and banging on my door, she'd turned from a scrawny kid into a woman with lushly captivating curves.

I'd found her amusing as a kid and admired her feisty attitude. I'd never allowed my feelings to go any further than that. Her home life had been shitty, but she didn't let that stop her. I'd questioned her choice of my brother. I loved the little brat, but he'd been bad news back then. Running wild, drinking, stealing cars. If it was on the wrong side of the law, he'd do it.

He and Emma had parted ways when a judge had given him the choice of jail or enlisting, and he'd done the smart thing for once and chosen the Army. Not as good as the Navy, mind you, but definitely better than jail.

As far as I knew, he and Emma had parted on friendly terms, and hadn't had much contact since. Still, my body's reaction to her was inappropriate at best.

Before I managed to get past the shock of her showing up on my doorstep in the middle of the night looking like all the hounds of hell were chasing her, she threw herself into my arms. Just the feel of her soft body crushed against mine jerked me back into the here and now.

"He's going to kill me!" She spit the words out in a terrified whisper, peering up at me. "I know he is."

"Who's going to kill you?" I frowned, automatically wrapping my arms around her. "And why?"

She hissed out a long breath with her teeth clenched and her hand went to her side. Blood seeped from the mangled material of her jacket.

Taking a step back, I lifted her arm so I could see

where it was coming from. An ugly gash plowed across the side of her rib cage, and the material of her shirt stuck to the oozing blood.

Bullet wound. She'd been shot.

That made no sense. The Emma I remembered always kept her nose clean and followed the rules. I'd kept casual tabs on her over the years and as far as I knew, Emma led one of the most boring lives around. School, work, more school, and then back to work.

"What happened?" I kept my voice calm. Scaring her even more wasn't going to help.

"This guy was shooting at me, and I think one of the bullets grazed me. I was scared, so I ran here."

"Why come to me?" While it made me feel good to know she came to me when she needed help, this still made no sense.

"I heard you joined a motorcycle club when you left the service. I thought you could scare him off. Or protect me. Or something."

Still didn't make sense. "Why was someone shooting at you? Who was it?"

"I don't know who it was. I was walking home, and I saw this guy shoot someone and he knows I saw him." Her voice rose to a hysterical pitch. "I think I might have screamed, and he turned and looked right at me. Then he pointed the gun at me, so I ran."

The blood was still oozing out of the wound. Damnit, not a good sign. Getting her some help was more important right now than trying to make sense of her story.

"I'm going make a quick call and get the club medic over here to fix you up." As gently as I could, I took her jacket off and pulled the shredded remains of her shirt away from the wound. Without touching it, I tried to assess the damage. It looked superficial, but I wasn't about to take any chances. "Okay with me taking a pic and sending it to Joker so he knows what to bring with him?"

"Joker?" she whimpered, her eyes going wide, and I remembered she wasn't part of my world. Normal people went to the hospital if they needed a doctor. Then again, normal people didn't usually have bullet wounds, and bullet wounds were reported to the police.

I still had no idea what we were dealing with. "The club medic. Do you want me to take you to the emergency room instead?"

She shook her head violently. "No. He might look for me there. Take the picture."

I picked up my phone. Snapping a picture, I sent it to Joker, followed with a quick text: *Need your help. My place. ASAP. Bullet wound.*

A second later, Joker responded: *Gimme five minutes.*

Joker wasn't a doctor; however, he'd been a medic in the SEALs, and seen more action than most of the high-level jerks that had sent us into those deadly situations. Bullet wounds were almost routine to him. He'd be able to fix her up, even put in a few stitches if she needed them.

My attention snapped back to Emma. "You didn't recognize the shooter or the victim at all? Maybe seen them around somewhere. Maybe at the bar where you work?"

She shook her head. "Don't know who they were."

Motherfucker. The terrified look on her face made a lot of sense now.

She swiped her hand across her face, smearing her mascara. "There were three guys, but I only saw two, and then one was dead, and I heard the other one talking to someone so there had to be three. Before one got killed."

She was starting to sound panic-stricken, and I needed her calm if I wanted more information. After being deployed multiple times, I considered myself good at getting information out of civilians.

Emma took a deep breath, and I could see how much effort it took to pull herself together. She ducked out from under my arm and crossed the room to stand by the ridiculous fake plant one of the brothers had given me as a gag gift last year.

Her hand went to the bloody mess at her ribs, and she winced. "Damn, that hurts. Never been shot before."

"Most people haven't. I'd say it's just a flesh wound, but that doesn't make it hurt any less. Just means it'll be easier to clean and bandage. No digging around to find the bullet."

A wry smile crossed her lips. "I suppose I should be happy about that."

I shrugged. "Not really, but it's something."

I watched the emotions chase each other across her face as she took a moment to digest that. "Yeah. I guess it is. Sorry for freaking out on you. I'm a little more rattled than I thought."

She carefully placed her arm across her chest so as not to put any pressure on the bullet wound. "Not every day I witness a murder. I got off work late, and I took a shortcut through Merrymen Park. I know it's not a great place to be after dark, but I was tired and my feet hurt. I didn't see anyone at first and I wasn't really looking, because, you know, it's dark in there in some places and I didn't want to trip and fall so I was looking at the ground more than anything. The streetlights don't all work, vandalism and whatever. Even with a full moon it can be tricky."

She looked so vulnerable; I had to resist the urge to pull her back into the circle of my arms. "Yeah. It can be dark in there." She wasn't trembling as much now, which was good. "So, what happened next?"

"I didn't see anyone before I heard the first shot. They were off to the side of the path, where it opens by that old band shell. Like I said, I was mostly looking down. When I did look up, this big guy was holding the gun still pointed at the other guy. I could see the outline of the revolver. The metal kind that shines in the moonlight, you know?"

She paused as if waiting for me to comment. I grunted my agreement. Some do, some don't, but I wasn't about to start a discussion on the finer points of identifying weapons. She said she saw a revolver; she saw a revolver. It didn't matter. The guy had a gun, and he took a shot or two at Emma. He'd pay for that.

"He shot the other guy two more times, right in the forehead. I guess he wanted to make sure he was dead. The back of the other guy's head just kind of disintegrated and blood and stuff went flying everywhere. He didn't make a sound, just crumpled to the ground in a pool of blood." She worried her bottom lip with her teeth. "His eyes were still open, and he looked surprised. Like he didn't think it was going to happen."

This was not good. The park was in Riptide territory, and we didn't take kindly to outsiders committing crimes on our home turf. The cops inevitably thought we were involved. By we, I mean the Riptide MC. We were a close-knit bunch, most of us closer to our club brothers than the families we came from. We protected each other and what was ours. I had no idea who these guys were, or what the hell they were doing, but they were doing it on our territory. Big mistake.

I strode across the room and placed my hands on Emma's shoulders, being careful not to hurt her. She looked up at me, her eyes wide. They were as beautiful as I remembered, deep green with flecks of gold. A man could drown in those eyes. It took a major effort to drag my attention back to the task at hand.

I knew she had an independent streak a mile wide, and she would detest being treated like a helpless wimp, so I didn't bother to sugarcoat. She'd grown up in the same neighborhood as me. She knew the world wasn't all unicorns and princesses.

"I need you to tell me exactly what happened after you saw the guy get shot. Don't leave anything out."

She took a deep breath. Her eyes lost focus as she related the whole damn thing from the time the shooter realized there was a witness until she stumbled onto my porch and pounded on the door. That included the fact that the shooter had fired at least three shots at her as she ran. The explanation definitely shed light on the terror-stricken expression she had when she arrived. I was impressed she'd managed to hold it together that long.

She slumped against me when she finished. "I didn't know where else to go. I remember someone saying you were in a motorcycle club, and one of the girls I work with, Katya, she pointed out your house one time when we were walking to the bar." She paused, peeking up at me from under her lashes. "She's kind of a bad guy junkie, and she was hoping to catch a glimpse of you. Except she called you Ace, instead of James."

Bad guy junkie? I'd seen my fill of those. Club whores that hung around the clubhouse, hoping one of the brothers would ask them to stay. Didn't matter which brother.

"Ace is my road name. No one's called me James in years."

"Ace?" Her forehead wrinkled in a frown. "You're into gambling?"

"No." My mouth curved up in a wry grin. "Ace because just when some asshole thinks he has me down, I always manage to pull an ace out of my sleeve."

She still looked confused.

"A solution. I always find a solution."

The blank look on her face gave way as she let out a delighted laugh, quickly followed by a yelp of pain. She pressed a hand against her injured side. "Damn, that hurts!"

I scooped her up in my arms and carried her to the sofa, careful not to touch her wounded side. She buried her head against my chest, and I felt a protective urge sweep through me. I just wanted to make everything all better for her. No matter how tough and independent she tried to be, everyone has a breaking point, and I suspected she was damn close to hers.

Sinking into the well-worn cushions, I kept my arms wrapped around her and pretended I couldn't feel her shaking as she sobbed quietly into my shirt. I kept a tight rein on my temper. There were so many things wrong with this mess.

I was not okay with someone committing murder on territory under Riptide's protection.

I was totally not okay with some idiot taking potshots at my Emma.

Yeah, my Emma.

From the moment I'd opened the door and stared into her panic-stricken eyes, all those feelings I'd squashed down when she was dating my little brother had come roaring back.

I didn't know who the shooter was yet, but he'd just signed his own death warrant.

Chapter Two

Emma

This was so not me. I didn't whimper and hide and beg for help. I was not a high-maintenance princess. I was smart. Tough. Independent. Asking for help just wasn't my thing. Whimpering solved nothing. I was more of a 'suck-it-up and get on with it' type of gal. Witnessing a murder and getting shot, though, was a little too much even for me.

It had been years since I'd had anything to do with anyone from the old neighborhood, but Ace was the first one I thought of when I realized how deep I was in over my head. Telling Ace what happened had helped. A bit. At least now I didn't feel quite so panicked. Truthfully, I felt more embarrassed than anything. I liked to think I wasn't good at playing the helpless princess, but here I was with my head buried against the chest of one very macho biker. The scariest part about it is how good it felt.

I peeked up at him from beneath my eyelashes. His face was set in stone with no emotion showing at all. I couldn't tell if he was annoyed at me for bringing trouble to his doorstep or if he actually cared about my predicament.

As if he could read my thoughts, he looked down, and a crooked smile brightened up his features. "Feeling any better?"

I bobbed my head without letting go of my death grip on his massive chest. "Yeah. My side hurts like hell, though."

"Getting shot will do that. Joker will be here soon. He can clean it up and give you something for the pain."

The sound of a motorcycle's engine echoed

through the air, the volume increasing as it drew closer. I swear I could feel the vibrations of the motor, it was that loud. "Don't those things come with mufflers? Or are you trying to warn people you're coming and give them time to hide?"

"Something like that. It's always handy to have the target too scared to think straight before you get to them." This time the humor went all the way to his eyes. "Or have the barista get started on your coffee. Depends on the circumstances."

I didn't have a snappy comeback for that one. I just blinked up at him.

The sound ceased, and moments later someone knocked on the front door in a strangely staccato rhythm. Maybe it was some kind of secret code the bikers cooked up.

Or maybe it was just a knock, and I was being paranoid.

"Gotta go for a minute, and let him in."

I reluctantly loosened my grip, and Ace slid out from under me and crossed to the door. I noticed him checking an app on his phone before he unlocked the deadbolts to let his buddy enter. So, probably not a secret code unless Ace was more paranoid than me.

The man called Joker swaggered in, looking every part the bad-assed biker. Six feet tall and muscular, he had shaggy dark hair and a five o'clock shadow. His leather cut had a badge on the front -- the name read Joker and below that was the word *Medic*.

Medic... was that a rank, or just a description? I assumed the leather bag dangling from his left hand had first aid supplies in it -- hopefully some high-powered painkillers.

"What's the story here?" The newcomer's gaze shifted from Ace to me and back again. "Last I heard, you were single. Suddenly you have a woman with a gunshot wound bleeding on your sofa at two in the morning?"

Ace pointed to me with his chin. "Emma. Used to date my little brother. Saw some guy get popped in the park, and the shooter took a few potshots at her. Just a flesh wound, I think. It needs to be cleaned up, and probably some stitches."

Joker's eyebrows shot up. Ignoring me, he asked, "As in Merrymen Park?"

"That's the one," I confirmed.

Joker frowned. "Inside Riptide territory."

Ace nodded. "I'm getting Rattler to check it out, make sure there's no dead bodies hanging around. We don't need to have the cops all riled up before we know what's going on. Could be a one-off thing or could be another club trying to move into our territory. From Emma's description, sounds more like an execution than a random shooting."

"I'd better get this gal patched up ASAP, then." Joker moved toward me. "Does the shooter know she's here with you?"

Both bikers turned their attention to me, and I shrugged, immediately regretting it when pain lanced through my side. "I don't know. I just ran. I could hear them behind me, but I'm not sure if they saw where I went or just heard noise in the bushes and followed the general direction. They know where I work, though. I heard the one guy tell the shooter he recognized me from one of the bars. It wouldn't take long to check out all the bars within walking distance of the park."

Joker eyed up my side. "The bullet pushed material into the wound. I'm going to need you to take off your shirt so I can clean that properly."

"Ummm…" I gaped up at Ace wildly. I did not

want to strip half-naked in front of a couple of bikers.

"My mistake. Didn't realize that would be an issue." A mischievous smile lit up Joker's face. "I take it you two are not in a see-each-other-naked kind of relationship?"

"Shut it," said Ace.

"You have a towel or something she can use to cover up with, Prez? I really do need her to take that shirt off."

Ace stalked off down the hallway. He came back with a towel and motioned Joker to move away from me. Ignoring the medic, he held the towel up like a big screen. "Get your top off. Bra too. Let me know when you're ready and I'll drape this over you."

Wow. A gentleman biker. I doubted I'd get this much consideration if I'd gone to the emergency room. More likely, some overworked nurse would have told me to suck it up and get over myself.

Taking my shirt off proved to be more difficult than I'd anticipated. Raising my left arm past my shoulder hurt like hell, pulling the wound on my side tight. After a few unsuccessful attempts, I realized this was not a one-woman job.

"Ace?"

"Yeah. You done?"

"Um. No. I think you'll have to cut it off me. I can't raise my arm high enough and there's not enough stretch in it for me to just pull it over my head. Plus, it's sticking to all that blood. Pulling it off is going to hurt even more than it already does."

He peeked over the top of the towel. "You sure you want to do that?"

"It's not like I'm going to be wearing this shirt out to dinner any time soon."

"Right. I'll go find something to cut it with."

The towel came down, and Ace headed toward the kitchen.

"So." Joker took a seat beside me. "You and Ace aren't an item?"

I shook my head. "No."

"I'm currently single as well." He grinned suggestively.

"Knock it off." Ace returned, a wicked-looking knife in his hand. "She's not here looking for a hookup."

Joker's eyes twinkled, and he smirked knowingly. "Thought so." He eyed up the knife. "I realize you're trying to impress her and all, but a pair of scissors would have worked just as well."

"Don't have any." Ace shrugged. "The knife is sharp enough."

"I'm sure it is. Be careful," said Joker, serious now. "She's lost enough blood already."

"She'll be okay, though? She doesn't need a transfusion or anything?"

"Relax. It's not as bad as it looks. Since we're cutting the shirt, anyway, just chop off the side so I can dress the wound. That way we won't have to worry about you being flashed with her titties."

The glare Ace directed at the medic would have made me laugh if I wasn't in so much pain. My antics in trying to get the shirt off had started the wound bleeding again and woke up every nerve along the gash. I gritted my teeth. "Can we just get on with it?"

Ace knelt down beside me. "Try to hold still and let me know if I'm hurting you."

He used that knife like he'd been born with it, slicing the side of my shirt off without applying any pressure to the throbbing bullet wound. That probably should have scared me, but I was just grateful he managed it.

"Get me a pail of warm water, and some towels." Joker rolled his sleeves up, his attention focused on my mangled side. "Rags if you have them. Bloodstains are murder to get out of fabric." He winked at me. "Get it? Murder?"

"And now you know why we call him Joker." Ace shook his head and headed down the hallway. "Despite all evidence to the contrary, he thinks he's funny."

"I'm going to give you a shot to freeze the area before I start. It should kick in pretty quick." Now all business, Joker opened the leather satchel and pulled out a needle and a bottle of liquid. "I'm used to dealing with a bunch of gnarly old bikers. I'll try to be gentle."

I'm not sure what was in that bottle, but within minutes my side was numb. He worked fast, cleaning the wound and applying some type of ointment on it before adding a few butterfly bandages in the worst areas, then covering it all with a loose layer of gauze.

"That should do for now." He shot a satisfied look at Ace. "The biggest worry is infection, so I'm going to give her a shot of antibiotics just to be safe." He turned his attention back to me, administering the dose so smoothly I barely felt it. "I'll check the wound again tomorrow to make sure it's starting to heal. Gunshot wounds can be tricky."

He pulled out another bottle from his bag of tricks; this one containing pills. "These are for pain. Take one every six hours, four hours if it gets really bad, but no more than that. The antibiotic shot I gave you is good for twenty-four hours. We'll decide if you need another one when we see how well you heal."

He snapped the bag shut and turned to Ace. "You bringing her over to the clubhouse?"

"Damn right. Safest place for her."

They were talking over my head, deciding my future as if I weren't sitting right there. "Excuse me, but do I get a say in this?"

Ace turned that icy glare on me that I remembered so well from childhood. He'd used it every time he caught his brother and I doing something he didn't approve of.

"No."

* * *

Ace

I felt better now that Joker had taken a good look at the wound and patched Emma up. He might like to play the clown, but under that act he was one hell of a medic. If it weren't for his PTSD, he could have become one of the top surgeons in the country. Well, his PTSD and his total lack of respect for anyone who hadn't earned it. That tended to include his superiors. Most of the brothers had the same issue.

Emma couldn't be in better hands.

Unless they were mine, of course. I wanted to get to know her better. Since shipping out over a decade ago, I'd managed to mostly put her out of my mind. Although I'd noticed her growing into a very sexy young woman, she was too young for me. I had a decade on her. And she was too fucking good for the likes of me. She deserved someone better than an ex-Navy SEAL who'd seen far too many dead bodies.

Despite that, my dick stood at attention just having her in the house. It really wanted to get to know her better. A lot better. But hell, she'd dated my kid brother. That made me some kind of perv for the way my cock got hard every time I gave her a sideways glance.

Or did it? Maybe she was one of those women that liked their men with a little more experience. I didn't see any rings on her fingers. Maybe I was just what she'd been waiting for. Might be worth a shot.

That was going to have to wait, though, until me and the club took care of the unknown gunman, and anyone else who might pose a threat to my woman. Her account of the park thing resembled an execution-style killing, leading me to question what was going on right under the noses of the club.

I risked a peek at the woman curled up against me on the sofa. She looked good there. Looked like she fucking belonged there. Deep down, below the level of logic and reason, when she needed help, I was the one she'd come running to.

That felt good. Real good.

I stuffed those feeling away to be considered later. Right now, I needed to understand the events of the night a little better.

A thought occurred to me, and I frowned. "Do you usually walk home from work this late at night? Where's your car?"

She sighed. "Damn thing won't start. Replaced the battery six months ago, so it's probably the starter this time. I just forked over all my cash for next term's tuition, so I can't afford to fix it before payday. Until then, I'm hoofing it." She managed to look everywhere except at me. "I knew taking the shortcut through the park was risky, but my feet were killing me, and I hoped luck would be on my side just this once."

She didn't need me to point out how badly luck had let her down. Again. The fact that she'd been forced to ask me, a guy she hadn't seen in years, for help was proof positive that Karma had it in for her.

Or maybe Karma thought it was time to do me a

favor.

I picked up my phone from the side table, keeping one arm wrapped around her in case she got the silly notion that she could leave. "I need to call a couple of the guys and get them to check out the park."

She glared at me and tried to pull away. "Check it out? You think I made this up so I could come play snuggle bunny with you?"

I smothered the urge to laugh. She was the farthest thing from a snuggle bunny as I'd ever seen. "Yes, I believe you. Pretty hard to fake a bullet wound. Issue is that dead bodies tend to attract the attention of the authorities. The last thing the club needs is to have cops swarming all over the place. Which they will, if there's a dead body found in a public park."

"So...? The cops will find the killer and then everything goes back to normal."

I raised one brow. "You can't possibly be that naïve. The first person they're going to suspect is the head of the local motorcycle club."

She winced. "Sorry. I didn't think of that. I didn't mean to get you into trouble. I can leave. Go home and call the cops from there. Leave you out of it. I just thought..." Her voice trailed off and she shrugged. "I don't know. I guess I thought you could protect me. You know. From whoever that guy was."

"And I can. But getting the cops involved is a no go. I'll make a couple of calls, and the guys will take care of it."

She blinked. "Okay. Thanks."

A tentative smile curved the corner of her lips as she pulled back a bit and looked up at me. Mascara and eyeliner had combined to create black streaks down both of her cheeks. God, she looked so young and vulnerable. "Can I use the bathroom?"

She must have realized I wasn't planning on going into details about how the guys would handle things. Or maybe she didn't want to know. Regardless, it let me off the hook.

"Sure." I loosened my arm to let her stand and pointed toward the hallway. "Second door on your right."

"Thanks." She took two steps in that direction and paused then turned back to look at me. "For everything. Thanks for being here. I know it's been years since we even talked, but you were the only one I could think of that might be able help."

"Go wash up." I growled the words out. It was all I could do to stay seated, not jump up and grab her and never let her go.

When I heard the click of the bathroom door closing behind her, I sent a quick text off to my second-in-command, Rattler, outlining the situation.

He replied immediately that he'd get back to me when he had something to report. Typical. A man of few words, Rattler was all action. If he said he'd do something, he did it.

I could hear the sound of the water being turned on, followed by splashing. When Emma emerged, she'd washed off her makeup and combed her thick mane of red hair into some semblance of order. She came back into the room and took a seat on the lounger across from me.

"I can't go home. They know who I am, or they will shortly. I told you the one guy recognized me from the bar, and if that doesn't clinch it, I lost my phone in the park. If they have that, they're going to know everything about me." Her eyes went wide. "They could know about you."

"How so?"

She toyed with hem of her shirt. "I have pictures on the phone. Some still on there from when I was dating your brother. You might be in some of them. From holidays, and you know, goofing around."

Damn. That made it tough. Not that I was afraid of some shit-assed murderer, but if they made me as the Prez of Riptide, then they'd know where to come looking for her. Hell, they could probably look my address up on the web. They'd have this place and the clubhouse.

"You're staying here tonight." I made it a statement.

"I don't think that's a good idea. I didn't think before I ran over here."

"It was a good plan. I have a spare room you can use. I'm not about to jump you, or any shit like that."

She frowned. "I didn't think you were. It's just… I've put you in danger and that's not fair."

I had to grin at that. "Life's not fair. I thought we all learned that back in the 'hood."

"Yeah." A faint smile lifted the corner of her mouth. "I guess we did."

I had to ask. "You still stuck on my kid brother? Is that the issue?"

She let out a derisive snort. "Hardly. We were never more than buddies, really. Being with him kept the bad asses in the school from bugging me and gave him an excuse when he needed one."

"Excuse?"

"Like, he couldn't possibly have broken that window, officer. He was with me all night." She batted her eyelashes in a poor imitation of a *femme fatale*.

"So, you lied for him?"

She nodded. "Not like he was dealing drugs or anything. Just pranks."

"You guys weren't...?" I wasn't sure how to ask if they'd been fucking around without sounding like a jealous old geezer.

She giggled. "Hooking up hot and heavy? Nah. He wasn't my type, really."

It took me a minute to digest that information. "Not your type?"

She shook her head. "He was a screw-up. I loved him like a brother, but that's it. I didn't need that kind of trouble."

I wasn't sure if I should be mad or insulted or relieved. At least I wasn't lusting after my little brother's leftovers, which made how I was feeling a whole lot less creepy. "Well, you haven't been with anyone else since, or so the local grapevine says. I was under the impression you were heartbroken when he joined the Army and left you behind."

She shrugged. "I can't help what people think, and in a way, it worked to my advantage. I want to get a degree, get a decent job, and get the hell out of here. I don't have time for all the drama that comes with a boyfriend."

She managed a faint smile. "Sorry. Nothing against Justin. We had fun, but it's not like I was wildly in love with him, and he was fine with that. He left. I moved on, and I imagine he did too. Still in the Army, isn't he?"

"He is. Says he's found his place in life."

Emma yawned, then winced, her hand going to her side. The freezing Joker put in was probably wearing off. Time to pack her off to bed for the night. Sadly, it wouldn't be my bed.

"The spare bedroom is at the end of the hallway. It has its own bathroom so you can take a shower without worrying I might come in without thinking. I don't happen to have any lingerie you can borrow, but you can have one of my T-shirts to sleep in." I eyed up her diminutive frame. "Should come down to about your knees. In the morning I'll have a couple of the prospects go over to your place and get you some things."

That elusive smile reappeared. "I take it there isn't anyone who's going to take issue with me wearing your clothes? I don't think I have the energy to fight off a jealous girlfriend."

"Nope. You're safe on that score."

For a moment, she looked surprised, then got unsteadily to her feet. "Thanks. I'm exhausted. A shower would be great but..." She gestured at the bandage on her side.

"Yeah. You need to wrap that in plastic if you really want a shower, but I'm pretty sure I don't have any. We'll get you over to the clubhouse in the morning, and you can shower there."

"Sounds like you've done this before."

"Once or twice." Or more. Active duty didn't come without risk, and I had enough scars to prove it. Luckily, they were hidden under my shirt. Didn't want to scare her off too fast.

Chapter Three

Emma

I woke up feeling tired and cranky and sore.

"Rise and shine, sleepyhead!" Ace's voice sounded from the other side of the door. "Coffee's on but I might just drink it all if you don't hurry up."

"Yeah. Yeah. I'm up," I mumbled. Not a brilliant comeback, but then I hadn't had any coffee yet. There might be another murder committed if it was all gone before I managed to get dressed.

Right. No shirt. Just the ragged bits left after Ace cut it off me.

I found the bottle of painkillers and downed two with a glass of water from the ensuite bathroom. Handy, but not exactly the setup you'd expect from a biker. Then again, what did I know about bikers? Hollywood clichés and rumors.

Gritting my teeth against the pain caused by moving, I rinsed my face and hands in the sink before pulling on my pants. I still had Ace's T-shirt on, and as suspected it fell almost to my knees. Much too long to wear out in public. Unfortunately, the alternative was to go topless, and I wasn't feeling that adventurous this morning.

Compromising, I rolled the shirt up to my waist and tied the front in a knot to hold it in place. Not exactly high fashion but it would do until I could get something of my own to wear. As a bonus, it didn't put any pressure on the bullet wound.

I gave my teeth a cursory brush with my finger and wandered out to the kitchen.

"Where's the coffee?" The heavenly aroma teased my nostrils.

Ace slid off the barstool and walked over to a

chrome appliance that bore no resemblance to any coffee maker I'd ever owned. "Made to order. How do you like yours?"

"Strong, with cream. No sugar."

He rolled his eyes. "Cappuccino? Latte? Americano? "

"Seriously? You can make all those?"

"I wouldn't offer if I couldn't deliver." He waggled his eyebrows suggestively. "I'm more than just a pretty face."

I wouldn't call the face pretty, more ruggedly handsome. The nose was off center a bit, hinting at a break sometime in the past. His dark hair had the slightly shaggy look of needing a trim, and that damn five o'clock shadow added a macho charm. The whole package was enough to send shivers of want down my spine.

"Cappuccino. With lots of foam."

I watched him fiddle with the shiny contraption on the counter, then pivot with a flourish to present me with the perfect cup of cappuccino, complete with a foaming cap.

I took the cup, inhaling the delightful scent. "What's that on top of the foam?"

He grinned. "My secret concoction of sugar and spices. Try it."

I lifted the cup to my lips and took a sip. Pure heaven. "Not bad."

He lifted one brow. "Not bad?"

I took another sip. "Okay. Quite good."

"It's perfect, and you know it."

It was, and I did, but that didn't mean I was willing to admit it. "Are you always this chipper in the morning?"

"Only when I've been up half the night rescuing

a damsel in distress. How's the side this morning?"

I made a face. "Should be better as soon as the pills I took kick in."

"Hopefully that will be soon. We need to head over to the clubhouse."

I cocked my head as a thought occurred to me. "I thought bikers all lived together, at a clubhouse. Yet you have your own house."

He shrugged. "We all have rooms at the clubhouse for when we party too hard and don't want to drive home, but some of us like to have our own places outside of the club property. I'm not exactly a social animal, and I like my privacy."

"So, this is your house? Like you bought it just for you?"

He inclined his head. "Yeah. I like to putter and fix things. As soon as I saw this place, I knew it needed me. That, and I got it for a good price because of the shape it was in."

I hadn't really taken in much the night before, but as I looked around now I could see all the personal touches. The moldings on the ceiling, the fancy frames around the windows and doors with stained glass inlays. He'd done an amazing job on it. "It's beautiful."

"Thanks." His phone chirped and he checked the screen. "Gotta take this." Putting the phone to his ear, he turned and headed into the other room.

I took the hint and sat myself down to finish the cappuccino. Out the window, I could see people bustling up and down the sidewalk on their way to work. Cars sped past, and it looked like any other day.

Except it wasn't. The man who'd been murdered in the park last night wasn't going to get up today, or any other day. I wondered who the dead guy was. Did he have a family? Children that would grow up without a father?

"Look at me." Ace was back in the room, standing right in front of me. I hadn't even heard him return. I lifted my chin to look up at him.

"It's over. Don't go back there. There was nothing you could do that would have changed the outcome."

How did he know what I was thinking? "I know. It's just…" My voice trailed off.

Ace shook his head. "Just nothing. Life sucks sometimes. You just shake it off and get on with it. For all you know that guy was a drug dealer, or a human trafficker. Maybe he deserved what he got. It doesn't matter. You're here and you're alive. That's what's important."

I took a deep breath. He was right. "So, what now?"

"Now we get you to the clubhouse where I know you'll be safe while we sort this out."

"Okay." I slid off the barstool, careful not to move my side too much. "But I'm scheduled to work tonight."

"There's no way you're slinging drinks until your side heals up some. That's on top of the fact that the murderer can probably find you there."

"How long?" Murderers aside, I needed a job to pay my rent, and get my damn car fixed.

Ace shrugged. "We can ask Joker when we get to the clubhouse, but I'm guessing a few weeks at least. Bullet wounds are messy. No neat lines to stitch together. As for the murderer, hard to say. Depends on how much of a danger he considers you."

"I can't take two weeks off work, let alone an indefinite amount of time! I need to pay my rent, buy books, fix my car."

"You've got an open wound on your side. If you don't give it time to heal it could become infected, which is going to keep you down a lot longer than two weeks. Plus, I'm guessing the bar isn't going to be thrilled to have their employee dripping blood on the customers. Or getting killed herself while on the job."

"Maybe they'll forget about me. And I can bandage it better. It's not bleeding now."

"We'll ask Joker. And you do what he says."

I muttered a curse under my breath. "I have to at least phone in and tell my boss I won't be there."

Ace held out his phone to me. "And while you're at it, you need to cancel your phone. I'll have one of the prospects pick you up a new one today, along with a clean SIM card. Android or iPhone?"

"Android. And I'll pay you back."

His eyes twinkled with sudden mirth as he swept me with a lustful glance. "Yes, you will."

"Not like that!" Although to be honest, the idea of having a hookup with Ace sent delightful shivers dancing down my spine. I just didn't want to it to be payment for something.

You want it to matter, my treacherous heart said. I quickly squashed that thought down where it belonged.

He immediately looked repentant, reaching out to stroke one finger down my cheek. "I was just kidding around. I would never make a woman pay for something with sex. I want you to have a phone so you can call someone if you are in danger. It will make me feel better, so it's really for me, not you."

Damn, the man had a way of turning things around to make me like him even more.

"Make the call to your boss, and I'll rustle us up some breakfast before we head out." He turned around, rummaging in the fridge.

* * *

Breakfast turned out to be eggs sunny side up, toast and hash browns with crispy fried bacon. The man was full of surprises. When he said rustle up breakfast, I kind of expected him to pull muffins or something similar out of the freezer. Maybe a box of stale cereal out of the cupboard.

We ate in companionable silence, and he insisted that I sit while he stacked the dirty dishes in the dishwasher and turned it on.

"Do you feel up to riding on the back of my bike, or do you want to use the truck?"

I hesitated. I really wanted to say bike, but I wasn't sure my side could take it. I'd never been on a motorcycle but the idea of the freedom it represented was tempting.

"How about we take the truck for now, and I promise you a ride on the bike as soon as you're feeling better." Ace's eyes narrowed. "Joker will skin me alive if I do anything to open your wound up again."

"Sounds like a sensible plan." I wrinkled my nose. "Some days I'm just not a fan of sensible."

Ace snorted. "Compared to the rest of us from the 'hood, you are the epitome of sensible!"

* * *

Ace

Damn, she looked good sitting beside me in my truck, even wearing my oversized shirt rolled up and tied at her waist. I kind of liked the fact she was wearing my clothes. Like she belonged to me, even if I hadn't put a cut on her yet.

Fuck. I needed to get myself under control. I was

too old for her, and she was too good for me.

Still, a tiny voice in my head murmured, *you know there's major sparks there, on both sides. You could just have a sizzling one-night stand and part ways. Scratch that itch and walk away.*

"The clubhouse is in town, right? I'm pretty sure I know where." Emma's voice dragged me back to reality.

"Barely in town." I braked to let an old man and his dog cross the street. "It's on the outskirts. More room, less nosy neighbors that way."

I had her full attention now. "Why? Do you guys throw wild parties or something?

"Both." Who knew how much fun it would be to tease her?

She tilted her head. "Both what?"

"Wild parties and something." I grinned. "We do both."

"What's something?"

I shrugged; the grin still plastered on my face. "You're the one that brought it up. You tell me."

"Drugs?" She didn't look happy at the thought.

"Nah. We have a strict rule against any of the brothers doing drugs. That always leads to trouble. Just liquor and beer. Not everyone is worried about privacy, though, so that might be an issue with nosy neighbors." I slanted her a sideways look. "You into watching?"

She lifted her brows. "As in watching other people have sex? No."

"Didn't think so." I tried my best not to laugh. "You're a little too prissy for that."

"I am not prissy!"

The outraged look on her face was too much. I burst out laughing. "You should see your face. It's hilarious. I was just kidding. About the prissy part, anyway. Some of the brothers do get carried away, and they aren't always discreet about it, so you might want to stay in my room if things start getting rowdy."

"I'm staying in your room?"

"You definitely are. Don't worry. I'm not going to assault you, but if you stay in my room the brothers will know you're off limits. They won't bother you."

That mischievous smile I remembered so well from the 'hood curved her lips. "What if I want them to bother me? It's been a while, and a clubhouse might be just the place to find a no strings hookup for a day or two."

A surge of white-hot jealousy threatened to choke me. Fuck that. If she really wanted a hookup it wasn't going to be with anyone else. "Not happening."

Her eyes widened. "I was just kidding. I'm not going to lead any of your precious brothers astray."

I felt like an ass. A certified ass at that. I wanted a lot of things from Emma that were never going to happen, but the one thing I didn't want her to feel for me was fear.

"Sorry." I mumbled the apology. "Didn't mean to sound like some kind of overprotective daddy. I'd just rather you didn't get involved with any of the brothers. It would be awkward."

"Because I used to date your little brother?" She sighed. "I get it. Don't worry. I'll behave myself."

No, she really didn't get it. It would be awkward because I'd have to beat the asshole she chose within an inch of his life. I sure as hell wasn't about to explain that to her. Luckily, we came to the gates of the compound. Thor and Tiny, two of the club prospects, were on guard duty. They recognized the truck and waved us through. The driveway curved to the left, behind a grove of trees that hid the clubhouse and outbuildings. Security wise, it was a great setup. Any hostiles who made it past the gate would be coming in blind, unable to see what was going on until they were within shooting range.

"This is beautiful!" The look of rapt wonder on Emma's face caused me to look at the clubhouse with fresh appreciation.

The main building was an antebellum mansion. It had enough rooms for all the brothers, plus a huge kitchen and dining room. The living room was more of a central meeting room, with lots of comfortable seats and a huge fireplace that we'd never used. It rarely got that cold in these parts.

"We like it." At some point before my time, someone had turned one of the main floor rooms into a game room with a pool table, foosball and a huge TV to watch sports on. A room for those that liked to play video games was down by the back door. The noise from those shoot-em-up games could drown out just about anything. There were several outbuildings that came in handy for working on bikes or cages, and one was set aside for church.

I doubted we could have designed a better club compound if we'd started from bare ground.

I parked beside a line of bikes, noting which brothers were here. Being early morning, none of them were due to work at the bar the club owned for a few hours yet. The only bike missing belonged to Deuce, the treasurer. Probably slept over at his old lady's place.

I sent him a quick text. *Church in an hour. Be here.*

Emma looked hesitant. Understandable. Taking her hand, I led her up the stairs and through the front door. I'd forgotten how imposing the clubhouse was on first sight, and I didn't have time to give her the grand tour right now. Maybe after the brothers and I discussed the murder and its likely fallout.

"Hey, Prez." Rattler eyed up Emma. "Who's the chick?"

"Emma. Old friend from the 'hood. Ran into some bad luck last night." I pulled her in closer to my side. "Bullet wound. Joker fixed her up, but I need him to check it out this morning."

"You shot her?" Rattler had the grace to sound shocked. "What the hell did she do?"

"I did not shoot her." I glared at my VP. "Some asshole in the park did and she came to me for protection. I'll explain it in church. One hour from now. Round up the rest of the crew. Thor and Tiny are on guard duty, and I want old Jake to keep an eye on everything in here. We can catch them up later."

"Church?" Emma looked up at me. "You got religion?"

I almost laughed at that. "No. Church is what we call it when the brothers all get together for a meeting."

Joker ambled into the room just then, a coffee mug in one hand. "So, how's my patient this morning?"

"Sore." She gave him a tired smile. "But those painkillers are working, so thank you for that."

He looked satisfied. "Good. I'll check it out a bit later to make sure infection isn't setting in." He looked up. "I take it she'll be in your room, Prez?"

"Just going to get her settled there now. Church in forty-five minutes. You can check her out after that."

Mom wandered in, her coffee cup in hand. She wasn't really my mother, or any of the other brothers' mother for that matter. Jake had brought her in with him one day and announced she was staying. I'm not sure we ever knew her given name. She mothered us all like a hen with a brood of chicks, so we started calling her Mom and it stuck. Right now, she was eyeing Emma with a lively interest.

"I heard tell you showed up with a chick, Prez. What's up with that?"

I felt Emma stiffen at my side, and I squeezed her hand to let her know it was okay. Mom wasn't the subtle kind.

"She's not a chick, Mom. Her name is Emma, and she's an old friend."

"She doesn't look that old. She your new side piece?"

I rolled my eyes. "I don't have an old lady, so how would I have a side piece? And no, she and I are not an item." I wanted to add yet, but wisely held my tongue. "She ran into a bit of trouble and came to me for help."

"So, she's fair game?" Mom was nothing if not direct.

"No. She's hurt, and she's under my protection. She's off limits." I glared around the room in case anyone misunderstood that.

Mom chuckled. "I see." She took a good look at Emma, noting the bulge where the bandage pushed her shirt out. "Don't worry, hun. They may look like a scruffy lot, but these are all good old boys. They'll make sure no one hurts you anymore. Boyfriend trouble?"

Emma shook her head but didn't elaborate.

"I need to get her settled in my room. I called church in forty-five minutes. I'll catch you and Jake up after that." I guided Emma over to the staircase, signaling the question-and-answer session was over. "Let's go."

Chapter Four

Emma

"There's only one bed in here." Emma looked around the room.

"It's big. I'm sure we can share it. We're both adults. "

"That's what's worrying me."

That hurt. "You think I'm going to force myself on you?"

She shook her head, slanting me a sideways look. "Just about the opposite."

"You're worried I might not force myself on you?" I frowned, confused.

She chuckled. "I thought you were smarter than that. I'm worried I might not be able to keep my hands to myself if we're both in that bed together. You know I've always had a bit of a thing for you."

News to me. "You have? I'm too old for you."

"You can't seriously believe that." She looked askance at me. "You're what, ten years older than me, maybe twelve?"

"Exactly. Too old and too fucking experienced."

She smiled, sidling toward me. "I'm not sure there is such a thing as too experienced."

Before I knew what was happening, she reached up to pull my head down and locked her lips on mine. Melting into me, she opened her mouth to let my tongue explore at will.

Well fuck that. I'm not a saint. When I wrapped my arms around her and pulled her close, she let out a startled whimper. Damn. Her side. I felt like the world's biggest asshole. If I'd done any damage, Joker would kill me.

Emma's one hand went to the bandage on her

ribs. "I'm sorry. For a moment there I forgot about the damn bullet hole in my side. We just have to be a bit more careful."

I stared at her in disbelief. "You're sorry? Are you kidding? I know better, not to mention the fact that I called church in less than…" I glanced at my watch. "Less than thirty minutes. If I ever make love to you, it is not going to be a quickie before I leave for some damn meeting." My eyes raked her from head to toe, my cock as hard as cement. "Make that *when*. When I make love to you, because we both know it's going to happen. And soon."

I separated myself from her as gently as possible, but I couldn't resist placing one last kiss on those tempting lips, now slightly parted and glistening with moisture.

I strode over to the door. With one hand on the knob, I turned back to her. "Stay here until I come back to get you. Right here. Unless the damn place is on fire, do not leave this room."

* * *

I watched Ace leave the room. Damn, the man looked good from the back side. Or the front. Or any side really. The soft click of the door closing behind him sent a pang of regret streaming through me. I'd blown my chance, at least for now. If it weren't for the damn bullet wound in my side, I could be writhing beneath that gorgeous hunk of man muscle.

I traced the outline of the wound with my finger. The pain was mostly masked by whatever pills Joker had given me, but only if there was no pressure on it. At least it hadn't started bleeding again, so it must be healing. How long did it take for a bullet wound to heal? Ace had said at minimum a couple of weeks, but he didn't sound too sure about that. Joker would know, and he'd be here to check it out sometime today. I'd ask him then.

A soft knock at the door jerked my attention. "Hello?"

"Can I come in?" A woman's voice.

"Umm. Sure."

The woman Ace had addressed as Mom closed the door behind her. I knew she wasn't Ace's real mom. I'd never seen this woman in the old 'hood. She must have read my mind, because she explained that right up front.

"I'm Alessandra, but most of the boys call me Mom. Easier to pronounce, plus I'm old enough to be their mother. I do the cooking and cleaning, and generally help Jake out with things. We're kind of a couple, without all the legal tags that go with it. Was married once. Not a fun time. I'd rather not repeat it."

"Hi." I took in her appearance. Plump, with soft blue eyes, and a cloud of gray hair, she looked like everyone's idea of the perfect grandmother. It was hard to tell how old she might be. Fifty? Sixty? She had one of those ageless countenances that made it hard to guess. "What should I call you?"

She tilted her head. "Might as well call me Mom. By the way Ace looks at you, I imagine you're going to be a permanent fixture around here."

"No." I shook my head. "We barely know each other. Hadn't seen each other for years, until last night."

"Oh, honey, time has nothing to do with it." Mom smiled softly. "These boys, they find their one and they know."

"I used to date his little brother back in high school." Now why had I blurted that out?

"But you didn't love him. I'm betting you never

even slept with him, did you?"

Damn, she was good. And right. "No. We were really more good friends than anything."

"And back then you had a crush on Ace, but he didn't even know you existed. Or he pretended he didn't."

I raised one brow. "You some kind of mind reader?"

Mom laughed. "No. I just have a bit of traveler blood in me, and I know the boys real good. And the way Ace looks at you, that ain't no two-day crush." She eyed me up shrewdly. "I bet he thinks he's too old for you."

I dipped my head. "He does. Keeps saying I deserve better too."

"Hang in there. He'll come around. But you better be serious because once he claims you, there ain't no going back."

"Claims me?" This wasn't the eighteenth century. Men didn't claim women. It's not like I was a stray dog or something.

"Yup. Once you and he do the horizontal naked dance, you're as good as hitched. He ain't never going to let you go. Of course, he's going to announce it to all the brothers, and get you a cut with 'Property of Ace' on it but that's just a formality."

"What's a cut?" I wanted to protest the property of Ace thing, but I'd take that up with him.

"A jacket with the sleeves cut off, hence the name cut. Although it's usually just a vest. But it will have the club logo on it, and all. It tells the world they'd better be nice, or they'll have to deal with Ace and the entire club."

"Oh." My side was starting to throb, and I realized it was time for more painkillers. Reaching for my purse, I pulled out the bottle of pills.

"Need some water?" Mom bustled into the ensuite and came back with a glass of ice water. "Hope it's not too bad. Ace said someone grazed you with a bullet. Joker will get you fixed up though. He could have been top doctor at that trauma clinic up North, but he's not so good at the bedside politics thing. Speaks his mind and all. Tends to piss off the suits."

I just about choked on a mouthful of water as I pictured Joker telling a bunch of snotty doctors what he thought of their politics. I managed to swallow. "He fixed it up last night, but he said he'd come check me out today. Something about bullet wounds being prone to infections."

"Well, he'd know. He's seen enough of them."

That didn't sound comforting. "The bikers get shot a lot?"

"No, in the SEALs." She shook her head. "He was a medic, active duty. Didn't Ace tell you that?"

I shook my head. "No. I knew Ace went into the Navy, but he never talked about it. That's actually why I ran to him when I got shot. I figured anyone who'd been deployed a few times would be able to protect me. But like I said, it's been a long time since we'd seen each other."

"PTSD. Joker has it, sometimes bad." She looked thoughtful. "Not sure if I should be telling you all this. The brothers, Riptide, they're all ex-SEALs. By invitation only. Came back from the service and knew too much, seen too much to fit back into the cookie cutter world back home here. So, they joined Riptide. One by one. Here with their brothers, they can be themselves. No one freaks out if they have an episode. No one questions their sanity because we all understand."

"Oh." I'd had no idea. "No, he didn't tell me."

"Well, now you know. These are good men. Honorable men. They served their country, and they still do."

I frowned. "They're still in the service?"

She shook her head. "No. But I've said enough. Ace can explain the rest to you when he's ready. Club business and all." A faint smile crossed her face. "You'll get used to that term. Club business. It's what the guys say when they don't want to tell you something."

The sound of doors opening downstairs interrupted my reply.

Mom got up and glided over to the door. "Church is over, so I imagine Ace will be up here any minute. He's one of the good ones. You're a lucky woman."

Ace appeared behind her. "Not so sure about that, Mom. But she's stuck with me."

* * *

Ace

I hadn't meant to eavesdrop, but I heard the last part of Mom's conversation with Emma. At least I wouldn't have to explain club business to her.

Well, maybe a little. Like the part about it being for her own protection. If she were ever questioned by the police, what she didn't know she couldn't tell them. Once I put a ring on her finger and signed all that legal shit, it would be even less of an issue. A wife can't be forced to testify against her husband.

Yeah, I'd jumped all the way from too old for her, to wedding bells. No one ever accused me of letting the grass grow under my feet.

"The bikers in Riptide were all Navy SEALs at

some point?"

I narrowed my eyes. "I see Mom's been spilling the beans."

"She seems to think it's okay because she's under the impression that I'm going to be one of the gang." Emma tilted her head. "Now why would she think that?"

I crossed the room in three long strides and captured her mouth with mine. The kiss was long and deep, our tongues tangling with each other in an erotic dance that had my cock swelling in anticipation. When we finally surfaced for air, I had to remind myself she'd been shot yesterday. It was a bit early for a wild naked playtime.

And frankly, I didn't trust myself not to go wild.

"She thinks that because she saw the way we look at each other." I ordered my cock to stand down. It didn't take the hint. "You want me. You just haven't admitted it yet."

"I see ego isn't one of your issues."

I chuckled. "It's not ego if it's true. I didn't hear any objections when I kissed you."

"I was in shock. I expected an answer, not to be attacked by your lips."

"You could have said no," I pointed out. "I've never taken a woman by force."

"I was in shock." She tried to look stern, but didn't quite pull it off.

"Because my kissing skills are so awesome?"

"They're not bad, but I would hardly call them awesome." She wrinkled her nose.

Yeah, she wanted me.

"Care for another round? Just so you can judge my awesomeness?" Without waiting for an answer, I seared another kiss across her lips. When she opened her mouth to protest, I took advantage, my tongue swooping in to conquer.

She tasted like sunshine on a Georgia summer's day. Sweet, bright and welcoming. Almost more tempting than a bike ride, along the coastal highway. Almost.

I let my hands slide down her back, careful to avoid the bullet wound. Cupping her perfectly rounded ass, I let out a low groan.

Fuck, I wanted to bury my cock, balls deep inside her and never let her go. Never. If my cock got any harder, it was going to explode.

Emma pulled her head away from me. "Ace?"

"Yeah?" I gazed into those beautiful eyes.

"You really do kiss remarkably well."

Fuck. Fuck. Fuck.

I couldn't believe she just said that. Especially while I was already hard as a rock, and unable to do anything about it.

A loud knock on the door forestalled any reply I might have been able to come up with.

"You all decent in there?"

Joker. Come to check on Emma. I hastily let her go and tugged my shirt straight. Glancing over at her, I saw the glazed look on her face.

"Saved by the medic," she whispered.

I wasn't sure if she meant her or me.

"Hello?" Joker knocked again. "You better not be doing anything to rip that wound open."

"Fuck," I muttered under my breath.

Three strides took me to the door where I jerked it open. "She's all yours."

Without waiting for a reply, I headed for the stairs.

* * *

"You're looking awful grouchy for a guy who just installed his old lady in his bedroom." Mom gave me one of those looks. The kind that lets you know your private life is about as private as the town square on the Fourth of July.

"Joker is checking out Emma's side."

"And he interrupted you making a move on her?" The laughter in her voice told me she didn't have any sympathy for my predicament.

"She got fucking shot yesterday. Can't make a move until she's healed up some." I knew I sounded like a bear with a sore ass, and I didn't care.

"You could if you took it really easy."

"Not sure that's possible." I glared at Mom, which seemed to amuse her.

"Then I guess you're just going to have to wait." She pivoted toward the stove. "Care for some grub? Most of the guys ate when they came in from church, but there's still a helping or two left."

"Please." I sighed. "Sorry for being so grouchy."

Mom dished up a plate of bacon, eggs and grits and plunked it down on the table. "Eat up. Some food in your gut will help settle you down a bit."

I doubted that, but I sat my ass down at the table and started shoveling the food in.

"You want me to order a cut for her?" Jake peeked over the top of his newspaper. Glasses askew as usual, he looked like a harmless old coot. I knew better. Before the accident that crippled him up, Jake had been President of Riptide. He might not be able to ride anymore, but that didn't make him any less dangerous.

"Naw. Don't want to jinx it." I took another mouthful of perfectly cooked eggs. "But thanks for the thought."

"Whatever." Jake disappeared back behind his newspaper.

I heard the sound of footsteps descending the stairs just before Joker appeared in the kitchen. Helping himself to a cup of coffee, he leaned against the counter and took a big gulp.

"Well?" Patience was not my strong point.

"No infection, and the wound is starting to heal. These kinds take time though, jagged edges and all." He took another sip. "I gave her some more painkillers, and rebandaged it. As long as she doesn't do anything stupid, it should be fine. It's going to scar, but there's not much I can do about that."

"What do you mean by anything stupid?"

A huge, cheeky grin lit Joker's face. "You can have your way with her, but be gentle. Maybe let her set the pace."

Mom snorted. "Have his way with her? What are we, a bunch of high society snobs?"

"Okay, he can fuck her brains out, but he has to do it gently." Joker drained the coffee mug. "I have shit to do. See you guys later."

I got to my feet. "You heard the man. She's good to go. Now I just need to convince her."

Chapter Five

Emma

Ace looked thoughtful, closing the door softly behind him. A far cry from his mood when Joker interrupted us.

"Joker says I'm healing up well." I lifted the shirt up to show off my newly bandaged side.

"Good to know." He came over and lowered himself to sit beside me on the bed. "Rattler checked out the park last night. No sign of a body. Shooter must have had a clean-up crew on call, which means this was targeted and professional. A random shooter would have left the body and made a run for it. Shadow is checking online to see if he can find out what went down. Until we know more, you stick to me like glue. If I'm not around to watch you, I'll assign one of the brothers or prospects to watch over you. I'll let you know first, though. You down with that?"

"I suppose I have to be." I wasn't happy about it, though. "I'm the one who brought trouble to your doorstep. Literally."

"Glad you thought of me." He reached out and gently tucked a stray lock of hair behind my ear. "You weren't kidding before? You really didn't know I had a thing for you when you were dating my little brother?"

"Hell no. I had no idea."

He kept his gaze locked on mine as he took my hand and placed it on his crotch to let me feel the outline of his rock-hard cock through the material of his jeans.

I opened my mouth to reply, and he slanted his lips over mine. Damn, the man knew how to kiss. The feel of his lips took the very breath from my lungs as his tongue invaded, claiming mastery.

Or maybe it was the way his cock twitched and grew beneath my hand, ramping up my desire. He hadn't been the only one who'd had fantasies back then. "Tell me what you'd like to do to me."

"I'd slide my hand under your bra and cup those perfect little tits of yours, feeling the nipples go hard when I tweaked them." He slid the shirt I'd borrowed from him up to my neck. My bra had been a casualty of the previous night, and my breasts were bare to his gaze.

His eyes glowed with lust as he surveyed the hard pebbled nipples. "Perfect!" He breathed the word out softly, reverently. Lowering his head, he snaked his tongue across one taut nipple before sucking it into his mouth. He took his time, lavishing attention on first one breast, and then the other.

He lifted his head, locking his gaze on mine. "Then I'd slide one hand down into your panties. You'd be wet, just waiting for me to slide into you."

"Yeah." I closed my eyes, savoring the feel of his rough hand as it slid over my belly and down to my mound. One finger slid between the lips of my pussy, stroking across my entrance. I whimpered, thrusting my hips up to meet it.

Ace chuckled. "You like that, do you? Tell me you like it."

"Uh huh." Actual words were beyond me as flames of liquid heat raced along every nerve. I was ready for him. More than ready. Eager.

He pulled back, and I opened my eyes to see him quickly shucking his boots, shirt and pants. Boxer shorts followed, to be tossed in a careless heap on the floor. Naked, he was a magnificent specimen of a male in his prime. Tattoos snaked over half of his body, winding down both arms and across his impressive abs. Just gazing at him took my breath away.

Someday, I might ask him to explain the intricate designs of those tats and what they represented. I knew there was meaning behind each one of them.

Someday, but not right now. His body was ready and primed for sex. I was right there with him. I wanted to feel that gorgeous cock sliding into me. *Now*.

"Much as I like seeing you in my shirt, it has to go." He dropped onto the bed and grasped the bottom of the shirt. I lifted my arms, allowing him to ease it up over my head. Part of me noted how careful he was not to disturb my freshly bandaged side. The rest of me just wanted to get naked.

I rose to my knees and wriggled my pants down over my hips. Ace gently eased me back onto the bed and pulled them down my legs.

Naked, I slid my tongue out to wet my lips, my gaze locked on the massive hard on staring me straight in the face. "I want to taste that."

"Not this time." Ace's nostrils flared as he stared at my naked body. "I'm too close, and I want to feel you wrapped around me when I come."

Reaching behind him, he slid open the drawer on the bedside table and pulled out a condom. Ripping it open with his teeth, he quickly sheathed himself.

Draping one arm around me, he lay on his back and sat me on his chest. "Don't want to hurt you or mess that side up so you get to set the pace. This time." His lips curved in pure devilish promise.

I blinked. He'd gone from blazing hot alpha male in charge to concerned lover in less than an instant. Still blazing hot, and so damn sexy to boot.

I reached behind me and wrapped my hand around his cock. Raising up on my knees I shuffled backward to position myself.

Ace grasped my hips in both hands, his expression suddenly serious. "You sure about this?"

I felt he was asking about more than just a quick roll in the hay, but I was too far gone to take the time to analyze his motives. I gave a curt nod of my head. "I'm sure."

His eyes shone with lust as he teased my aching pussy with his cock. He held me there for an endless moment, while I squirmed and wriggled in an attempt to impale myself.

Then he slowly lowered me onto that stiff shaft, one achingly sweet inch at a time. When his balls snugged up against my ass, he let out a low groan. "Damn, woman, you are tight. Almost thought you were a virgin."

Almost. I licked my lower lip. "Not quite. Just haven't had time for much horizontal play lately."

He rocked his hips and sent a blaze of heat rippling through me. "Lately?"

"A year or two," I admitted. "Maybe more. Between work and school, I keep busy."

"You were telling the truth when you said you and my little bro never had sex?"

"Yeah. Gospel truth. And before you ask, I've only ever had one serious relationship and frankly it didn't set off any fireworks in the sex department. He said I was frigid and left me for a blonde bimbo who, and I quote, knew how to make a man feel like a man."

"Bastard. He didn't deserve you." He started to rock his hips in a slow steady rhythm. I closed my eyes and leaned back. Resting a hand on either side of his thighs, I matched his pace, sliding up and down on that pole like I was riding a horse. One hell of a well-hung horse.

Ace moved faster, pistoning in and out of me, his

hands holding my hips steady and guiding my movements.

"Open your eyes."

I obeyed. My gaze locked on his.

"I want you to be looking at me when you come. I want us to be staring at each other." He slid his hand between us and stroked the little bundle of nerves at my entrance.

The surge of heat sent me plummeting over the edge into the biggest climax I'd ever experienced. I stared up at him as I screamed my release, my channel tightening around his cock as spasm after spasm rocketed through me.

Ace let out a roar as my release triggered his own. I collapsed on top of him, his cock still buried deep inside me. We lay there, in companionable silence, our breathing heavy in the still air.

"Well, that proved one thing." He reached up and smoothed my hair away from my face.

"It did?"

"You are definitely not frigid."

He held me cradled on top of him, my head snuggled in the crook of his shoulder. His lips slid across my forehead in a tender kiss, and I closed my eyes to savor a feeling I'd rarely experienced. Belonging.

Deep down, I knew I belonged right where I was. Not in the clubhouse of some motorcycle club but snuggled up against the one guy I'd never quite gotten out of my system. Strange, since we'd never dated or openly expressed any interest in each other, but it felt like I'd belonged to Ace forever.

This. The sex. The snuggling. The togetherness. We were like two halves of a whole.

And that scared the hell out of me.

* * *

Ace

I could feel her stiffen up, start to withdraw from me and there was no fucking way I was going to let that happen. That was not only the best damn sex I'd ever had, but it made my fantasy pale in comparison.

I'd given her an out, asked her if she was sure and she'd said yes. She was mine now and there was no way I was going to let her go. I just had to deal with the little matter of the murder she'd seen in the park and then we could live happily ever after. Maybe have a kid or two or three. Fix up my house or buy a new one if she wanted something with a big backyard. You know, for the kids to play in or maybe host BBQs for the club.

I'd get her whatever she wanted. Hell, I'd get her the moon if she asked for it.

I just wouldn't fucking let her leave.

"I have to run into town this afternoon. You can stay here with Jake and Mom. A couple of the prospects will be at the gate, and Joker will be here. Rattler and a couple of the other brothers are coming with me."

"What if I don't want to stay here? I've already missed a day's pay, and I need some fresh clothes." She glanced over at the pile of discarded clothes. "Your shirt doesn't exactly fit me."

"I thought it looked great." I shifted so we were practically face to face. "I can send one of the prospects over to your place to get some of your things. Just make a list of what you want."

"I want to go get my own clothes, and I want to go home."

"No."

She looked stunned. "No? Do you seriously expect to toss out orders and have me follow them?"

"Yes," I replied calmly. "You came to me for protection, and that's what you're going to get. I can't protect you if you're not here, so no, you are not going home unless you're prepared to have me and half a dozen of my brothers stay with you."

"My place is not that big."

Understatement of the year. Her place was a converted garage. Four hundred square feet max. Defense wise, it sucked. There were numerous ways for people to sneak up on it without detection.

"No, it's smaller than a fucking walk-in closet, so staying here makes more sense."

It did have off-street parking, but not much else to recommend it. I'd had one of the prospects check it out, and he'd managed to jimmy the locks and get inside in under five seconds. No way was I letting her go back to that death trap.

"But…"

"No buts. You stay here."

So much for the warm fuzzy snuggling. Emma wrenched herself out of my arms and reached for her discarded clothing. She hesitated at putting my shirt back on, but unless she planned to parade around the clubhouse naked from the waist up, she didn't have much choice. She turned to glare at me. "Fine. I want my own room."

"No." I managed not to chuckle at the mutinous set to her lips.

"Why not?"

"Because I'm not planning on fighting with one of my brothers over you, and if you have your own room, it's as good as declaring you're now fair game."

"You're saying I have to stay here, and I have to

bunk with you?"

"Yes."

"Fine!"

It didn't sound fine, but I was willing to overlook that.

"Can I come with you to get some of my stuff?"

I considered saying no again, but I was smart enough not to push it too far. "Okay, but you need to do what I say. No questions. I'm not trying to be an ass but until we know exactly what we're up against, I don't want to take any chances."

"Thank you."

The meek answer had me giving her a sharp look, but she just smiled innocently.

I did not believe in innocent Emma.

She did that thing again where she tied my shirt at her waist and made it look like a fashion statement instead of a sloppy oversized shirt. My cock stirred at the thought of what lay beneath it.

"When do we leave?"

I made a few quick mental calculations. The boys and I had a meeting with our FBI contact to make, but there should be enough time to run Emma to her place and back without being late. If things went south, I could always have Rattler and a couple of the prospects escort her back to the clubhouse while I made the meeting.

Tigger and Tiny had been with us for quite a while, and were close to being patched in. I'd trust them to keep her safe. "Give me five minutes to brief the guys, then we go."

"On your bike?"

I liked the hint of excitement in Emma's voice when she asked that. It told me she liked the idea of riding behind me, even with her messed up side.

Unfortunately, it wasn't going to work this time, not if she had a bunch of shit to bring back. Besides, my bike was still at my house, and her side might not take too much riding at the moment either.

"I think we'd better stick to the truck this time. Need room for your stuff."

"Right." She grimaced. "Sometimes it sucks to be a reasonable adult."

I managed not to burst out laughing at the note of regret in her voice. "Yeah. Sometimes it does."

* * *

We arrived at Emma's place a little before noon. As soon as I pulled up in front, she put her hand on the door handle, prepared to jump out. I reached over and stopped her. "Let the guys check it out first."

"Oh, right." She let her hand drop back into her lap.

Tigger and Tiny parked their bikes behind the truck and approached the little studio from opposite sides then they paused. When nothing happened, Tiny motioned to Tigger, who promptly disappeared around the back. Minutes later the front door popped open, and Tigger poked his head out.

He motioned all clear, and I reached over and opened Emma's door. "Not to rush you, but make it quick."

"Aren't you coming in with me?"

I shook my head. "Tigger is inside. I'll keep watch out here to make sure no one disturbs you."

"You know you sound paranoid, right?"

"Paranoid is what's kept me alive all these years, girl," I said. "Now go get your stuff before I change my mind. I'm being nice. I could just have Tigger dump things into a garbage bag for you to sort out back at the clubhouse."

"You are not sending some kid to paw through my underwear!"

Tigger was hardly a kid. Not sure he ever had been, but it was fun to see the outrage on Emma's face. "So go!"

She turned and stomped up to the front door. Tiny bobbed his head deferentially to her. Good. Word had got around the brothers that she was mine. Whether or not she liked it, it blanketed her with an extra layer of protection.

I had to hand it to her. Less than five minutes later, she came back out dragging a roller bag. Tigger followed close behind carrying a contractor sized garbage bag which he hefted into the back of the truck. He placed the roller bag in with a bit more care, then turned to jog back to the house.

I raised one eyebrow at Emma.

She shrugged. "Don't have a lot of fancy luggage. Garbage bags are big, tough and waterproof."

I let out a quick hoot of laugher. "I think I see some of the old 'hood peeking out from wherever you stuffed it down. Glad to know it's still there."

"Not everything about the 'hood sucked." She smiled softly. "Remember the nights everyone in the neighborhood would sit on bleachers in the park because it was too hot to go home and be cooped up inside?"

I remembered them all too well. I remembered how I'd sometimes join the gang in the park. I'd wanted to make a move on her, but knew it was all kinds of a lousy fucking idea. "Yeah. It wasn't all bad, was it?"

"No." She climbed in awkwardly and buckled the seat belt.

"Here." I pulled a new cell phone out of my

pocket and tossed it to her. "I programmed my number in, and Joker and Rattler and the clubhouse. Shadow, the IT guy, set up the security on it, so it can't be hacked. You'll have to set the rest of it up yourself."

She caught the phone, regarding it as if she expected it to bite. "This thing must have cost at least a grand. I can't afford that. I expected one of the cheap models. Didn't think I had to say that. You know I'm on a hell of a strict budget, and with having to miss a couple of weeks of work I'm going to have a tough time just making rent this month."

"Consider it a gift." I shrugged and put the truck in gear. "I want to know you can call for help if you need it, so it's really more for me than for you."

Emma rolled her eyes. She was doing that a lot these days. I took it to mean the discussion was over.

She played with the phone for a few minutes, then shot me a puzzled look. "It says I'm on the Riptide network. You have your own telecom system?"

"Sort of. The detailed answer falls under club business, so we'll just go with yes for now."

She frowned, shaking her head. "Mom said you use the phrase 'club business' when you don't want to have to explain something."

I chuckled. "Mom's been doing a lot of talking, but she's partly right. In this case, the details really do fall under the heading of things you're better off not knowing. Can we leave it at that for now? You needed a phone. Now you have one."

"Thank you, then." She smiled wryly. "I guess I'd better call my boss and let her know I'm out for more than just one night."

"No need. Joker called as your medical practitioner and informed her. Sounds more official that way, and he used his Navy credentials, so no one can trace that back to club."

"You really are paranoid, aren't you?"

"You say that like it's a bad thing." I slid one hand over to rest it on her thigh. "You'll get used to it."

She snorted. "You think so, do you?"

But she didn't move my hand.

Chapter Six

Emma

"I have a meeting to get to, so Tiny is going to be your shadow while I'm gone." Ace stopped the truck in front of the clubhouse to let me out.

Tiny, who was anything but, was waiting for me on the wraparound porch, and saluted Ace. It looked a bit corny between two bikers, but made sense after learning about their military background.

"You mean he's my bodyguard?"

"'Shadow' sounds so much nicer."

"At least you didn't say he was my jailer."

"That would be silly. You're not under house arrest."

"No, but I can't leave without permission. Or a keeper. Or possibly both."

Ace grinned that infuriating grin. "Exactly. For your own good."

I wrinkled my nose. "Makes me sound like a difficult-to-control toddler."

Heat infused his eyes as they swept over me. "Possibly difficult, but definitely not a toddler."

I sighed. I wasn't going to win this one, and he did have a point. I'd asked for protection, and he was providing it. "Who are you meeting?"

"Club business." He reached over and opened the door for me. "Should be back within an hour. Two at the most. Tiny can carry your crap up to my room so you can get it sorted. Beast is going to drop me off at my place after to pick up my bike."

I rolled my eyes as Tiny obediently grabbed the suitcase and garbage bag out of the back of the truck. I noticed he waited for me at the door, until Tigger came out and replaced him. They took this bodyguard stuff seriously.

I slid out of the truck. I didn't consider myself to be short, but the ground was a good two feet below my toes. Just as I regained my balance, Beast rounded the side of the house and headed for the truck. He nodded at me and grunted, waiting for me to get out of the way before climbing into my just vacated seat.

"Hi to you too," I grumbled. I swear I saw the tiniest ghost of a smile cross his face.

I waved at Ace. "Have fun at your meeting."

Ace didn't bother to answer, throwing me a smoldering look before taking off.

I watched the truck until it disappeared behind the bend in the driveway. Damn. I wanted him to stay, and that made me grumpy. I thumped my way up the stairs to the porch.

"You mind telling me what's with the 'club business' thing?" I threw the question at Tigger, not really expecting an answer. One thing had become glaringly obvious from the time I first set foot in the clubhouse, and that was the way these guys covered each other's butts. I thought it was an admirable trait, until it kept me closed out.

"Not sure, but I imagine it has to do with the murder you saw."

I threw him a surprised look. "You know about that?"

His head bobbed. "Yeah. Prez filled everyone in at church this morning."

"I thought you weren't supposed to tell me what happened at church." I frowned.

He held the door open for me to enter. "You already know about that, so it doesn't count."

"What exactly does count?" I asked.

"Nice try." A wide grin stretched across his face,

instantly shaving years off his appearance. "Everything else."

I obviously wasn't going to get any more answers out of him about the meeting, and I honestly wasn't sure I wanted to. I was suddenly too tired to care. Not sure if it was the overwhelming events in the past forty-eight hours, the throbbing bullet wound, or the effects of the painkillers. Probably a combination of all three.

Tiny deposited my gear in Ace's room. I looked around. There was a dresser against the far wall, but I felt reluctant to open the drawers and squish his stuff to make room for mine. It wasn't like I was moving in or anything. And it felt like I'd be invading his privacy.

I'd left the door open, and I turned as I heard grunting noises. Tiny and Tigger appeared, hauling a second dresser between them.

"Mom said you'd need this. Where should we put it?"

I gaped at them.

"Not trying to rush you, but this damn thing is heavy." Tigger put his end down. "How about right beside the other one?"

"Umm. Okay." I managed to close my mouth.

The two burly bikers maneuvered the dresser through the door and placed it beside the current one. Tiny dusted his hands off on his pants. "Anything else you need?"

I shook my head, at a loss for words. My stay at the clubhouse suddenly looked a little less temporary. "No. Tell Mom thanks."

"Sure. If you need anything, just holler." They headed out the doorway.

As they left, I realized I only heard one set of footsteps going down the stairs. I stuck my head out the door and saw Tiny lounging on a chair in the hallway.

He looked up. "You need something?"

"No." I cocked my head sideways. "Are you making sure I don't escape?"

He laughed, a deep-down belly type laugh. "Hell no. Just the opposite. I'm making sure no one gets past the guys downstairs and gets to you. Prez would not be happy if we let anything happen to you while he's gone."

"Oh." What was I supposed to make of that? There was protective, and then there was crazily paranoid over the top protective. I should probably be upset, but it felt kind of nice. "You guys do this a lot?"

"No, at least not this personally." He squinted, as if trying to decide how much to tell me. "Sometimes we do protection, but this *is* personal. You belong to Prez, and he wants you to be safe."

"I don't belong to your Prez." That made me sound like some kind of prized pet. "I just asked him for help."

Tiny didn't look convinced. "You're in his room. And he put you off limits. You and he can figure out what you want to call it, but from where I sit it looks like you belong to each other."

Belong to each other.

I kind of liked the sound of that. Except our expectations from life were so very different. He was top guy in a biker gang, and I was desperately trying to get myself out of the ghetto and into a respectable profession. The two were not compatible.

Were they?

"How did you end up a Riptide prospect?" I asked.

"Just luck, really. My family life was shit when I

was a kid, so I joined the Navy as soon as I made the age thing." Tiny squirmed around in the chair to face me. "When I made it into the SEALs, I felt like I finally had a home, and a family. Prez was my platoon sergeant. All the guys were close. So, when I got out I kind of didn't do so well. Felt like I was back where I started. Alone. Then Prez showed up and offered to get me into Riptide. Saved my life, really."

"Offered to get you in?" I tilted my head. "Oh right, Mom told me you had to be sponsored or something like that."

"Yup. Riptide is by invitation only." He shrugged. "You have to have someone sponsor you, and then you have to prove you deserve the patch."

"So, a prospect is not quite a member?"

"I guess." He looked thoughtful. "I've been here over a year now. Prez is trusting me with more shit. It's a real honor being asked to watch his old lady."

"Old lady?"

"That's just what you get called if you're like claimed by one of the brothers. Mom is Jake's old lady. It's a term of respect."

It didn't sound that respectful to me. I did not consider myself old. Still, it was one more thing to take up with Ace. Or not. Once this murder thing got cleared up, I'd be on my way. I wouldn't be here long enough for it to be an issue.

Why did that thought not make me feel happier?

"Guess I'd better get unpacked. Thanks for the dresser." I withdrew back into Ace's room and stared at the new dresser. Putting my clothes in it would make this seem real, seem like I planned to stay.

My side was starting to ache again. Hopefully I hadn't overdone it. I downed a couple of the magical painkillers and laid down on the bed while I waited for them to kick in. I could always unpack later.

The sound of a dozen or more Harley engines pulled me out of a fitful sleep. It was no doubt Ace returning from his mysterious meeting. Minutes later, the clubhouse erupted with sound downstairs as the bikers all jostled their way inside.

I sat up, rubbing my eyes and glanced at the alarm clock. I'd been out for over an hour, but it sure didn't feel like it.

"She okay?"

My heart skipped a beat at the sound of Ace's voice. Much as I didn't want to admit it, I was happy he'd come back, and happy he worried about me.

"Yes, sir. She's been in your room the whole time. She didn't close the door so when things got real quiet I peeked in and found her passed out cold on the bed. Been through a lot lately, I guess. Must have tuckered her out."

"I'm sure it did. Thanks for watching her for me. Joker been around to see her?"

"No, sir. Not while you were away. Thought maybe he went with you."

"Can you go tell him to come on up when he has a minute?"

"No problem."

I heard the rattle of the chair as Tiny left to find Joker.

Ace loomed in the doorway. God, the man was gorgeous. Not fancy magazine type gorgeous, but the rugged, scarred kind of gorgeous that told you he knew how to look after himself and anyone he cared about.

He ran one hand through his thick mane of hair as he stared at me. "Woman, you are trouble."

I propped myself up on one elbow and tucked

my feet under me. "How so? I did exactly what you told me. I stayed put and didn't even leave this room while you were gone."

He stalked across the room, lowering himself to the bed beside me. Placing one hand on my thigh, he shook his head. "What you saw was an execution by a rogue club from Atlanta, and intel is that they plan to run drugs through Riptide territory. This is our town, and we like to keep it clean. No way we're going to sit back and let them set up shop here."

"How do you plan to stop them?" I had the sickening feeling I already knew the answer.

"We'll throw some friendly clues their way. Let them know their presence isn't appreciated. Hopefully they take the hint and move on. There are other towns around they can spoil with their presence."

"Then why did they decide to use this one?" There had to be a reason, especially if it would have been easier to avoid it.

"That is the fucking million-dollar question." He reached up to trace the outline of my lips with the rough pad of one finger.

"What does this have to do with the guy I saw get murdered?" I tried to ignore the tingle in my gut as his finger slid down to my neck.

"Intel says he was a drug mule, and he tried to keep some of the product for himself. That kind of shit never goes well."

Still didn't make sense to me. "How do you know the guy was a mule?"

"Club business, but you can count on it. Our source is reliable." He quirked the corner of his mouth.

The butterflies in my belly stirred to life. "I'm still in danger?"

"Not as long as you're with me."

"Fun as that sounds, what about my life? My job? School? Friends?" Frustration had me clenching my fists, and the pain in my side did nothing to calm me down.

Ace looked thoughtful. "Your job is a dead-ender. If you want to sling drinks, you can do it at the club's bar. Plenty of protection there, and the girls make good tips." He chuckled. "Assuming you're any good at it."

"At flirting with guys for money? I'm really good at that. Just come watch me some night."

A thunderous expression crossed his face. "I don't think I'd like that."

"It's really not up to you, is it?"

"Actually, it is. You're under my protection right now so you might want to be careful."

"Or what? You'll throw me out?"

"Worse." His smile held no warmth. "I'll have you locked in, with a twenty-four seven guard on you."

I gaped. "You wouldn't dare!"

He stood and stalked over to the dresser. Pivoting, he pinned me with a glance. "Try me. You asked for protection, and I promised you'd be safe with me. I never promised you'd like it."

A giggle escaped my lips. I couldn't help myself. Standing there, with his hands on his hips and that cold, don't-fuck-with-me expression on his face, he reminded me of the godfather in some Mafia movie. All he needed was a couple of menacing bodyguards to back him up.

Oh right. Tiny and Tigger.

He closed the gap between us in two long steps, grasping me lightly around the waist. "Care to share the joke?"

"You."

Brows raised he studied me. "Me?"

"Yeah you." I managed to get my laughter under control. "You looked like the godfather from a Mafia movie. All stern, and in control."

"Well, I am the Prez of a powerful motorcycle club," he pointed out.

"True." The throbbing in my side was increasing painfully. Laughter and gunshot ribs were apparently a bad combination. "Sorry. I blame the drugs." I glanced at the doorway behind him. "Speaking of which, is Joker around? I really hurt, and the drugs don't seem to be working as well as they did yesterday."

"Yesterday you weren't jumping all over the place. I think you need to lay down for a bit. Tiny should be back with Joker soon."

I raised my eyes to his. "Can you lay with me? Just for a little while." Wow, those drugs might not be handling the pain, but they sure killed my inhibitions.

"Thought you'd never ask. Just let me have a word with Tigger first." I clutched my injured side, watching him stride to the door.

Returning minutes later, he closed the door and lowered himself to the edge of the bed. He rubbed his hand gently down my arm, waking my inner sex fiend. Hopefully he wasn't aware of her voracious nature.

"This is serious, you know. Those guys play for keeps."

"I know. And I'm sorry. I didn't mean to get you involved in something dangerous." I paused, running the events of the yesterday in my mind. "I guess I didn't think past escaping from the shooter."

Ace smoothed a lock of hair away from my face. "Don't feel bad. I'm glad you came to me. The club will take care of this, and then we can work out the future. For now, you stay here where I know you're safe."

"Did I ever say thank you?" I ignored his assumption that I'd do what he decreed, or that we had a future.

"Not necessary." He slid onto the bed beside me, stretching out to full length. "Turn over. You don't want to sleep on your hurt side."

I did as I was told, for once without complaint, and was rewarded when I felt his warm body mold itself against my back. I could feel the hard length of his cock pressing into my butt, and suddenly I wasn't sleepy anymore.

Ace's hand slid around my waist. I hadn't bothered with a bra, and he reached up to fondle my breast. I let out a low moan, and he chuckled. "I love how sensitive you are." He scored his thumb across my nipple, and my breath caught in my throat.

I heard footsteps outside in the hallway, and a muffled conversation. The realization that what Ace and I were doing could be clearly heard by anyone wandering down the hall jerked me out of the lustful haze. "I can't do this."

"Do what?" Ace's hands paused in their exploration.

I struggled to sit up, to extricate myself from him. "I can't stay here. Like this. With everyone able to hear what we're doing. It's degrading." I took a deep breath, willing him to understand.

"You can't go home." Implacable iron was in his voice. "Not until we know it's safe."

I knew he was right. Going back to my place would be tantamount to suicide. "We could go to your place?" More of a question than a statement.

Ace was silent for a long moment, and I regretted

blurting that out. Just because we had sex, I had no illusions. It's not like we were suddenly an item, despite what the rest of the bikers thought. We were just scratching an itch, and when it was satisfied, we'd go our separate ways. Asking him to take me to his place was over the line. I opened my mouth to apologize, but he cut me off.

"That might work. Shadow already has a security system in place, cameras and all that shit. Yeah. We can do that." He shifted to capture my gaze. "You'd be stuck with me though. Just me. Here you have Mom and the other guys to talk to."

"I'll survive." The thought of being closeted with Ace didn't frighten me. Maybe a few days of isolation would help to get him out of my system.

A wry smile curved his chiseled features. "I can see you're thrilled with the idea."

"It's just…" I gestured at the door. "I'm used to some kind of privacy, and here everyone knows exactly what we're doing."

"If we go to my place, they're going to assume that's what we're doing. Not much difference." To his credit, he said that with a straight face.

"But they won't get to listen. Besides," I tried to voice my feelings. "I'm used to living alone. Quietly. No one else. This is just too much all at once."

He held up a hand to stop me. "I get it. After Joker checks out your side, we can move your shit to my place. I'll have the prospects go check it out, establish a perimeter."

"Establish a perimeter?" My brow furrowed.

"Sorry. Military talk. Make sure there's a safe zone around the house and set up patrols." He touched my neck, a feather light caress. "These guys are serious bad guys. They know who you are and where you work. So far, I'm not sure they've connected you to me, but when they do, they will come after you with both barrels loaded. Unless we get to them first."

"Or the cops pick them up." I had to hope that was still an option.

"I wouldn't count on that. They probably have one or two in their pocket."

"Oh." That hadn't occurred to me. How had my life gone from boring, nothing but work and school, to this in less than a week? No wonder my head was spinning.

A knock on the door interrupted our discussion.

"You guys decent?" Joker asked.

"Yeah, come on in." Ace let go of me and levered himself off the bed.

Joker stepped into the room, his medic's bag hanging from his hand. "And how's my favorite patient today?" He exchanged a hooded look with Ace.

"Sore." I scooted over and swung my legs over the edge of the bed. "Any chance you've got some stronger painkillers in that bag?"

"No. And you wouldn't need them if you'd obey doctor's orders and avoid any strenuous exercise." He gave me one of those looks usually reserved for naughty toddlers.

"I've been good," I protested.

He didn't look convinced. "Pull off that shirt and let me take a look." Placing his bag on the bedside table, he squatted down beside me and waited for me to expose my side.

"We're planning on moving over to my place." Ace outlined the plan to Joker. "You think she's okay for that?"

"It's healing well, so yeah. I can come check her out over there, or you can come into the clubhouse. I'd like to keep an eye on it daily until I'm sure it's well on the way to healing." Joker finished his inspection and rewound the bandage to hold the gauze in place.

Ace nodded. "Good. I'll get the prospects on it." Pulling out his cell phone he moved to the doorway and started barking orders out.

"He's a good man." Joker looked at me intently.

"Yes, he is." I paused. "We knew each other growing up."

"Ah. That makes sense then. Thought this was a bit quick."

I cocked my head. "What was?"

"Him falling for you. He's never shown much interest in the groupies who show up for parties, other than a quick lay. Suddenly he brings you in and he's all over you like you'd been together for years. Pissed as hell that someone has the gall to threaten you and ready to start a turf war over it without approval."

"Approval from who?" Confusion caused me to frown.

"I think Joker's said enough." Ace pocketed his phone, glaring at Joker.

"Sorry, Prez." Joker ducked his head and glanced at me. "Club business. Forget I said anything."

I looked from one to the other. Club business? What? That the other bikers thought Ace had the hots for me, or that he didn't have the final word on anything that happened? My head was spinning already, without wondering if the club was a democracy or a dictatorship. To be honest, it didn't matter to me.

"The prospects are going to set things up at my place." Ace eyed up the unpacked baggage stacked in front of the new dresser. "Since you haven't unpacked much yet, it should be an easy move."

Chapter Seven

Ace

The move to my place didn't take much. The prospects did the grunt work, and one of them made a grocery run to stock up the fridge with enough food to keep us fed and happy for a couple of weeks. If Emma wanted something special, I'd let one of the prospects know and they could run out and get it for her.

Fuck, I didn't even know what Emma liked to eat. Or if she liked to cook. Or if she even knew how to cook. We'd both grown up poor enough to know twenty ways to serve cheap noodles. Pretty sure she hated them as much as I did at this point.

This might turn out to be a good thing, shacking up and getting to know each other.

I glanced at my watch. I had a couple of hours to spare.

I had a meeting scheduled with the Feds this afternoon. I needed to let them know Emma was permanent.

It was a given that they'd run a background check on her. Kind of a pointless exercise since I had no intention of letting her go, but they had their protocols, and they followed them religiously. Dumb as fuck, and just one of the reasons Riptide cut the umbilical cord decades ago.

Originally Riptide had been formed as a ghost organization for the FBI, and occasionally the CIA. Totally controlled. They'd owned our asses, carefully recruiting guys who knew how to handle themselves in risky missions. Guys willing to take on those nasty undercover missions that might get them killed. Ex-Navy SEALs fit the bill perfectly, or so the desk jockeys thought.

Problem was, we weren't so good at blindly taking orders or we would have stayed in the SEALs. We had our own values, and we stuck to them. We asked questions. We refused to compromise our honor. It wasn't long before we refused to be a ghost organization under the Feds' control. That did not make them happy.

A lot of shit went down at first. Threats. Posturing. The Feds didn't like to be told no. In the end, though, we came to an understanding. Riptide became an independent group.

If the Feds needed something done quietly, they'd contact us. If we all agreed on the mission, we'd do it on a contract basis. They paid us. We kept their reputation lily-white for them. Sometimes justice needs to be served, and you know the pansy-assed legal system just isn't up to the task.

That's where Riptide came in.

Part of the arrangement though, was letting them know about any newbies in the group. Paranoid bunch, those Washington desk jockeys. Seemed to think we could be tricked into taking a spy into our club, someone trying to get to them.

As if we'd just pick up a stranger and let them into our clubhouse. They did not understand the brotherhood, the bond we shared, the family we'd become.

Hell would freeze over before that would happen. Yeah, they could check Emma out, but it meant fuck-all. She belonged, part of the family.

I lay down beside her and wrapped my arms around her, carefully avoiding the gunshot wound. Lowering my head, I nibbled at the tender skin on the back of her neck.

* * *

Emma

I woke up wrapped in my lover's arms.

I tasted the word, rolled it around on my tongue. *Lover*.

Yeah. It felt good. I'd never relied on anyone else, and the thought was terrifying, but I was okay with having a lover.

Ace had made love to me last night. Making love was totally different than fucking. Everything he did, every move he made, he made with my feelings uppermost.

I blushed all over again when I thought about how many times I'd climaxed.

I stretched, smiling when Ace grumbled in his sleep and snuggled closer.

Dropping an affectionate kiss on the top of his head, I slipped out from under his arm and headed to the bathroom. I hadn't had time or energy to unpack my stuff the previous night, so I rifled through the contents of the garbage bag to find something to put on. I wasn't comfortable cavorting around Ace's house in the nude. I was well aware that one or two of the prospects were lurking in the shadows to protect us.

Donning a pair of jeans and a comfy sweatshirt, I wandered out into the kitchen.

I wanted a coffee, but that chrome monster did not look like something I could figure out. Maybe with an owner's manual. And a couple of hours of instruction. And a butler. That might work to coax a drinkable beverage out of it.

Frankly, the thought of attempting to use it had me opening cupboards and searching for a substitute. Ace didn't look like the tea drinking kind of guy but looks could be deceiving.

I managed to find some mugs in the cupboard beside the sink, and a dubious looking can of hot chocolate. By dubious, I mean it looked like it had been purchased when I was in grade school and jammed into the back corner of the cupboard.

Maybe I could just go with hot water and pretend it tasted like coffee?

A knock on the door interrupted my explorations. Abandoning the search for life saving caffeine, I padded out to the front room and peered out the peephole.

Thor stood on the front porch, balancing a tray of takeout coffee in one hand and a paper bag in the other. Saved!

I fumbled with the deadbolt and threw the door open. "Come in!" I snatched the tray of caffeinated goodness from his hands and turned to find Ace glaring at me.

Clad only in a pair of boxers, he looked like an avenging demon. A deliciously well-appointed demon. His hair, tousled from a night's sleep only made him look sexier. Hands on his hips, he narrowed his eyes as he clipped out the words. "You. Do. Not. Go. Near. The. Door." He made it sound like the verdict at a murder trial. Harsh and final.

"But it's Thor. And he had coffee." I frowned in confusion, stretching out my arms to show him the tray.

"Um. I should go." Thor shuffled his feet, his gaze firmly locked on the floor.

"Go." Ace didn't take his eyes off of me.

Thor beat a hasty retreat, pulling the door closed behind him.

"What the heck?" I shouldered past Ace to place the tray down on a side table. "I looked first. I knew it was one of your minions. It's not like I'm an idiot." I picked up one of the cups which had my name scrawled on the top. "Do you think I'm an idiot?"

"No. I just don't think you realize just how deadly the people who are after you can be. What if they were waiting for you to look through that peephole so they could shoot you? What if they had a gun on Thor just out of sight of the door?" His stance relaxed just a tiny bit, and I hated that I noticed the way his biceps flexed.

"Wouldn't they have had to get past your guard dogs first? You told me you had guys patrolling the perimeter." My temper was starting to get the better of me. I put the coffee cup down and turned to face him, my hands on my hips.

"I do." He took one step closer to me, and I could suddenly smell that scent that was peculiarly Ace. "That's not the point. Someone could take them out. Or slip past them. These are not rebellious kids we're talking here. They're hardened killers. Assassins."

"You expect me to just sit here and not even answer the door when I know who's there?"

"That's exactly what I expect. I intend to protect you from everyone, including yourself."

"What if I don't want your protection?"

"You asked for my protection."

It just angered me more, him pointing it out like that. "That was when someone was shooting at me, and I thought they were going to kill me."

"And you think it's over now?" He stared pointedly at my side.

"I think I can handle it. I can disappear. Maybe move or something." I knew I was being unreasonable, but I didn't care. No one got to dictate to me, not even a sexy biker who could make me wet just by looking at me. "I hear California is nice this time of year."

Ace laughed. Actually laughed, a deep-down belly laugh. Damn him. When he stopped acting like a dictator with total control over me, he was irresistible. I couldn't stop the side of my mouth from curving up in the beginnings of a smile.

"What's so damn funny?"

"The thought of you in California." He didn't bother to wipe the silly grin off his face. "You aren't nearly laid back enough for that scene."

I sniffed. "I can be laid back."

Heat shone in his eyes, and that grin took on a predatory look. "Yes, you can. As a matter of fact, I'm thinking of laying you back right now."

He pounced on me so fast, I didn't have time to dodge. As if I actually wanted to. I squealed as he scooped me up in his arms and carried me to the kitchen. Setting me down on the counter, he kept his arms wrapped around me. It amazed me that he could do all that without putting any pressure on my side. He slid his hands up under my shirt, tracing the curve of my spine.

I shifted, attempting to shed the top and he obligingly grasped it by the bottom and pulled it over my head.

Naked from the waist up, I shivered in anticipation.

"Damn." He stared at my breasts; my nipples hardened into stiff peaks. "You are so beautiful."

I chuckled softly. "You're a breast man, are you?"

He didn't bother to answer, leaning forward to stroke his tongue across first one, and then the other.

Scooting closer to the edge, I arched my back. He responded by sucking one breast deep into his mouth, his tongue tracing a blazing circle around the nipple.

I took a deep breath, inhaling his warm musky scent. God, how I wanted him. Wanted to feel him inside me. On top of me. Surrounding me.

In his arms, I felt safe, secure. Contented.

I didn't want to explore that too deeply. This was just temporary, until the danger was over.

He moved his attention to the other breast, and I gasped. Wrapping my arms around his neck I pressed up against him, spreading my legs to grind my aching groin into him.

He tore his mouth away from my breast and hooked his thumbs in the waistband of my jeans. "Lose them."

He tugged downward, and I quickly unzipped them and wriggled my way free. Tossing the pants aside, he slid one hand down to cup my center. His eyes locked on me, blazing heat. "Shit, you're ready for me, wet as fuck."

I bobbed my head, not trusting myself to speak.

Liquid heat washed through me as he slid one finger through the folds and inside me. I whimpered and ground myself against him. Wanting more. Wanting him inside me.

"I need to taste you." He lowered his head, his hands grasping my hips as he swiped his tongue across my pussy, while inserting a second finger.

To say I went ballistic would be an understatement. I fisted his hair, holding him against me as he tongued me, and finger fucked me at the same time. I rode his fingers and his tongue, mindless of anything but the heavenly feel of him between my thighs.

He twirled his fingers, finding that spot that had me whimpering as darts of white-hot lust burned through me.

He pumped his fingers in and out, rotating them to make sure I felt every single move he made. His warm breath trailed over my naked body. "Come for me, Emma. Let yourself go."

His tongue swirled around my clit, and the sensation sent me screaming over the edge. My pussy tightened around his fingers, as wave after wave of intense pleasure washed through me.

Ace lapped at the liquid dripping from my pussy, his tongue scooping up every bit of moisture. He kept his fingers inside me, moving in silent rhythm as the aftershocks slowly faded.

"Better than coffee," I muttered as I slumped against him. "Who knew?"

He chuckled. "You mean sex?"

I mumbled, my eyes still closed. "Yeah. Morning sex is better than morning coffee. I don't think I can move now."

"No problem. I'll do the moving." He stepped back, and I immediately felt bereft of his warmth.

I opened my eyes and saw him toss his boxers aside. My gaze tracked lower, and I gulped at the size of his erection.

"What's wrong? Did I hurt you?" Concern flashed across his face.

I shook my head. "No. It's just, that is… I didn't get a good look at you. Before. You're huge!"

He grinned. "Now that's what a guy likes to hear." He ripped open the condom he'd produced as if out of thin air and quickly sheathed himself. Stepping forward, he positioned the tip of his cock at my entrance. "Just relax and enjoy yourself. I'll do all the work this time."

I spread my legs wider, as if cradling him

between my thighs would somehow help ease him in.

"This time? You plan on making a habit of this?"

"Morning sex in the kitchen? Hell yeah."

I leaned forward. "Kiss me."

He shook his head. "Not yet. I want to see your face when I come inside you." He held onto my hips, his movements slow and rhythmic. His cock eased its way in, and he kept the gentle rhythm up, pushing deeper and deeper until his balls were tight against my ass.

Pleasure danced across every nerve ending. I felt deliciously full. Closing my eyes, I tilted my head back, moaning softly.

"Like that?" He nibbled on my earlobe.

I gasped, unable to form a coherent sentence. Hooking my heels behind him, I matched him thrust for thrust as he picked up the pace. Faster. Harder.

I couldn't hold back, I came first, muffling my scream against his shoulder.

My muted shout triggered Ace's own climax, and he didn't bother to try and hide it. "Fuck, woman! You are amazing!" He thrust one last time before collapsing against me.

He rested his chin on my head, and we snuggled there for a few moments, panting softly.

I felt content, complete. I didn't want to move, to speak. It just felt so right.

Ace's phone rang, breaking the spell. He pulled out of me and picked the offending tech up.

"What?" He barked out the single word.

I couldn't hear the other side of the conversation, but the look on Ace's face told me our morning tryst was over. He glanced over at me, mouthing an apology before he strode out of the room.

Club business. I was beginning to hate that phrase.

* * *

Ace

I wasn't about to tell Emma how close someone had come to breaching the perimeter. Fuck!

The prospects caught him sneaking in the shadows, but they'd been a little overzealous. Guy was out cold. Hard to get answers from someone who wasn't conscious. I checked to make sure Emma was distracted for the moment and slipped out the back door. Thor met me outside and led me to the garden shed where they'd secured the intruder.

"Don't look like anyone I've ever seen around, and he's not wearing a cut." Thor shrugged his shoulders. "Might have taken him for a guy in the wrong place at the wrong time, except we found this in his pocket." He handed me a folded slip of paper. It had my address on it, along with instructions to kill the girl and anyone who got in the way. Clipped to the top corner was a grainy picture of Emma. Now where the hell had they got that?

I pocketed the paper, and hit quick dial to Beast, the club enforcer.

"Yeah?" Beast was a man of few words.

"Got an intruder. Need you to find out what you can from him."

"Location?"

"My place. Thor has him trussed up in the back shed."

"On it."

The connection went dead, and I pocketed the phone. "Beast will be here shortly. Do whatever he says. Let me know when you have any info for me."

"Yes, sir." Thor nudged the intruder with the toe of his biker boot. "Tiny is checking the perimeter to make sure there aren't any other nasty surprises waiting for us."

Already regretting letting Emma talk me into staying here, I nodded curtly. The clubhouse was way easier to defend. I pivoted on my heel and headed back to the house.

When I entered, I found Emma pacing back and forth in the mudroom. At least she'd had the sense to stay in the house. She halted; her arms crossed. "Well?"

"Well, what?"

"You tell me it's 'club business,' leave the room, then sneak out the back door. So, what the hell is going on?"

I sighed. "Someone tried to slip past the prospects and get into the house." I handed her the piece of paper Thor had found on the guy. "Looks like they've connected us. I didn't think they'd manage that quite this quick."

She studied the paper. "That's my college ID photo."

Damn. They knew where she worked, where she went to school, and her name. It wouldn't take much to find out her home address and anything else they'd need to track her down. "This information is public? Anyone with a computer or smartphone would have access to it?"

She frowned. "I guess. All they'd have to do is search the university website."

"What else is on that website? Your address? Phone number?"

She shook her head. "No. But it would list my classes, and it wouldn't take much to get from that to where I'm going to be, and when." Realization flickered across her face. "I can't go to school until this is over, can I?"

"Sorry, babe, but no."

"They'll boot me out of the program if I'm a no show for too long."

"How long is too long?"

She shrugged. "I'm not sure."

"How about if you have a medical reason for not showing up?"

Her hand went to the wound on her side. "You want me to tell them I was shot?"

"No." I reached out and pulled her toward me. I couldn't resist touching her any longer. "Shadow is our tech guy. He could hack in and place something on your record that shows you have a medical reason for not attending. Maybe meningitis, or some type of disease that requires you to quarantine. How much time is left in this semester?"

She squinted. "It just started, so almost four months until exams."

"Perfect," I said. "Meanwhile you stay with me."

"I can't miss months of classes and expect to pass an exam."

"Shadow can have lessons sent to you. How about we just have him insert a vague doctor's note for now and see what happens? Might fix this quick."

The frown on her face told me how likely she thought that was. Too bad. Until we had this thing under control, she'd just have to learn to trust me. Meanwhile, it gave me a chance to woo her. "Want to go out to dinner with me? Somewhere fancy?"

She blinked at the sudden change of subject. "What?"

I used one finger to tilt her head back so I could skim a quick kiss across her lusciously pink lips. "Dinner. With me. Fancy-ass. Not a cheap take-out joint."

"Why?"

"Because I'm irresistible?"

She snorted. "Try again."

"Because you're stuck with me for the next while, and we can't spend all our time in bed. We should probably get to know each other better. And I'd really like to take you out on a date."

"Like a real date? Okay."

It was my turn to look confused. "Okay? Just like that?"

A gorgeous smile lit up her face. "Just like that. Remember, you said fancy, so I expect you to deliver."

"Done!"

"So where are we going?"

It was my turn to grin. "You'll have to wait and see. It's a surprise."

"Fair enough. Just tell me, do I need a ballgown, or will a dress and heels suffice?"

I pretended to consider. "I think a nice dress and some heels will work."

"And just when is this fancy date taking place?"

"Tonight is as good a time as any. Say six thirty?"

Her jaw dropped. "Tonight? You know those kinds of places need reservations, don't you? Like weeks ahead of time? Especially for a Saturday night."

I gave her a smug look. "Not a problem. I know a guy. "

Chapter Eight

Emma

Why on earth had I agreed to this? For one thing, I hadn't bothered to grab any dresses when I'd been home. Didn't exactly think I'd need them, bunking in with a biker and all. When I mentioned it to Ace, though, he'd sent one of the minions over to my place to grab some dresses and my pitifully scant array of shoes.

I eyed up my three choices they'd brought back. In their defense, I only had four dresses, and the prospects had brought three of them back along with all four of my pairs of shoes. I picked up the green sheath and held it up in front of me.

Nope. It made me look like a cucumber on steroids. Not sure why I'd never turfed it. The pink one was out as well. A typical bridesmaid dress, it was much too frothy for a dinner date. That left the sky-blue cocktail dress with the back pretty much missing. I'd never actually worn it anywhere outside of the house. It showed a little more skin than I was comfortable with, but if I could come up with a sweater or a wrap to wear over it, it would suffice.

If the man expected to be dazzled, he needed to give me more than a couple of hours to get ready. Hanging up the chosen dress on the back of the bedroom door, I headed into the ensuite to fluff and buff as best I could in a strange bathroom.

An hour later, after some serious primping, I was ready. Butterflies fluttered in my gut. Why, I'm not sure. This was Ace. I'd known him forever. He'd seen me with pigtails, with mud caked on my clothes, and probably worse. Hell, he'd seen me naked less than twenty-four hours ago. So why was I nervous about seeing him with my hair and makeup done properly and a pair of three-inch heels?

Because you like him, and you want him to see you as something other than his little brother's playmate, whispered the demon on my shoulder.

Well, we'd done the horizontal nasty already, so I doubted he saw me as a kid anymore, but the little demon was right. I liked Ace. A lot. Maybe more than I should.

This was different than the crush I'd had on him as a kid. He made me feel safe. Secure. I couldn't think of when I'd ever felt this comfortable with another person. And that was the problem. I'd worked so hard at getting out of the crappy neighborhood I'd grown up in, getting on the path to a degree and the possibility of feeling I belonged in the respectable community. I couldn't just throw all that away because my knees went weak when I saw Ace's eyes darken with lust.

Was there a way to reconcile my world to his? Did I even want to?

I grabbed my purse and headed to the living room. I intended to enjoy tonight. Tomorrow was soon enough to worry about reality.

"Wow!" Ace scanned me from head to toe. "You clean up good, babe!"

"As do you." In clean black jeans with a button-down shirt stretched tight across that massive chest, Ace looked downright classy. Even the leather cut didn't distract from the look.

"Do you wear that everywhere?" I gestured at the leather vest.

"Yup. It bothers you?"

I shook my head. "No. But it might be a problem if we're going somewhere fancy."

"It won't. The owner is a friend of the club."

I digested that in silence. He'd said somewhere fancy, so I'd assumed it wasn't related to his club. The fact that the owner was chummy with a motorcycle club had me curious as to exactly where we were going. "So not Red Lobster?"

Ace hooted with laughter. "Red Lobster isn't even close to this."

"You're not going to tell me, are you?"

He smirked. "Nah. I'm having too much fun." He turned to open the door, and I glimpsed a shoulder holster under the cut.

"You're wearing a gun."

He raised one brow. "Problem? I have a permit for it."

"I'm just not used to going out with guys who carry on a date."

"Better to have it and not need it, than to need it and not have it." He stopped and turned to me. "You do know I'm a biker?"

I blushed. "Point taken." Somehow, the gun made the whole situation a little more real. As if the wound on my side wasn't enough of a reminder.

He opened the door with a flourish. "After you."

"Such a gentleman!" I slid into the passenger side of the truck. "When do I get to see your bike?"

"When Joker says your side is healed enough." Ace circled the front of the truck to climb in the driver's side. "Until then, you'll have to make do with the cage."

"Cage?"

"It's what we bikers call cars and trucks. You are surrounded by metal, in a cage. As opposed to being free to feel the wind whistling past like you do on a bike."

"Oh." I suppose that made sense. In a twisted sort of way. "What kind of bike do you have?"

He looked over at me and waggled his brows. "A big one."

I laughed. "You are incorrigible!"

"Is that a really big word that means sexy?"

"No. It's a really big word that means smart-ass."

"So, you've noticed my ass?"

I had, but I wasn't about to admit it. I turned my head to look out the window. "I don't recognize this part of town." It looked like one of those old areas that had been gentrified to garner top dollar on the real estate market.

Ace slanted a look at me. "Change the subject much?"

"When it suits me." It was my turn to smirk.

He pulled the truck into a parking lot beside a big old brick building. I looked around but couldn't see anything resembling a restaurant.

"We're going to picnic in the parking lot?"

"Nope." He came round and held the door open for me.

"So?"

"Wait and see." He elbowed the door shut. Sliding an arm around my waist, he led me across the parking lot to the back of one of the buildings. Concrete steps led down to a door at basement level. Throwing a mischievous look at me, he knocked on the bulky oak door.

* * *

Ace

Emma couldn't look more tempting if she were standing beside me stark naked. That little blue number she had on covered a minimal amount of skin while hinting at the delights to be had when I managed to get her out of it. Standing behind her, I could see all the way down her naked back, and the flared skirt dancing across her buttocks was just begging me to slide my hand under it.

Fuck, did she do this on purpose just to tease me? My cock had been in a semi-permanent state of erection ever since she'd stumbled into my house.

Had it only been a few days ago?

Within moments, the door was opened by Stanley, an old buddy from my military days. Dressed in black pants and waistcoat over a white button-down shirt, with a bow tie to finish, he looked like a butler out of some damn movie set. It kind of worked here though. Made the place seem classy. Hard to believe he'd been the one of the best hand-to-hand combat veterans less than a decade ago.

Bowing low from the waist, Stanley beckoned us in with a sweep of his hand.

Emma tilted her head, sending me a quick look before preceding me inside. I wasn't sure if that look meant she was impressed, or wishing she'd knocked on someone else's door that night.

The entryway was dimly lit and opened into a hallway decorated in old world elegance. The flickering lights on the wall were reminiscent of the gaslights in vogue at the turn of the century. Stanley and his partner, Geoff, had done a good job of staging the place. Geoff was a renowned chef, and this was their dream come true, to work together in an upscale restaurant that catered to a few select customers at a time.

Stanley led us to a room at the far end of the hallway. A real wood fire crackled in the fireplace, casting a flickering glow over the rich decor. The walls were painted in a muted green, with expensive looking landscape pictures hung at strategic spots.

The table, clad in crisp white linen, took center of the room, with two plush chairs arranged around it. Set with sparkling crystal glassware, gleaming silver utensils, and delicate bone China, it screamed high end quality. A fresh floral arrangement held two tapered candles, giving the room a romantic touch.

Holy shit. I turned to Stanley and caught the faintest hint of a smirk on his expressionless face. He hadn't been kidding when he said his place would wow my new lady.

I gave him a discreet thumbs up, before turning to pull out a chair for Emma. Pacing to the opposite side of the table, I sat down. "Impressed?"

Her eyes went from the artwork to the perfectly set table. "It's beautiful. Seems a little upscale for someone in your line of…" She hesitated, "Work. How did you find it?"

"Stanley here is an old Navy buddy." I inclined my head. "Stanley, meet Emma."

"Delighted." He swept an approving look over Emma. "About time this old dog settled down. Would you like to start with something to drink?"

I decided to ignore his assumption that we were a couple. It actually felt good. I glanced at the bulge under Emma's scanty dress where the bullet wound was bandaged. "Did Joker say not to mix the painkillers with alcohol?"

"He didn't say, but probably safe to steer clear." She smiled sweetly up at Stanley. "Nice to meet you. I'll just have a glass of sparkling water."

"A beer for me please."

By the flicker of disapproval on Stanley's face, I got the feeling most of the patrons did not order beer.

"Very good, sir." He turned and glided out of the room.

Emma looked around, nodding her approval at the elegant décor. "What is this place?"

"It's known as The Cellar. I had to call in a favor to get us in on short notice. It's reservations only, and they book weeks in advance."

"Well now it sounds expensive." She lifted her head and inhaled deeply. "Not sure what that is, but it smells wonderful."

I loved the way her feelings showed on her face. "Whatever Geoff cooks, I'm sure it will taste great. And you are worth every penny."

She looked uncomfortable at the compliment, and I made a note to keep the sweet talk to a minimum. Didn't want to scare her off. She was under the impression this thing between us was going to burn itself out quickly. I knew better.

Stanley returned with a crystal glass of sparkling water and a fancy stein of beer. Classy touch. No bottled crap here. I waited until he departed to lift my glass in a salute. "To old friends, and new beginnings."

Emma lifted her glass and tapped it against mine. The emotions playing across her face were easy to read. She was happy but scared at the same time. I wondered if the fear was of me, my club, or the feelings that she couldn't ignore.

Time to put her at ease. I could be charming if I put my mind to it.

"What are you studying at university?"

"Medicine." A ghost of a smile played around her lips. "The plan is to get licensed as a paramedic, and then study to become a doctor. I'd love to specialize in pediatrics."

"That's a children's doctor, right?"

"Yeah." She toyed with the stem of her glass. "I know it's a tough specialty, watching kids in pain, but I think I could make a difference. If I could take that pain away from them, that would be great."

The passion in her voice when she talked about working with kids wowed me. "That's a really damn cool ambition. I know you'll make it too. You can do anything you set your mind to."

She wrinkled her nose. "Not sure about that. It's expensive, and it takes dedication. That's why I don't have time for this." She gestured at the two of us. "I can't let myself be distracted."

I reached across the table and captured her hand. "The right guy wouldn't be a distraction. He could help you."

I saw the trapped look in her eyes, and quickly let go of her hand. "Tell me about your job at the bar. If you plan on becoming a doctor, why did you decide to take a job like that? Wouldn't it make more sense to do something in the medical field?"

She retracted her hand, moving it out of reach. "Not much to tell, really. The tips can be good most nights, and the hours don't conflict with my school courses. Money and time are both big issues. After a day in class, it's refreshing to just do something without having to think a lot." She took a sip of the water. "What about you? How did you end up the President of a motorcycle club? I would have thought you'd make a career in the Navy SEALs."

"I considered it." And I had some good memories of those days, right up until that last mission went sour. "I re-upped a couple of times. Really enjoyed the comradeship and the feeling of family, you know? Then there comes a time when you know you need to get out, so I got out."

She gazed at me soberly, and I appreciated her not asking for details. I was not ready to discuss that. Maybe I never would be.

Stanley glided back into the room and placed a dish in front of each of us. "Your appetizer. *Foie gras.*" With a deferential nod of his head, he quietly left the room.

Emma's brow wrinkled as she eyed up the dish.

"You don't like it?"

She tilted her head up. "I've never had it. What is *foie gras*?"

I chuckled. "No idea. I usually eat at those take-out joints on the highway, but they didn't seem like a good place to take a date I wanted to impress."

She took a tiny spoonful of the mixture and put it in her mouth. Looking surprised, she met my gaze. "It's good."

Relief washed through me. This was the kind of place where you ordered in advance of the date, and I hadn't known what the fuck we'd get to eat. I'd opted to let chef decide on the meal. Left to me, we'd have a two-course meal consisting of steak for the main and chocolate cake for dessert.

The meal progressed slowly. I'd never thought to ask how many courses it might contain. My eat-in restaurant experience was sadly lacking.

"I love fish." Emma beamed at me when Stanley placed the plate in front of her. For the main course, Geoff had cooked some kind of fish. Sea bass, Stanley informed us, pan seared to crispy perfection.

Emma's eyes shone softly in the flickering light. I wanted to lean across the table and kiss her. "Me too." I picked up a fork and took a bite. "Usually, mine is cooked over a fire beside the stream where I caught it."

"You like to fish?"

"Yes. Didn't do all that shit when I was a kid, so I've been making up for lost time."

She sighed. "Yeah. I sometimes wonder how it would have been if I'd had a normal childhood."

"Not much point in trying to rewrite the past." I couldn't keep my hands to myself any longer. Reaching out, I stroked a finger down her cheek. "The future is what counts, and it's what we make of it."

"True, I suppose. That's why I'm determined to make something of myself." The melancholy look on her face tugged at my heartstrings.

"You ever think about having kids of your own?" I'd honestly never considered it until this moment. I could picture a mini-Emma running around, pigtails flying behind her.

"No." She gave a negative shake of her head. "I'm barely managing to hold my own, or at least I was until now. Adding a kid to the mix is not a good idea."

"Maybe not now, but someday?"

She picked at the food on her plate, avoiding meeting my eyes. "I decided a long time ago that I would not put a kid through the kind of childhood we had. When and if I decide to have kids, it's going to be when I know they will have a chance to be happy."

I understood her decision. I'd seen too many kids get into gangs, drugs or alcohol just because they didn't get the love they needed at home. Hell, half of Riptide could tell you horror stories about their childhoods, and they were the lucky ones. "So, you have thought about it."

She shrugged. "Yeah. I know all about the biological clock running out, but that doesn't change my mind. If time runs out, and I can't have kids of my own I could always adopt. We both know there's a ton of kids in the foster system that could use a stable home life."

"True." But I still liked the idea of a little mini-Emma.

"You haven't explained how you made the jump from upstanding Navy SEAL to biker."

"Not as hard as you might think." I squinted as I considered how much I could safely reveal. "I got to talking to another ex-SEAL and he told me about Riptide. Got me an invite to see what they were about, and I liked what I saw. I felt comfortable with them. They're a family, in a good way. We look out for each other."

Emma forked the last of the fish into her mouth, swallowing. "Sounds like you found a home."

"I guess I did." I thought of all the things I'd learned from Riptide, the way they'd helped me transition back to life in the States.

"I always thought of all motorcycle clubs as criminal. You know. Murdering, pillaging, drug running. That's not what your club is like though, is it." She made it more of a statement than a question.

"No. Those clubs are known as the one-percenters. The other ninety nine percent of us are mostly law abiding. We don't have anything to do with drugs, and I think pillaging went out of style a few centuries ago with the end of the Viking raids."

"You didn't mention murder?" she pointed out.

"Do I look like a murderer to you?"

She grimaced. "Nope. And I have a very current item to compare you to. I really must ask, how do you support yourselves if there's no drug money and no murder for hire?"

"We run a bar in town, and we have investments. One of the guys is a whiz with the stock market thing. We all work the bar, and it's packed most weekends.

The customers like to rub shoulders with us bikers. Kind of gives them a kinky thrill. Weeknights are slower, but still bring in cash."

"Huh." She looked thoughtful.

"Is that a good 'huh'?"

"It's just not what I expected. You're not what I expected."

"I'll take that as a good thing."

We were interrupted by Stanley returning with dessert. He set the dish between the two of us, and the scent of rich dark chocolate wafted up to tease us. He set a spoon down in front of each of us, indicating the dessert would be a shared event.

"Chocolate lava cake!" Emma squealed in delight.

"Chocolate fondant," Stanley corrected her, with a faint smile curving his lips.

"What's the difference?"

Stanley chuckled. "The price." He turned to me. "Would you and the lady like coffee or tea?"

I looked at Emma, who shook her head. "No, thanks. I'm already full, but I'm going to give dessert my best shot."

"As you wish." Another bow, and he departed.

"Is this like that spaghetti scene in the movie with the dogs?" Emma picked up her spoon and scooped a mouthful of chocolate from the dish. "Like we each start on our side and meet in the middle?"

I picked up the other spoon. "Only if I get to lick the chocolate off your mouth at the end."

Chapter Nine

Emma

I'd never seen this side of Ace before. As a kid, he always seemed grim and unapproachable. Hot as hell, but with that don't-touch-me vibe. We'd finished the chocolate lava cake -- yes, I was still going to call it that -- and lingered for a while before heading back to the truck.

I climbed in and scooted over to the middle of the bench seat. "Thank you." I placed a hand on his leg. "That was amazing. I swear I've never been in a place that fancy before in my life."

"You're welcome." He covered my hand with his and glanced over at me.

We drove in companionable silence for a few miles. The sun was just setting, spreading a golden red glow across the landscape. Everything was going well at the moment, and I refused to spoil the mood by thinking about how screwed up my life was right now.

Turned out I didn't have to. Ace spoiled it for me.

"Hate to get serious again, but we need to talk about living arrangements for the next little while."

"I thought I was staying with you?" I swallowed nervously.

"Yes," he said as he navigated a sharp corner, "but much as I love having you all to myself, it would be a hell of a lot easier to keep you safe if we were at the clubhouse."

I studied my shoes, not wanting to meet his gaze. "I really don't want to go live in a house full of macho guys who can hear everything we do." I tried to pull my hand back, but he kept it captive on his leg. "For one thing, morning sex in the kitchen would be out."

"That's your only concern?" He actually had the nerve to laugh. "Because I could place the kitchen off limits for an hour each morning if you feel it's necessary to ravage me on a regular basis."

I yanked my hand free and scuttled to the far side of the seat. "It's not that, you idiot. It's my life. Me. You put me in there and it makes me feel like a kid who can't take care of herself. Like when I used to get caught doing something my mom didn't approve of, and she locked me in my room." I made imaginary quotes in the air with my fingers. "'For my own good.'"

"Not quite the same thing. I'm trying to keep you alive." He grimaced. "The murderer knows way too much about you. Where you live. Where you work. And you saw that paper Thor found on the guy who tried to break in. They put a hit out on you. A contract on your head. Dead. Not dead or alive. Dead."

"Yeah. I got that but your guys stopped him." I swallowed hard. "I can't hide forever. I need to get on with my life."

"Hopefully we can figure this out and put a stop to it soon. Then you can do whatever the fuck you want. Until then, you need to be smart." Ace gripped the steering wheel so tight his knuckles were going white. "I need to know you're safe, and the best way to do that is to have you at the clubhouse. It could take more time than I originally thought to put an end to this." He pulled into the driveway and saluted the prospects on perimeter guard.

Right. "Time. The one thing I don't have a ton of. Actually, one of two things, cash being the other. I need to figure out how to keep my life on track while all this goes down. I can't go to work, and it sounds like I can't go to school either." How the heck had my life become such a train wreck?

"I said I could get you a job at the bar the club owns, and I meant it. You'd be safe there, and you'd make some money. For later." He held the front door open for me.

"Sure, I guess that works." I sighed loudly. What choice did I have?

"I'd say I need to get you a set of keys, but you're not supposed to be out without alone." Ace came up behind me. Putting his hands on my shoulders, he gently turned me to face him. "Hey. I know it sucks, but it's not forever. We'll take care of your problem and then things can go back to normal."

"I don't think so," I said softly as I reached up to trace my fingers across his lips. "Normal isn't what it used to be, is it? At least not between us."

The look he gave me was pure molten lust. His hands dropped to my ass, and he pulled me tight enough to feel his rock-hard cock pressed against me. "No, it's not, but is that such a bad thing?"

He lowered his mouth to claim mine, his tongue demanding entrance. He proceeded to kiss me thoroughly, his tongue stroking over mine as his fingers sank into my hair and held me in place. His scent filled the air around me, warm and muskily male.

I gave myself up to the primitive urges flooding through me as Ace's hands roamed down my back to cup my ass. Heat danced across every nerve ending, and a low moan escaped my lips. I melted against him, silently surrendering.

"I want you. Now." I muttered the words against his lips.

Scooping me up, he strode down the hall to his room and kicked the door open.

He placed me gently me on the bed and stood

looking down at me for a long moment before he methodically stripped his clothes off, tossing them carelessly aside. His posture screamed raw sexual appeal.

I propped myself up on one elbow to admire the show. His chin was covered in a day's worth of scruff and his hair was mussed up from me running my fingers through it downstairs. His eyes, normally slate gray, were darkened with lust, and muscles covered his whole body, as did a multitude of tattoos.

They were truly awesome, but right now I was more interested in his cock. Long and thick, it jutted stiff and hard from a nest of dark curls, promising an evening of carnal delight.

I ran my tongue around the circle of my lips, my nostrils flaring to capture his scent as he stalked naked across the room.

"Strip. Now." Low and gravelly, his voice sent shivers of want and need snaking down my spine. Normally I'd object to being ordered around like a puppy but the way he said it made it sound like more of a promise than an order.

I shifted to my knees and lifted the dress up over my head, careful not to disturb the bandage that still covered my side. Keeping my eyes locked on Ace, I tossed it to the floor and reached behind me to unhook my bra. The lacy confection slid to the bed, freeing my breasts to his hot gaze.

Posing before him in nothing but a thong and a pair of high heeled shoes that laced all the way up to my knees, I lifted one finger to my mouth and slowly sucked it in while peeking at the hulking biker from beneath my lashes.

Ace pounced with the speed of a hungry wolf, taking me down to the bed in one smooth movement.

"Tease," he said as he slipped his fingers beneath the lacy thong and ripped it off me. Even then, he managed to avoid my wounded side as he towered over my prone form and lowered his head to suck one taut nipple into his mouth.

Still sucking on my breast, he lowered his hand and slid one finger inside my slick pussy. "You're wet. So damn fucking wet."

Reaching past me, he opened the drawer and fished out a condom. Ripping the package open with his teeth, he quickly rolled it down over his impressive length.

"I want you." I reached up to run my hands across the sexy scruff on his chin. "Now. Fuck me now."

He chuckled, a dark growly sound that sent heat curling through my belly. Scooting down, he settled himself between my thighs. His tongue was pure magic, sliding in and out of my wet pussy, making me twist and squirm. He inserted one finger, pumping it in and out with a circular twist that drove me crazy.

My breath escaped in a tortured hiss as he found that one spot that had me melting into a pool of liquid heat. I bucked my hips up, wordlessly begging for more. Faster. Harder.

He feasted on my pussy like a man facing starvation. His tongue. His fingers. His mouth.

I could feel myself getting close. I begged him not to stop, whimpering shamelessly as he upped the pressure on my most sensitive parts.

"Come on, babe. Come for me." He lifted his head to spear me with his gaze. "I want to taste your desire."

I couldn't answer, couldn't form a sentence. I was so lost in the feeling of his mouth on me. His fingers stroking inside me. His masculine scent surrounding me, a mixture of lust and sweat and desire. He knew exactly what it took to drive me insane with want, to make me crave him with every fiber of my being.

My orgasm washed over me in intense waves, and I arched up against him, grinding myself against his face.

Ace lapped at the moisture dripping from me, the evidence of my pleasure. When I finally stopped squirming against his mouth, he lifted himself over me and stared into my dazed eyes. "You good?"

I nodded. "Yeah. But I still want you. Want to feel you filling me up with that massive cock of yours."

"Fuck, babe. Don't have to ask me twice." Reaching down, he took himself in one hand and positioned himself at my entrance.

I closed my eyes and let myself revel in the feel of him, the anticipation of what was about to happen. He paused, the tip of his cock barely inside me, and I opened my eyes to find him staring down at me. Wordlessly, we looked into each other's eyes for a long moment before he bucked his hips and speared me with one massive thrust.

I gasped, my breath hitching in my throat as he thrust in and out, fucking me with a delicious abandon. I gave myself up to the feeling of Ace in me, on top of me, surrounding me with his presence.

He rolled over, taking me with him and suddenly I was on top, in charge of the pace. A sense of power surged through me as I rode him fast and hard, like a wild horse running free on the mountain ranges. Our sweat mingled, and he grasped my hips, holding me but letting me set the pace.

I threw my head back and felt my hair cascade

down my back. I sucked in a deep breath, then let out a cry as another orgasm, more intense than the first washed over me in waves. My channel clenched around his shaft as a series of aftershocks pulsed through me.

Moments later, I felt a surge of heat just as Ace let out a roar, signaling his own release. I arched my back, riding him with eyes closed as I reveled in pure feelings.

I collapsed on top of my burly biker lover, my head resting in the crook of his shoulder. A thin sheen of sweat covered both of us as our breathing slowly returned to normal. Warmth and an unfamiliar feeling of belonging washed over me. Despite everything that had happened, everything that I thought I wanted or didn't want, this felt so good. So right.

Ace nuzzled the top of my head, skimming the lightest of kisses across my forehead. "This is where you belong, where we belong." Just as he reached up to brush a stray lock of hair off my face, the sound of shattering glass echoed from the front of the house.

"Now what the fuck?"

* * *

Ace

I knew we should have gone back to the clubhouse. Why had I let Emma talk me out of it? Grabbing my pants, I pulled them on commando style and yanked my cut on over my naked chest as I raced out into the living room.

The front window was destroyed, shards of glass covering the floor, and in the middle of the living room floor sat a flat black box with wires wrapped around it, and an alarm type clock duct taped to it.

Fuck! Fuck! Fuck!

I'd seen enough shit to know what it was. A homemade bomb. The alarm clock would be the timer, since it hadn't exploded yet. No idea how long before it went off, and I didn't waste any time trying to find out.

Pivoting sharply, I raced back to the bedroom.

"We need to get the hell out of here. Now!" I grabbed a blanket, wrapped it around a naked, stunned Emma and threw her over my shoulders.

"What the hell?" Emma squirmed against me.

"Bomb. No time." Pausing to grab my pistol and tuck it into my waistband, I raced to the back door and threw it open.

Hopefully there were no hostiles outside waiting for us to emerge. A quick glance showed me one of the prospects pistol-whipping a guy, who collapsed to the ground unconscious. Hopefully the only one. I raced across the lawn, yelling at the prospects as I went. "Bomb! Get back!"

Tiny left the unconscious perp where he'd landed and raced to intercept me.

"Bomb?"

I nodded, setting Emma on the ground carefully so as not to disturb the blanket. "Someone threw it through the living room window. Didn't stop to check details. Looked like a timer strapped to a brick of plastic explosive. Don't know how much time we…"

The rest of my sentence was lost as a spectacular explosion rocked my house. The force of the blast pushed Emma back against me, and I wrapped my arms around her, resting my chin on the top of her head as I watched my house disintegrate.

"Holy shit." Tiny stared at the wreckage.

"Where's Thor?" I craned my neck to see if I could spot him.

"He was patrolling the front. Should have been far enough away when the blast went off." A frown furrowed Tiny's forehead. "Hopefully he didn't go inside looking for you when he heard the window break."

"Fuck." I didn't want to let go of Emma. No telling what threats lurked outside the range of sight. "Go check up on him."

"No need." Tiny gestured with his chin. "Here he comes."

Thor limped across the grass in our direction, his figure outlined by the fire slowly engulfing my home. Flames shot out the windows, and thick black smoke curled skyward. Even at this distance I could feel the heat.

A look of total shock covered Emma's face, and she clung to me like a drowning victim clinging to a life raft. I tucked her against me, pulling the blanket up snug to her chin.

Sirens sounded in the distance, the pitch increasing as they got closer. Emma didn't need to be caught up in this mess.

"Can you get her to the clubhouse?" I glanced over at Thor. "I don't want her to have to deal with the authorities when they start in on the questioning. You know they're going to make assumptions when they realize it's my place."

Thor straightened, nodding in the affirmative. "Sure thing, Prez. I came on my bike, but it got toasted in the blast. I'll get one of the other prospects to bring in a cage."

I smoothed Emma's rumpled hair back from her forehead. The shock was clear on her face as she looked up at me. "I want you to go with Thor. He'll take you to the clubhouse and I'll meet you there as soon as I deal with this. You okay with that?"

"Don't I have to stay and talk to the cops when they get here?"

I shook my head. "Not a good idea. As far as the authorities are concerned, I was home alone when this happened. You've got enough to deal with right now."

"Are you sure?" She looked doubtful. "I don't want you getting into more trouble for me."

"I'm sure." I glanced down the road. The sounds of the fire trucks were getting louder, but they weren't in sight yet. "Trust me, you don't want the authorities to link you to this. As soon as they realize it's my place, they'll likely put it down as some kind of biker turf war. Probably won't even bother to investigate it."

Emma tilted her head, and I dropped a swift hard kiss on her lips before releasing her. I watched as Thor led her away in the opposite direction. Even if his bike had survived the blast, he'd have to call for someone to bring a cage. No way she'd to be able to ride on the back of his bike wearing nothing but a blanket. Suited me just fine. The uncivilized caveman part of me didn't like the thought of my Emma riding on the back of another man's bike, her arms wrapped around his waist and her legs spread wide against him.

Thor led her around the corner onto the side street. Smart guy, making sure she was out of sight of any incoming authorities before he called for a cage. I made a mental note to look into letting him patch in soon.

With Emma safely taken care of, I turned my attention back to my house. By now, the flames were shooting out the roof and one side had collapsed into itself. There must have been some fucking high-powered accelerant in that bomb for the structure to be fully engulfed so quickly. My guess was they'd hoped to catch me asleep. If the initial blast didn't kill me, I would have been overcome with smoke before I regained consciousness.

Too bad for them, I'd been awake and alert. If I hadn't been intent on making love to Emma, both of us would be dead by now.

The fire truck careened around the corner and screeched to a halt in front of the house. Firemen poured off it and stopped to stare at the blazing inferno. One of them raced over to me. "Anyone in there?" he asked without taking his eyes off the blaze.

I shook my head. "No. I live alone." I gestured at Tiny. "My buddy and I were in the backyard when the bomb went off. Just shooting the shit. Lucky timing we weren't inside."

"Good." He nodded. "Looks like an unstable structure. Since we don't have to worry about anyone inside, I'm going to have the guys establish a perimeter and take steps to contain the fire to the one structure. Stay put. I'll talk to you once we have it secured." With that, he started yelling directions to his crew, who hooked up hoses to the nearby hydrant and began to soak the adjoining structures before directing their efforts to outside of the house. Given the way the roof was sagging, and the fact that they knew the place was empty, I doubted they would attempt to enter. Luckily, I didn't have much that I'd worry about losing. My most prized possession was my motorcycle that I'd restored by hand, but since I'd used the truck for my date with Emma, the bike was safely stowed at the clubhouse. The truck was insured, as was the house. I had no emotional attachments to either.

I stepped back to let the firemen work, waiting to answer the inevitable questions once they had the blaze under control and felt the area was safe.

I watched as the fire crew worked to minimize the damage. By the time an hour had passed, they had contained the fire to my property and were mopping it up. Not much left to mop up though. The building had collapsed completely in on itself. A smoldering pile of ashes surrounded the brick chimney which was all that was left standing.

These guys played for keeps, and it was sheer dumb luck that Emma and I were safe.

"Mr. Maclean? "

I turned to see the same fireman I'd talked to earlier. "Yeah?"

"I'm Chief Placket. Sorry about your home." The chief rubbed an ash covered hand across his forehead, leaving a black streak. "There was nothing we could do to save it. The structure was already fully engulfed when we arrived."

I nodded curtly. "I know. But thanks. At least you managed to keep the neighbors' places from going up too."

"Any idea what started the blaze?" He squinted. Probably already had a good idea.

"Someone threw a bomb through the front window." I shrugged. "We heard the glass break, but the place exploded before I had time to see what the fuck was going on. The house went up like a torch within minutes."

The chief nodded slowly. "Sounds consistent with how fast things went. That makes it arson. The police are going to want to talk to you. Any idea who is responsible?"

"Could be several people. Comes with the territory some days." I turned so my cut was visible. "Some people just don't like bikers."

"True." He glanced at his watch. "It's late, and

the arson experts are probably all home with their families. I'm going to make sure all the hot spots are out, and as long as you promise not to take off, you can go down to the police station in the morning and fill out a report. I'll send in a summary later tonight, so they know what to expect. That work for you?"

"Sounds like a plan. Thanks."

The chief shook my hand before heading back to his crew, directing them to water down the few hot spots still smoldering.

I pulled my cell phone out and called the clubhouse to have one of the prospects come pick me up. No way in hell was I going to ride bitch on Tiny's bike.

As if he could read my mind, Tiny pulled up beside me. He eyed up the pile of rubble, shaking his head. "Fuck."

"Yeah."

"Same guys that did the murder in the park?"

"Yeah."

"We voting on war?"

I regarded him soberly. "Yeah. Soon as I get back to the clubhouse, church. Time to clean this shit out of our town."

Tiny nodded and kicked his bike into gear. "See you back at the clubhouse, Prez."

Chapter Ten

Emma

What kind of hell had I landed us in? By us, I meant me and Ace and the whole damn Riptide club. I'd gone from witnessing a murder and having someone take potshots at me, to someone tossing a bomb into the house I was supposed to be safe at, and damn near killing me and Ace both. A bomb!

Talk about the shit hitting the fan. It took all my willpower not to break down into a blubbering mess. Thank God I still had some clothes up in Ace's room here. I'd been literally buck naked, wrapped in nothing but a damn blanket when Thor drove me here. It was the middle of the night, so Jake and Mom weren't anywhere to be found. I pulled on an old pair of jeans, and one of Ace's sweatshirts. I had a few shirts of my own, but I wanted the comfort of something that had touched him wrapped around me.

I sat down on the edge of Ace's bed, with my arms crossed, and took a deep ragged breath. What was I supposed to do now? I had nowhere left to run. Nothing to fall back on. I wanted Ace so bad I ached, but what if he'd changed his mind? What if he didn't want the issues that came with me?

I practically oozed problems, and he'd sent me away with Thor when I needed him most. I wasn't good at this relationship thing. What if that meant he was done with me? I couldn't blame him. Hell, I hadn't seen him in years, and when I finally did, I was nothing but trouble. What did they call that? High maintenance. Yeah. I was about as high maintenance as you could get.

I lay on the bed, huddled in a pathetic pile with my knees pulled up to my chest. I couldn't stop shivering. I pulled the blanket I'd been wearing over myself, inhaling deeply. It smelled like a mixture of Ace and me, and that just made me feel worse. Was there any chance for Ace and me?

We came from the same place, but our paths had taken such different routes. Could I be part of his world, his club? It felt like family, and that was one thing I'd never had. A family. These guys counted on each other, covered each other's backs. They trusted each other. I wasn't even sure I knew what trust was.

Except for Ace. I trusted him without question, without thinking it through. Was that enough to base a life on? Did he even want a life with me, or was he just scratching an itch?

A soft knock on the door sounded, and I attempted to pull myself together. "Come in?"

The door slid open, and two teenage girls entered hesitantly. I frowned. "Do I know you?"

The taller one, a lithe brunette, shook her head. "No, but Thor told us Ace's woman was here and probably needed another woman to talk to, so we thought we'd come up and see you." She crossed the room and held out her hand. "I'm Jasmine, and this is my sister Jewel."

I sat up, the blanket still wrapped comfortingly around me. "I'm Emma. And I'm not Ace's woman, we're just…" I paused, not sure how to explain Ace and me.

"You're in his room, wearing his shirt, and Thor says you've been staying at his house with him." Jewel wrinkled her nose. "That kind of says you are his woman."

I shrugged. "We're just temporary."

Jasmine giggled, and her sister elbowed her in the ribs. "Whatever. Are you going back to sleep for a while, or do you want to come up to the range with us?"

"The range?"

"Shooting range. We like to get in a bit of practice a couple times a week. It makes our dad happy. Beast is our dad. I think you met him." She smiled. "He likes to know we can take care of ourselves if we have to. He worries too much."

I shook my head. "I don't know how to shoot, and besides, I should wait for Ace to get back."

Both girls looked shocked. "You don't know how to shoot? What if you need to protect yourself?" asked Jewel.

"You don't want to have to count on some guy to protect you, do you?" Jasmine sat down beside me on the bed. "We can teach you. It's not hard and besides, as soon as he gets back the Prez is going to call church, so you won't see him for a while. Only the guys go to church."

"Ace told me about church. It's when the guys hold a meeting, right?"

"Do you want to come learn how to shoot?" The two girls bounced up and headed for the door.

"Sure. Why not?" Given the last week of my life, learning how to handle a firearm suddenly seemed like a good idea. "Except I don't have a gun."

"No problem," insisted Jasmine with a grin on her face. "You can use ours for now. Ace can get you your own later if you want."

The pair's enthusiasm was hard to resist. I shrugged the blanket off before I realized I didn't have any shoes.

"What size are you?"

"Sevens usually? Maybe seven and a half."

The two exchanged a look. "I bet there's some in

the box."

"The box?" I was beginning to suspect there was a secret language only these two were privy to.

"It's where Mom and Jake throw all the extra bits that people leave behind when there's a party. Jackets. Shoes. Shirts. That kind of stuff. She throws out the underwear. Says no one's going to want used underwear."

Good call. Just the thought of wearing someone else's underthings made me shiver. Yuck. "Kind of like a lost and found?"

"I guess. People don't usually come back for the stuff so it's just extra. Mom washes it before she puts it in there. It's in the coat closet."

I let them lead me downstairs and to the back door. Jewel opened a door to the left and gestured at a rack of shoes and boots neatly arranged by size. "Pick something that fits."

I picked a pair of ankle boots in serviceable black leather and tried them on. They fit and were well worn in, so they felt comfortable. Hard to believe no one had come to claim them. Did they go home barefoot?

While I was busy getting footwear, Jasmine disappeared and came back with a long-barreled gun and a box of ammunition. "This one's easy to start with. Lighter than some of the big guns, and it doesn't pack as much of a kick. It's got a sight on top too, so it's a good one to learn on."

I eyed it doubtfully. "What is it?"

Jasmine hefted it up. "Twenty-two semi-automatic. The magazine can hold ten rounds, so you don't have to reload quite as often. That makes it better for target practice. And the cartridges are small, so they're cheaper. You don't want to waste money on expensive ammunition just to practice with."

We exited the back door. A prospect I hadn't met yet was sitting on the back porch.

"Dodge, meet Emma. She's with Prez. We're going to do some target practice." Jewel gave the young guy a dazzling smile as the three of us tripped down the steps and headed toward a field behind the clubhouse.

"He's new around here, and Jewel thinks he's cute." Jasmine laughed when Jewel growled at her.

"He is cute, but Dad would kill him if he looked at me sideways so there's not much point in getting to know him any better." Jewel sighed. "Sometimes it sucks having a biker for a dad."

"You live with your dad full time?"

Jasmine nodded. "Yup. Mom and he split up and she shacked up with a creepy guy from Atlanta, so we opted to stay with Dad."

Before I could ask, Jewel chimed in. "Mom's boyfriend is a banker, and he'd expect us to act like perfect little southern ladies. Not our style. I think everyone was happy when we said we wanted to stay here. We still see Mom a lot. She comes down, or we go up there for holidays. It works as good as anything can."

"How old are you?" My guess was eighteen so when Jewel said fifteen, I was taken aback. "You look older than that."

"Thanks." Jewel laughed. "We try. Dad is kind of strict about us not wearing much makeup and staying out of sight when the club hosts parties. I think he wants us to stay his little girls forever."

"Sound like a nice guy." I couldn't keep the note of envy out of my voice. The last time I'd seen my father he'd been heading out the door and I'd been six years old.

"So how old are you?" Jewel threw the question out innocently enough.

"Twenty-three."

"Wow. "

I raised one brow. "Wow?"

"I thought you'd be older. Ace is like over thirty."

"We're not permanent."

She didn't look convinced. "Ace sounded pretty sure when he told the guys you were off limits. That means he doesn't want any of his brothers fooling around with you. And that means he thinks you're permanent."

She was young. Probably believed in happily ever after and all that crap. Far be it for me to disillusion her. Time to bring the subject back to the task at hand.

"Tell me how this shooting thing works?"

Jasmine motioned me over and showed me all the parts of the gun -- the safety, the magazine, the barrel, the stock. "This one is really easy to use." She demonstrated how to load a cartridge into the chamber. "This will also eject the spent cartridge, the one you've already shot."

She picked up the magazine and held it up for me to see. "This is a 10-shot magazine. You fill it like this." She slotted a few of the cartridges in, then handed it over to me to finish. When she was satisfied that I had done it correctly, she showed me how to insert the magazine into the rifle. She stressed how to check that the magazine was empty, and not to ever point the barrel at anything I didn't intend to shoot.

"Most firearm accidents are caused by guns that the person thought was unloaded." Jewel shook her head solemnly. "Always check for yourself. You do not want to be that person who shoots their best friend."

When it came to firearms, both of the girls dropped the giggly teenage personas and became deadly serious.

Satisfied that I knew the basics, Jewel set up a target against an old hay bale and showed me how to stand, how to hold the stock snug against my shoulder to minimize the kickback, and how to sight down the target. My first few shots went wide, but by the time I'd emptied the first magazine, I was hitting the target, although not the bullseye.

Both girls looked impressed.

"You're a natural," Jasmine said. "Ace is going to be very proud of you."

"Yes, he is."

I turned to see Ace striding across the field toward us. Making sure to keep the muzzle pointed at the ground, I handed the twenty-two to Jasmine and raced to throw myself in my lover's arms.

Yeah. I was ready to admit he meant something to me. At least for now. Maybe. Or for a long time.

Why did life have to be so confusing?

* * *

Ace

Emma threw herself into my arms, and I caught her tight against me, inhaling her sweet scent. I couldn't believe I'd been so fucking stupid as to think I could protect her without the full weight of the club behind me. Last time I made that damn mistake.

She lifted her head, staring up at me like I was some fucking kind of hero. Not hardly. Me and my ego had almost got her killed. I tightened my arms around her and seared a possessive kiss across her soft lips. She parted them, just enough to let me slide my tongue in. I took advantage, kissing her like we were the last two people on the earth.

I could hear the twins sniggering over by the gun range, but I didn't care. Not like this was the worse they'd ever seen. They lived here with their father, Beast. Their mom had bailed on them a few years back. Found herself a guy who didn't carry a gun all the time. He didn't like kids and they sure as hell didn't like him. It worked out. Despite his name, Beast was a great dad, and he adored the twins. They say it takes a village. Well in this case, it took a club, and I think we're doing a pretty good job of looking after those two.

When I finally managed to lift my head, Emma had that dazed look on her face that I liked to see. It usually followed me fucking her long and hard, but maybe my kissing skills were improving.

"Eww! Get a room!" Jewel shouted across the field.

"Plan on it." I wrapped my arm around Emma's shoulder and led her back to the clubhouse.

* * *

Kicking the door to my club room closed behind us, I stripped off my cut and tossed my gun on the side table. "The twins were teaching you how to shoot?"

She nodded. "Yeah. Not something I ever thought of trying but it was kind of fun."

I raised my brows. "Fun?"

"Yeah. It was a challenge trying to see if I could hit the target. I was doing pretty good at it. By the end there, I was hitting the target every time. I bet if I had more practice I could hit the bullseye."

"I'll have to make sure you get more practice then. Kind of like the idea of my woman being a crack shot. What caliber?" By this time, I'd stripped down to my boxers, and the tenting in the front left little to the imagination.

"Huh?" Emma raised her eyes to my face.

Couldn't help the smirk on my face. What guy didn't like the sight of his package straining to get out distracting his woman so much she lost track of what was being said? "The gun. What kind was it?"

"Oh. A twenty-two. Semi-automatic with a ten-shot clip."

Impressive. She'd remembered details.

Raising up on her knees, she scooted across the bed and reached for the waistband of my boxers. "You have too many clothes on."

"What do you suppose I should do about that?"

"This."

I stood still and let her slide the material down my hips. My cock sprang free, hard and ready for action.

"Much better."

I kicked the offending clothing to the corner of the room as Emma circled my stiff shaft with one hand, gently cupping my balls with her other. Lowering her head, she swirled her tongue around the tip before sucking it deep into her mouth.

For a girl who professed to have little interest in sex or dating, she sure knew how to give a man the blow job from heaven. She licked and sucked, taking me so deep in her throat she almost choked. Her tongue danced up and down the sides, and I closed my eyes as emotions washed over me.

I could have lost her tonight. We both could have died. I needed to put a stop to those assholes before this went any further.

Emma scored her teeth gently down the sides of my cock, and I let out a low groan. "Enough, babe." I grasped her hair and pulled her off me.

The dazed look on her face showed how invested she'd been in that blow job.

I pushed her back onto the bed. "I want to come inside you. I want to look into your eyes when I come, and I want to taste your lips when you scream my name."

Her eyes darkened with desire, and she struggled to shed her clothes.

I helped, pulling her jeans down over her hips, and tossing them to the floor. Her shirt went next, tossing it behind me. I lowered my head and sucked one lace covered breast into my mouth, teasing the nipple with my tongue. Reaching up, I unsnapped the front clasp and freed her gorgeous breasts. Her nipples were perfect, round pebbled hard peaks. Scoring my teeth across first one, then the other, I worshipped them with my mouth and hands.

Emma squirmed beneath me, and I kissed and licked my way down from her breasts to her bare mound. Her skin, smooth as silk, tasted like heaven. I regretted every year I'd kept myself from chasing her, from claiming her as my own. Had I known she and Justin weren't really into each other I might have made different choices, but regrets were a waste of time. She was here now, and I intended to make sure she never left.

Sliding a finger through the damp folds guarding her entrance, I slipped it inside her. "Damn you're wet. Ready for me."

"Always."

"I'm going to fuck you till you can't walk."

"Less talk. More action."

I chuckled. "Yes, ma'am."

"I'm not a ma'am."

"No?"

"Definitely not."

"What are you then?"

"I'm…" She paused. "Not sure, but a ma'am wouldn't be laying on a biker's bed with her legs spread and his finger buried inside her."

"Good point." I removed my finger and inserted it in my mouth. "Fuck that tastes good."

Spreading her legs wider, I buried my head between them and feasted, using my mouth and my tongue to make her twist and wiggle against me. Swirling my tongue around her clit, I was rewarded when she screamed my name, and a warm gush of liquid bathed my tongue.

Pulling myself up over her, I reached into the nightstand and grabbed a foiled condom. Ripping the package open I quickly rolled it on and positioned myself at her dripping entrance.

"Ace." She breathed my name out in the sexiest whisper I'd ever heard.

"Yeah, babe?"

"I think I might be falling for you."

"I sure hope so, cause I'm sure as hell not letting you go."

I sank into her, savoring how tight she was, how her slick channel gripped my cock. Heaven couldn't be any sweeter than this.

She lifted her legs and wrapped them around me, hooking her heels at my back. The slight change in angle let me plunge even deeper and my balls slapped against her bare ass. I enjoyed the feel of her surrounding me for a delightful minute before I started to move, rocking my hips to slide in and out. Fucking had never felt so damn good.

I captured her lips with mine and ceased to think

about anything at all except for how well we fit together. She was so fucking wet; it drove me crazy. I moved faster and faster, wanting to drag this out but unable to slow myself down. I fucked her hard, in and out, watching as her eyes rolled back in her head and she muttered my name, her fingernails plowing deep furrows down my back.

"Oh God, Ace!" She moaned my name as her channel clamped down on my cock, pulsing and rippling until I couldn't hold back any longer.

I buried my face in her hair and bellowed loudly as I shot my load. I moved a few more times, milking every ounce of pleasure as ripples of aftershocks rocked us both. She clung to me, her legs still wrapped tight around my waist, holding me against her, in her.

I felt at peace, not a feeling I was used to. Her body was a haven for me, and I didn't want the moment to end. But it had to. The threat wasn't over yet. I needed to deal with that so Emma and I could get on with our lives. Together.

Chapter Eleven

Ace

"What have you found out?" Shadow was the best IT guy in the business. If there were something to be found, he'd find it. Right now, he didn't look so happy.

"They knew she was at your place, so the hit was on her, but they were willing to take out the Prez of the Riptides to get to her. That shows a disrespect for our club that you can't ignore."

"You know that for sure?"

He pulled up a file on one of the monitors in front of him. "This is a text convo between their president and the guy Thor clocked in your yard. The guy who threw the bomb."

I scanned the conversation.

Yeah. They knew who and what I was, and they assumed Emma was my old lady. Not that she was yet, but they'd believed it and tried to take us both out. That amounted to a declaration of war on Riptide.

I nodded soberly. "What else you got?"

His fingers flew across the keyboard as he brought up the club's name, its membership, location, police records, strengths and weaknesses. If there was anything to be found online or on the dark web, he'd found it. Not a pretty picture. These guys were into drugs, arms deals and human trafficking. The worst of the worst.

"Thanks. Church in half hour. Be prepared to fill the club in on all this shit."

Shadow nodded. "Yes, sir."

* * *

Emma

I watched the guys troop out to the little cabin out back. An air of solemnity surrounded them. There was no smiling. None of the usual laughing or banter. The prospects held back, watching as the patched members entered in single file. They entered last and closed the doors behind them.

Jasmine had told me that's where they held their club meetings. She also told me they all got to vote on anything important, and going to war with another club had to be considered important.

Who would have thought a motorcycle club would run on democratic rules?

"I feel like this is my fault." I stared at the closed door of the cabin. "If I hadn't gone to Ace that night, Riptide wouldn't be involved in this. Someone could get hurt badly, maybe even killed. Hell, it's amazing no one has gotten hurt to this point what with bombs going off and all."

Jasmine shook her head. "Wouldn't have made any difference. You just gave them a heads up. Those guys are trying to move into Riptide territory, and my men wouldn't stand back and let that happen. This just sped up the agenda." She slanted a look at her sister. "Especially if there's human trafficking going on. No way they'd stand for that kind of shit going down in their town."

"Aren't you worried your dad could get hurt? Or worse. If they go after these guys, it's not going to end well for someone."

Jewel shrugged. "Life's a crap shoot. Sure, Dad could get hurt, but he could also get cancer. Or have a heart attack. Or live to be a hundred and five. We don't know what the future holds, we just have to live our lives as best we can so when our time comes, we have no regrets."

Jasmine nodded her agreement. "It's true. No regrets is the best way to live. These guys have a saying. Death before dishonor. And they live by that. If they die defending something they believe in, they consider it a good way to go. They don't care if what they need to do to preserve their honor is considered illegal by society. Dad always says justice and the law are two entirely different things."

I shook my head. "That is one of the deepest, most profound things I've ever heard. How did you two get to be so wise so young?"

Jewel giggled, and suddenly looked her age again. "You could credit our awesome dad, but I prefer to think it's from watching all those television shows. You know, the ones with the hunky young heroes in skintight pants and no shirts, who always save the day."

"Definitely. Ever watch Captain America? Or the Avengers?" Jasmine pretended to fan herself with her hand. "Hot!"

I smiled despite the tension in my gut. "You two are crazy."

Jasmine grinned cheekily. "We try."

"Ace is good at what he does. You don't have to worry about him. He'll slay the dragon and be back in time for supper." Jewel wagged her eyebrows knowingly. "Or you, if that's what he's hungry for."

I felt my face heat up. The walls around here weren't soundproof, and Ace and I hadn't been all that quiet. I hadn't considered who might be within earshot when we made love.

"That was quick."

I followed Jasmine's gaze and saw the bikers all trooping out of the church building, heading back to the clubhouse. I wanted to get up and run to Ace, find out what was going on, but I resisted the urge. If I was going to try and fit in here, I had to do things their way.

Huh. When had I decided to try and fit in?

Ace came through the doorway and paced over to me. He held out his hand. "We can talk upstairs."

I looked at the twins, who nodded silent encouragement. Placing my hand in his, I followed him up the stairs and into his room. He closed the door quietly behind us, still holding my hand. Crossing to the bed, he sat and pulled me down onto his lap.

"You're going to war with them." I made it a statement.

"Best defense is a good offense." He stroked my hair. "They're going to keep coming at you and at us unless we do something. You witnessed a murder, and they want you out of the way. To them, that means dead. They know you're with me. They know you're mine. They knew I was the Prez of Riptide when they bombed my house. Can't let that fucking shit go. We have to respond."

"They'll expect you to do something. They'll know you're coming at them." I pointed out the obvious.

"Maybe. Probably." Ace shrugged. "But they won't know when or how we plan to attack."

Attack. I didn't like that word. "When are you going?"

"Waiting for a couple of the guys to get back here." He ran his hand down my thigh, and I shivered. "Deuce and Preacher went up to Atlanta for some downtime, but that's over now. I messaged them to get their asses home. Should be back tomorrow. Soon as they are here, we go at dawn. Hopefully we'll catch them when they're just getting up. Not awake and or organized yet."

Made sense. I wrapped my arms around his neck and buried my face in his shoulder. His scent surrounded me. Warm. Male. Comforting.

"I just found you. I don't want to lose you." The words were muffled against his shirt.

"Don't plan on getting killed." He gently pulled me away from him. Cupping my chin in his hand he stared into my eyes. "This is me. This is the life. I know you got thrown in the deep end, but if we're going to make this work you have to understand club culture. There are some things I've just got to do, the club just has to do."

I nodded soberly. "I get it. I really do. Death before dishonor. Duty and all that crap. I just don't want you to die."

"I'm not that easy to kill." He ran his hand down my back. "You're going to stay here with Mom, Jake and the twins while this goes down."

"I am?"

"Yeah. This whole place is on lockdown until this is over. No runs to town. The outside help can keep the bar going for now. The manager isn't part of Riptide, and he doesn't ask questions. He just takes orders. It's too risky for anyone attached to us to show their face in town until this is over. We don't know who all's with the other club and we can't risk having anyone taken and tortured for information."

"They would torture someone? Like really torture?" My head was spinning. You would think witnessing a murder would have clued me in, but this was so far outside of my tidy little world. I'd somehow thought murder was the exception, not the rule.

"Without hesitating. That means you're here for

the duration as well. No running into town, and no contacting anyone. You down with that?"

It didn't sound like I had much choice, but since I'd been shot, I didn't have a lot of places to be either. Work was out, and my home was definitely compromised. I'd been too busy trying to get a degree the past few years to have any close friends. Lockdown or no lockdown, I basically had nowhere to go. A little depressing when you thought about it.

"A couple of the prospects will stay behind and man the gates. You know how to shoot, and I want you to keep a gun with you at all times. Just in case."

I nodded slowly. I'd never considered whether I could pull the trigger to kill another human. Not even sure I could kill an animal if it came to that, but Ace had enough to worry about without me getting into that with him. Chances were, it would never come up.

"Thanks, babe." He wrapped an arm around me and pulled me in for a quick hard kiss. "Knowing you're safe means a lot to me. Makes things easier."

He leaned back on the bed, taking me with him.

I lay on top of him, resting my chin on a propped-up hand. I took in those gorgeous eyes of his, that unruly mop of hair that never quite stayed in place, that mouth that could make me melt into a puddle of pure need.

When had he become so important to me? "This is insane, you know."

"Us, or the situation?"

"Us. You're a biker."

"You knew that when you came to me for help."

"True."

His mouth twisted into a wry smile. "Rethinking your choices?"

"Maybe."

"Don't. I may be a biker, but I'm dynamite in the sack."

I burst out laughing. "You don't have an ego problem."

"Not an ego. Just the truth."

He pulled my head down to sear a kiss across my lips, and suddenly I didn't feel like talking anymore.

If he might die tomorrow, then I didn't want to waste today.

* * *

Ace

What I hadn't told Emma was that I needed that extra day to run this war vote past my contacts at the FBI. While the club was no longer controlled by that organization, we had an informal agreement to keep them apprised of any projects we undertook that might involve their interests. Going to war with a club that sold drugs, ran guns and trafficked in women and children? That absolutely qualified as being of interest to them. While we didn't have to abide by any orders they threw our way, we acknowledged that it wouldn't be in anyone's best interests if we inadvertently fucked up a mission they might have spent months or even years setting up. If they had undercover agents in place, we could get them killed.

I left Emma sleeping soundly in my bed and headed to the communications room. Shadow looked up when I entered, not bothering to remove his feet from his desk. A glance at the monitor in front of him showed a fantasy landscape with monsters and dragons wandering through a forest littered with purple and blue trees.

He nodded at the vacant chair on the far side of the room. "Your woman sleeping?"

"Yeah. Should be down for a while. All this shit is new to her."

"Saw her talking to the twins yesterday. Seemed like she's a good one. She going to stay?"

"Fuck, yeah. Just not sure if she's aware of it yet." I crossed the room and sat down. "Encoding and protocols set up?"

Shadow nodded. "Affirmative. Line connected faster than most times. Got the impression the boys in Washington were expecting you to contact them."

"They are not dumb. If they knew who was moving into our territory, and I've no doubt they did, they'd expect us to respond."

"Not to mention your house getting blown up. Can't possibly have thought it was an accident." Shadow sat up straight and killed the video game feed. His hands moved over the array of blinking lights and buttons in front of him. "Closing all the incoming and outgoing lines except the one you're using. Don't want to chance a security breach."

"Yeah. Wouldn't want that." I leaned forward and waited while the computer completed a retinal scan. A few moments later my contact's avatar appeared.

"What's up?" His conversational skills did not include social niceties such as hello and how's it going.

"The club we discussed a few days ago is moving into our territory." Might as well get right to the point. "My old lady witnessed a murder, and they've got a hit out on her. Blew up my house. Just lucky no one got hurt. We plan to take them out for good. ETA twenty-four to forty-eight hours."

"The top brass is aware of your housing situation. They send condolences. Haven't finished the background check on your old lady yet. That murder she witnessed is not on our radar either." There was a brief pause. "Mission anticipated, and conditionally approved. Sooner the better. Intel has it they have an arms shipment coming in the next day or two. We would prefer that didn't happen. Our wish list also includes termination of their President, Vice President and Enforcer. All three are extremely dangerous and we do not, with emphasis on DO NOT, want to give them the grandstand of a public trial. This is not a sanctioned hit, but there will be bonuses if things go well."

What he didn't say was that they were willing to pay us to take these guys out. Diplomacy required the situation be handled with finesse.

"Wish list noted. Will pass on to my guys."

"Appreciate that. You need any hardware or boots on the ground?"

"Nah. This is just a heads up. When they bombed my home, it became personal. Club tempers are running a little hot at the moment."

"Totally understand. Let us know if you need our help. Pre-Op or mop-up."

"Will do. Ace out."

I shut down the connection and set the headset on the desk.

"Good to go?" Shadow glanced over at me.

I nodded. "Yup. When Deuce and Preacher get back, we move out. Bit of a rush on it now. Arms deal going down, and our friends would prefer that doesn't happen."

"Sounds good. Enough of that shit on the street already." Shadow resumed his pose with feet on the desk and turned the video game back on. Picking up the discarded video controller, he turned his attention to the screen in front of him. "Need to kill a few more

Orcs before dinner time."

I nodded. "I'll let the others know."

Shadow smirked. "About the Orcs?"

"Asshole." I threw him a side eye.

Chapter Twelve

Ace

Waking Emma up from a nap was becoming my new favorite thing. I spooned her from behind, one hand splayed across her warm belly.

"Mmmmm." She wriggled around so she was laying on her back. "Thought you had a call to make."

"Done." I reached over to leisurely explore her warm lips.

She squirmed against me, wrinkling her nose. "I need a shower."

"I can help you with that." I leered suggestively.

A slow smile lit her face as she stretched and ran a hand from my chest down to my cock. "I was hoping you'd say that."

Almost an hour later, we were dressed and ready to face the rest of the day. "So, what's happening?"

"We're waiting for Deuce and Preacher to get back. The plan is to attack their base at dawn."

"Their base?" She frowned.

"They're from Atlanta, so they don't have a clubhouse here. They've established a base of operations that they are working from on the far edge of town. An old farmstead that's been vacant for over a decade now. There's a lot of cover around it, meaning it won't be easy for them to defend. Most of the guys are in the main building. The barn has half the boards missing and the floor may not be solid enough to hold the weight of a full-grown man."

"How do you know all that?" Her brows shot skyward.

I grinned. "Shadow. No such thing as privacy where he's concerned. Co-opted one of the satellites to spy on the place."

Emma shook her head. "I'll keep that in mind. No sex in the woods for you."

"That was on the table?" I pretended to look surprised.

"Not now it's not." She gave me a stern look. "I'm not into exhibitionism."

"Noted." I grabbed my pistol and checked the safety before tucking it into the holster at my hip. "You ready?"

"For what?"

"Thought we'd see how well you do with a bigger gun. The twins had you using a twenty-two which is great for target practice, but I'd feel better if you had something along the lines of a thirty-thirty if you I'm not around to protect you."

She frowned. "A handgun?"

"No." I shook my head. "Rifle. Handguns are harder to handle and take a lot more practice to get proficient with."

"Okay." She didn't sound too sure about it but took my hand as I headed downstairs to the gun locker.

We referred to it as a locker, but the gun room was actually a reinforced vault with an electronic lock. I punched in the code to disarm it and stepped inside. Dropping Emma's hand, I selected a Winchester thirty-thirty from the rifle rack, along with a box of cartridges. This model had a magazine in the barrel and held five shots plus one in the chamber. If she got off that many, anyone on the receiving end would be good and dead.

A quick check assured me it was unloaded, and I handed it to her.

"This is a thirty-thirty?"

"Yes. Big enough to kill a deer, or a person, but

not enough punch to bring down a moose or a bear unless you're a damn good shot and hit it just right."

"Good to know." She hefted it, moved it from hand to hand as if assessing the weight and balance. "It's lighter than it looks."

I locked the vault behind us, and we headed out to the rifle range. I'd never taught a woman how to handle a gun before, or any newbie for that matter. The twins had done a good job of showing her how to brace her feet, and how to snug the stock up against her shoulder to cushion the kick.

I showed her how to load the magazine, then emptied it so she could try it herself.

"Like this?" She automatically checked to make sure the safety was on, and the gun was empty when I handed it to her. She was going to be a natural.

She looked down at the rifle. "This isn't a semi-auto kind of gun. How do I get the cartridges from the magazine to the chamber?"

I explained the lever action, making sure to warn her not to get hit by the spent shell being ejected, watching as she chambered the first round.

"Yup. You got it." Not that I ever wanted her to be in the position to have to use it, but being able to defend herself would make both of us feel better.

I stood behind her as she took a stance and aimed. "Squeeze slowly, don't jerk the trigger."

"The twins already told me that." She placed her finger on the trigger and took the first shot.

"Shit!" She lowered the muzzle toward the ground and shrugged her shoulder. The Winchester had a harder kick to it than the twenty-two she'd been using the day before. "You could have warned me."

"Sorry." I stepped up to massage her shoulder. "Didn't think about it. You snugged it up like a pro."

She rolled her eyes. "Nice try. You're going to pay for that later."

"Hope so." I grinned at her.

"One track mind!" Stepping back up to the firing line, she readied herself to give it another try. She worked her way through the remaining rounds in the magazine before stepping back.

I was proud of the way she'd handled the changes in her life. They'd come fast and hard, and instead of constantly whining or complaining she just adjusted.

"I didn't hit the bullseye a single time." She glared at the rifle as if it were somehow to blame.

"You hit the target though, and that's good enough." I dropped an arm around her shoulder and pulled her in close to drop a quick kiss on her lips. "If you're shooting at someone, that's enough to scare them, even if you don't injure them. Aim for the chest. It's your best option. I want you to keep this rifle by your side while I'm gone. You take it wherever you go. Always within hand reach. Understand?"

She nodded, a frown marring the perfection of her forehead. "Okay. I will."

"Promise," I insisted. "I want you to keep it handy, and have it loaded. These guys are fucking nasty, and I won't rest easy until I know they've been cancelled."

She nodded, more firmly this time. "I will. I promise."

The sound of motorcycle engines echoed loudly in the distance, increasing in volume as they roared up the driveway. I cocked my head, and heard the creak of the gate as the prospects opened it to let them enter.

Deuce and Preacher were back. The mission was a go for daybreak.

* * *

Emma

"It's time."

Ace wrapped his arms around me, devouring my lips in a kiss that seared me to the very bottom of my soul. I wanted to hang on to him, keep him with me, tell him not to go. I'd just found him, just discovered how much I could care about someone if I let myself. And now he was leaving and might not come back. It wasn't fair.

I fought back the tears that wanted to spill from my eyes. I had to be brave. For him. Ace. I didn't want his last sight of me to be a hot mess of tears and red-rimmed eyes.

I let myself melt into the kiss, firmly refusing to dwell on the what ifs. After too short a time, Ace put his hands on my shoulders and lifted his head.

"I will be back. I promise."

"You can't promise that."

"I can. I've just found you and nothing is going to keep me away from you."

I wished I could believe him.

He let me go and slung a leg over his motorcycle. Lifting his arm, he signaled to the rest of the Riptide gang and a feeling of total loss swept through me as he rode away, his red taillights disappearing into the horizon. Then, one by one, the rest of the crew roared off down the driveway and out of sight.

Biting my lower lip, I turned to find Jake standing behind me. The sympathy in his eyes was almost my undoing.

"Does it get any easier?"

"Not really." He shook his head. "But you know they're doing something important, something not a lot of people are capable of. Because of them, our world is a safer place."

"I suppose." I admitted it reluctantly. "Except I want Ace to be safe."

Jake took a step closer and slung a fatherly arm around my shoulder. "If he hid from danger, if he didn't do what his conscience told him needed to be done, he wouldn't be the man you fell in love with, would he?"

"No." I rested my head on Jake's shoulder as we wandered back toward the clubhouse. "But he might get killed."

"I doubt it." Jake chuckled. "He's not that easy to kill."

"Yeah. He told me that already."

"See. He's smart too."

That drew a reluctant smile from me. "I guess he is."

Jake tousled the hair on the top of my head. "Of course he is. He found you, didn't he?"

We stepped into the clubhouse, and the smell of freshly brewed coffee wafted out of the kitchen to greet us. Mom must have known we weren't going to be able to go back to sleep.

"You didn't come to see the guys off. How come?" I knew she thought of the bikers as her kids in a way.

"Too hard." Mom shook her head. "If something happens, I want my last sight of that person to be a happy one. Eating. Drinking. Carousing with buddies. Not heading out to his doom."

A cold shiver ran down my spine at her words, the sight of Ace leading the string of bikers out of the gate flashing through my mind.

"Here. Drink this." She handed me a mug of

coffee with lots of cream. Just the way I liked it.

"Did you used to watch when Jake left?" I asked.

Mom shook her head. "Jake had already retired when we got together. Didn't have to worry about that."

"You would have stared longingly after my awesome ass," Jake piped up.

"Awesome ass?" Mom rolled her eyes. "You are delusional."

Jake turned and slapped his butt before sauntering over to the coffee pot and pouring a mug for himself.

I laughed, almost choking on a mouthful of coffee.

Looking fondly at Jake, Mom addressed me in a stage whisper, "His ass is kind of awesome, but don't tell him I said that. His ego is big enough as it is."

Jake turned, smirking suggestively before stalking across to Mom and pulling her in to smack a big kiss across her lips.

"Maybe I should leave you two alone." I forced a smile as I headed for the front door. "I could use a walk to clear my head."

Jake held out a restraining hand, all trace of playfulness gone. "Lockdown. Sorry, lass. Means you're staying inside until the guys get back and say otherwise."

"Seriously?" I frowned. "Like I can't even go outside and get some fresh air?"

"Nope. You stay in the clubhouse." He gestured at the rifle I'd propped in the corner of the room. "And you take that with you wherever you go. Loaded and ready, within arm's reach, at all times."

"Yeah, Ace already told me that," I groused. But Jake and Mom had been good to me, and I didn't want to start an argument with him. Or worse, get him in trouble when Ace returned. "I guess I'll just go play with the plumber and his buddies."

Mom gave me a blank look.

"*Super Mario World*. Silly little Italian plumber trying to save the world?"

Jake snorted into his coffee.

Mom nodded. "Good idea. Take your mind off other things."

I doubted it, but standing here worrying wasn't going to help either. Video games were one way to distract myself.

* * *

The games room was large, with lots of oversized furniture staged around the biggest television screen I'd ever seen. There was an assortment of game systems hooked up to a central switching station, and at least a dozen different controllers perched on chargers sitting on a shelf down the side of the room. Considering the clubhouse only had two inhabitants under the age of majority, it seemed a bit overdone.

I chose one of the controllers and thumbed through the vast array of available games. Instead of *Mario*, I chose to play *Spyro the Dragon*. The silly little cartoon dragon had captivated me decades ago when it first came out. Although I wasn't much of a video game enthusiast, I still found this game to be my go-to when I wanted to kill time without having to think.

I tried to forget everything bad that had happened as I loaded the disc and flew Spyro to the first world in need of conquering.

The look on the face of the murder victim just before he fell.

I barreled Spyro into a herd of unsuspecting sheep.

The sounds of the gunshots aimed in my direction.

I jumped Spyro through the portal into the next world in need of saving.

The sound of the window shattering as the bomb landed in the living room.

I let Spyro flame a few monsters. It felt good. It had been a while since I'd played, but I was starting to get back into the hang of things. I freed the statues in the first world and moved on to the next.

Really, my biggest issue wasn't with the murder. It was with Ace.

I wanted him to want me. Not because he had some kind of hero complex and thought he had to protect me. I wanted him to want me for myself, because he found me irresistible. I wanted him to want me so bad he couldn't even think about another woman. Silly, stupid romantic shit, huh? I flipped the controller to dodge an attacking Orc who was trying to smash Spyro with a big-assed club.

My side was healing well, and I assumed the rival gang was in the process of being crushed by the attacking Riptide bikers. But what if Ace decided there was no reason to keep me? We were so different. We lived our lives in separate worlds. His was full of guns and missions and loud motorcycles. Mine was full of books, and work, and stress. I still wanted to finish up my degree. I want to be a doctor. I want to help people. I want to help kids.

Hell, at some point I might decide I did want to have children of my own. Could I do that if I linked myself to a biker? And not just any biker, but the president of a motorcycle club? Would it be fair to kids to have them knowing their father is a biker? That he could die at any time? Would they grow up hating me for my choices, just like I blamed my parents for theirs?

Despite my doubts, a mental image of a mini-Ace distracted me, and Spyro paid the price. Luckily, he managed to respawn back to his last save point. Too bad people couldn't do that.

I managed to kill a few hours with Spyro before the game got too easy. Then I switched to *Mario vs Donkey Kong*, determined to keep my mind off what might be happening to the club.

To Ace in particular. Having him injured or worse didn't bear thinking about.

I heard the back door creak open. Great. I was under house arrest but obviously it didn't apply equally to everyone. As heavy footsteps approached, I hit pause on the game and twisted in my seat to see who was immune to the lockdown edict.

Lounging against the doorframe, his beady eyes gleaming with an unholy light, was the murderer from the park. "Bet you never thought you'd see me again."

I surged to my feet and opened my mouth.

"I wouldn't do that if I were you, bitch." He quickly raised his arm, aiming a revolver directly at me. I wondered if it was the same one he'd used to kill the guy in the park. "I'll pull this trigger before you can draw another breath, and after I shoot you, I'll kill whoever comes thinking they're going to save you."

I couldn't let him hurt anyone else. Hopefully Mom and Jake hadn't heard him come in. "There's no one else here. They all left to take on you and your buddies."

"Yeah, nice try," he said, "But I'm no fool. I've been watching this place for days now. I know those two old farts are here somewhere."

"Don't hurt them! They have nothing to do with this."

"Oh, it's not them I'm interested in hurting," he

growled. "Just keep your mouth shut and do as I say and maybe I'll let them live."

I snapped my mouth shut. How the hell was I going to get out of this one? I swept the room with my eyes, looking for something, anything that could help.

"Yeah. That's better." He took a step into the room and gently closed the door behind him. "Don't want anyone interrupting us, do we? You've given me and my buddies a whole lot of trouble."

From the corner of my eye, I could see the rifle where I'd left it, beside the chair. I resisted the urge to look at it directly.

Damn. If only it were a tiny bit closer, like leaning against the chair. If I bent down to get it, he'd put a hole through me before I could grab it. No way he'd miss from that close.

I started to edge my way back toward it.

"Stay right where you are." The asshole took a step further into the room. "You're a pretty little piece. Maybe we can make a deal. You'd like that, right?" He reached for me, grabbing my arm and dragging me toward him.

I shuddered, struggling to get free.

He laughed, backhanding me across the face.

I swallowed a scream, staggering backward. I put out a hand to break my fall, and the asshole took a step forward and kicked my side.

Pain lanced through me as his foot connected with the still tender bullet wound.

"Yeah. Winged you there, didn't I?" He grinned. "You're a slow learner, though. You be nice to me and maybe I'll let you live. For a little while."

I just bet he would. More likely he'd rape me and then sell me to the highest bidder. I remembered Ace saying the rival club was into human trafficking.

His eyes scanned across me as I tried to get to my feet. "Strip. Let's see what you're worth."

I whimpered. Maybe I could grab the gun while pretending to strip.

Hooking my fingers in the waistband of my pants, I slowly shimmied them down my legs, bending my knees as I did so.

I swear the asshole was drooling. His gun hand hung loosely at his side while his other hand went to his crotch.

Ignoring the pain, I threw myself sideways, grabbing the rifle and rolling to come up with it pointed directly at the bastard. I squeezed the trigger.

Nothing happened.

We both froze for a split second, and then he let out a sickening bray of laughter. "Forgot to load it, you little bitch?"

I thumbed the safety off and squeezed the trigger again. The noise of the shot was deafening in the enclosed space.

A look of shock crossed his face as a red circle bloomed in his chest.

I flipped the lever back to load another round and fired again.

He sank to his knees.

I fired again. And again.

It was like I couldn't stop myself until the magazine was empty. Even then, with his eyes glazed over in death, I kept pulling the trigger.

Chapter Thirteen

Ace

One. Two.

Fuck! Rifle shots. Inside the clubhouse. Sounded like the rifle I'd left with Emma.

Three. Four. Five.

Fuck! Full magazine emptied in rapid succession.

Pulling my gun as I ran, I spied Jake and Mom in the kitchen, shock written on their faces.

"Where is she?"

"Games room." Jake pointed down the hallway.

I pushed him out of the way and raced down the hallway. The door was shut. Locked. I raised my booted foot and kicked the fucking thing open.

Emma, my Emma, was sitting on the floor with the thirty-thirty I'd given her held so tight her knuckles were white. A clicking sound kept repeating itself as she pulled the trigger on the empty magazine. On the floor in front of her was a mountain of a man, his eyes staring lifelessly at the ceiling, his chest a mass of blood and gore.

A thirty-thirty Winchester can do a lot of damage at point blank range.

I went to Emma and gently liberated the rifle from her hands, setting it down on the floor. Coaxing her to her feet, I led her to the sofa and sat her down onto my lap. She melted into me, letting out a long shaky sigh.

Jake entered the room, followed by Tiny.

"Get rid of the trash." I gestured at the corpse with my chin.

"Yes, sir."

The two grabbed the corpse by the head and feet and carried it out.

I turned my attention to Emma, wrapping my arms around her shaking body. In a perverse way, I was proud of her for doing what she had to do, protecting herself but I knew it never should have gone down like this.

I should have been here. I should have protected her. I should have killed the fucker, so she didn't have to.

As soon as we'd hit the enemy base, I knew something was off. We did our job. We took out the top three assholes just like we'd been asked to but none of them matched the description of the murderer that Emma had given me that night. I'd stayed with my brothers, done my duty, made sure there was no remaining threat from the Atlanta crew, but a sick feeling in my gut told me it wasn't enough.

I'd hiked it back to the clubhouse double-time, only to hear those shots the moment I set foot on the front porch.

Fuck! Fuck! Fuck!

Would she ever be able to forgive me? Would she ever be able to trust me again? I had no idea what I'd do if I lost her. In just this short time, she'd become my whole world.

She took a deep breath and lifted her face to look into my eyes. "He's dead."

"Yeah. He's dead."

"I killed him."

"Yeah, babe. You killed him."

"I'm glad he's dead." She shuddered as she laid her head on my shoulder. "It's over now, isn't it?"

"It's over. We took out the head guys. Anyone left standing hightailed it back to where they came from."

"He kicked me. My side hurts."

I suppressed a blaze of white-hot anger. Asshole was already dead. I wished I could bring him back to life just so I could kill him again. Slowly this time.

I lifted her shirt to take a quick look. The bandage didn't show any sign of blood, so I decided to leave it until the club medic could take a look at it.

"I'll have Joker look at it as soon as he gets here. You hurt anywhere else?"

Her hand went to her cheek. "Probably going to have a bruise here. He slapped me pretty hard."

I ran a gentle finger over the area, and she flinched. "We should probably get some ice on that."

She didn't say anything, just nodded and snuggled in tighter against me.

Rattler and Beast came into the room, quickly followed by Shadow.

"Your woman okay?" Rattler eyed up the bloody mess on the carpet.

"A few bumps and bruises, but she'll be okay. Joker can check her out."

"She did a fine fucking job on that asshole."

"She did. I'm damn proud of her right now." I made sure Emma heard me. "That's one piece of shit that's not going to hurt anyone ever again."

"Good shooting." As always, Beast used as few words as possible, but they conveyed his approval.

"You want me to open a line to our friends to let them know how it went?" Shadow phrased the question carefully, but I was done with hiding shit from Emma.

"Send the Feds a message to let them know it's done. I'll talk details with them later."

"Will do." Shadow turned and left the room.

I rested my chin on Emma's head and inhaled her sweet scent. I could have lost her tonight. But I didn't. Hell, we didn't lose any of the guys. I had a cut on my leg where a knife had bit through my leather chaps, but the bleeding wasn't all that bad. Joker could throw a few of those butterfly strips on it for me. A couple of the guys had minor wounds but only one required a trip to the hospital. I credited the element of surprise coupled with good old-fashioned teamwork for the lack of casualties.

As if she could read my mind, Emma's lifted her head, her hand going to my thigh. "You're hurt!"

"Not a big deal. Joker will take care of it."

Emma sat up straight, her face drawn in determined lines. "Take your pants off. I want to see how bad it is."

Behind her, I could see Rattler and Beast grinning like idiots. Apparently watching their President get ordered around by a woman amused them. I glared at them.

"How about we do this up in my room?" I lifted her chin with one finger.

She pursed her lips. "Okay." She slid off my lap and waited for me to stand up. "Anyone else hurt?"

Didn't look like she planned to waste any time feeling guilty over killing a man. That boded well for when we had the talk about the future. Our future. Not saying she'd have to do it again, but the possibility was there.

It also pointed to the fact that she understood the difference between the law and justice. The law would have that asshole out on bail in under a day. Justice made sure he'd never hurt anyone again.

"Tiny took a strike to the ribs. Flak jacket stopped the bullet, but the impact bruised his ribs up something fierce. Blast went down with his bike on top of him, so he's pretty bruised up. Going to have to rest up for a week or so while he turns pretty colors. Nothing too bad though. Deuce is the worst hit. Took a nasty slash to his face. Those guys were fond of their knives. He's in emergency getting it stitched up. Missed his eye, but not by much."

"He'll be okay, though?"

I felt a twinge of jealousy at the concern in her voice. Yeah, I was that far gone. Like a caveman, drag her home by her hair and lock her up just for me gone. Of course, she'd kick my ass if I even tried to lock her down, so I just shrugged. "It'll probably leave a scar, but he'll be fine. It will give him something to brag about at the next club party."

I took her hand and shouldered our way past Rattler and Beast who seemed to be fascinated by her quick recovery. I twisted my head back as we headed out of the door.

"You guys might want to do something about the carpet. Bloodstains ain't coming out of that one."

We climbed the stairs in silence, holding hands like we'd been doing this for years. When we entered my room, Emma closed the door behind me with a gentle click. "Get those pants off."

* * *

Emma

In my head I knew I should be more worried about having killed a guy. Hell, I could go to jail. Or worse. Did Georgia still have the death penalty? Self-defense was a good reason, though, right? Ace told the guys to clean up the mess. Did that mean they were going to hide the body? Or dump it somewhere? Did that make them accessories to murder? I didn't want to get anyone else in trouble.

I took a deep breath and ordered myself to

ignore the whole shooting thing. Ace and Riptide would take care of it. That's what they did: they took care of things, and they protected people.

Some punk had sliced Ace's leg. I needed to make sure he was okay. The dead guy would still be dead tomorrow, and frankly if I had to do it over again, I wouldn't do it any differently. It had been him or me, and I wasn't ready to die yet. I had too much to live for.

Ace. I had my future with Ace to live for, and no two-bit pimp was going to take that away from me.

The knife wound on Ace's leg might not look to be bleeding badly but I wasn't going to be happy until I saw for myself. "Get your damn pants off!"

Amazing how my vocabulary could deteriorate when I was scared.

"I'm okay." Ace hopped off the bed, pulling his gun out of its holster and placing it on the side table. "It's just a flesh wound." He kicked off his boots and undid his pants, sliding them carefully down to his ankles.

I dropped to my knees, putting me at eye level with the knife wound. It really didn't look that bad. The leather chaps, and the heavy denim of his pants must have taken the worst of the blade's bite. Although more than a scratch, I doubted it would need stitches. Some antibacterial cream and a bandage to keep it clean would probably take care of it. Joker could take a look to make sure.

Reassured he wasn't in imminent danger, I inhaled a deep breath, sinking back on my haunches.

Ace reached down and captured my hands, drawing me to my feet. He kissed me then, long and thoroughly. When he lifted his head, a gentle smile played across his face. "Believe me now?"

"Yeah. I just had to see for myself." I fell silent.

"I get it." He sank down onto the bed, pulling me into his lap.

"Does stuff like this happen a lot?" I hadn't considered this part of dating a biker as thoroughly as I should have.

"Stuff like this?"

"You and the other guys going out and maybe getting hurt or killed?"

"I got to be honest." He caught my gaze and held it. "We do what we need to. You know we provide protection services, and we take contracts that aren't always legal. We run ops for the government that they aren't okay sending their own guys out on. Sometimes justice means playing hard and fast with the legal side. If things go bad, they can deny they knew anything about it. Sometimes it just means looking scary, so people think twice about what they plan to do. But when we need to fight, we fight. When we say death before dishonor, we mean it. That's just the way we live our lives. If we're going to give this thing between us a chance, you need to be okay with that."

I saw the truth in his eyes. He meant every word. And deep down I realized it didn't matter. I loved him, and part of that was loving a man who was willing to put himself on the line for his country, and for what he felt was right. And I knew beyond a shadow of a doubt that he would fight to the death if anyone dared to threaten the Riptide family he and his brothers had formed. I loved him even more because of that.

"Yeah." I reached up to trace the line of his chin. "None of us know how much time we have. I can't say I'm okay with you getting hurt, but I adore your willingness to put yourself on the line for what you believe in."

He pulled me in close, kissing me so thoroughly I could barely breathe. Damn, the man knew how to kiss. His hands slid down my spine to cup my ass. "So now that we got that out of the way, we going to discuss the other things?"

I tilted my head. "What other things?"

"You. Me. Marriage. A home. A little mini-Emma running around."

My brows shot skyward. "You're asking me to marry you?"

"Hell, yeah. I know I'm supposed to go down on one knee and all that shit, but I figured since I'm wounded and all I could get away with just sitting here."

"Marriage is a big deal. It's like, forever." Did he mean it? We'd only been together a short time.

"I know. And I'm sure. I was sure from the moment I opened my door, and you fell into my arms." He reached over me and plucked something out of the drawer in the bedside table. "When I got back here today and heard those gunshots, it was the worst moment of my life. I'm not sure how I would have survived if I lost you."

He opened his hand to expose a burgundy velvet jewelers' box.

"You're kidding. You have a ring already?"

"Bought it the day after you came back into my life. Knew I was going to keep you."

He flipped the lid open to reveal a diamond surrounded by emeralds. "To match your eyes," he explained.

My heart felt near full to bursting. The ring couldn't be more perfect if I'd picked it out myself.

"Well?" I saw the doubt in his eyes. As if he thought I could ever turn down a chance to be at his side, share his life.

"Yes, of course I'll marry you!"

He crushed me against his chest, claiming my lips with a searing kiss that deepened into a soul-sucking caress. The feel of his hands and lips on me sent heat curling down to my toes.

I could get used to this.

When we came up for air, a thought occurred to me. "Your place is gone, and mine's just a rental and frankly it's barely big enough for one of me. I don't think the two of us would fit. It would be a bit awkward to live here at the clubhouse. Everyone could hear everything we did." My cheeks flushed with embarrassment as I thought of all the things I wanted to do with my big bad biker.

"We can buy a house." He dismissed my concern with a wave of his hand. "I've already got a guy lining a few places up for us to look at. Or we can have one built if we don't find anything you like."

"That would take a long time!"

He chuckled. "We've got forever, babe."

I wrinkled my nose, trying not to beam from ear to ear. "Yeah, I guess we do."

A knock on the door interrupted us. "You guys decent? Mom sent me up to check on your leg, Ace. She said you took a knife wound?"

"Come on in, Joker," Ace said.

I tried to stand, but Ace held me firmly in place on his lap.

The door swung open with an abysmal creaking sound. I made a note to get it oiled.

Joker entered and let out a hoot of laughter as he took in the scene. "You don't look like you're in pain, bro."

I realized Ace didn't have any pants on, and the

tent in his boxer shorts didn't leave anything to the imagination.

"Hell no. You can be the first to congratulate us." Ace boomed out the news, "Emma's agreed to marry me."

Epilogue

Six Months Later
The Wedding

Ace and I held our wedding in the back yard of the clubhouse. With a huge lawn, and lots of room for dancing and entertainment, there was also the added attraction of lots of bedrooms for people to sleep off a little too much partying. Or retire to for more private pursuits. Bikers aren't known for their restraint when it comes to party activities.

Since we didn't have a minister, Preacher, the newest patched member, scrambled to get registered to officiate the ceremony. He'd been a topnotch sniper in the SEALs but spent his spare time studying the bible. He said killing on command and trying to live by Christian values just didn't jive together, so he'd mustered out. Organized religion didn't hold much appeal for him either, more politics than good deeds, or so he said. And rules. He didn't like blindly following rules any more than the rest of them. He asked too many questions.

Then he'd found Riptide, and fit right in. It didn't take much to sweet talk him into officiating at our wedding.

The twins took care of decorating the yard. They had the guys haul enough chairs out for everyone to sit on, and they coaxed Beast into making an arch for them to decorate with fluffy white flowers. I swear they were more excited than Ace and me.

Rattler surprised us by announcing he knew a caterer who could take care of the food, and a couple of the prospects found a canopy to set up for shade. Georgia can be a tad warm in the middle of the summer.

Finding a dress suitable for a biker wedding had me stressed out, though. Since I didn't have a best friend to talk to, I decided to consult the twins.

"White." Jasmine pursed her lips. "But not the flouncy kind of dress you see in magazines. That would just look silly."

"White leather," Jewell stated firmly. "With white leather fuck-me boots."

"What are fuck-me boots?" I wasn't sure I wanted to know the answer.

"You'll see." Jasmine giggled and looked over at her sister. "Sassi Elegance?"

"Definitely! My favorite store!" Jewell grabbed my hand. "Let's go shopping."

Their enthusiasm was contagious. After all, what could go wrong?

Two hours later I stared at the stranger reflected back to me in the mirror. The skintight white leather sheath had a plunging neckline studded with shiny rhinestones. The side was split clear up to my hip, showing off the fuck-me boots and a lot of skin with every step I took.

I loved those boots!

The groom wasn't supposed to see the bride before the wedding, and Ace surprised me by holding to that quaint tradition. It felt strange, waking up without him. Lonely. Almost panicky. I'd become addicted to the feel of his warm bulk against my back, protecting me from the big bad world.

Once I'd had my coffee and a luxurious hot shower, the twins helped me do my hair and get dressed. Giggling and grinning, they made me feel like a princess getting ready for her coronation.

They'd agreed to be my bridesmaids, and I'd asked Mom to be my maid of honor. Since I didn't have a father to give me away, Jake stepped up to walk me down the aisle. I may not have any blood relatives to share my big day with, but I had a family. A family made up of people who cared about me and for each other as much as any biological family, maybe more because they'd chosen to be family.

Now here I was, getting ready to hitch myself to one of them, a man who would love and cherish me for the rest of my life.

I stepped outside and linked my arm through Jake's. Someone started the music, and I held my head high as we walked between the rows of chairs.

Ace stood waiting for me at the end of the aisle. Dressed in his best black jeans and shirt with his leather cut polished to perfection, he took my breath away. His eyes tracked my progress, his love shining for all to see.

We reached the archway. "Welcome to the family, Emma." Jake gave me a quick hug before handing me off to the love of my life.

Ace took my hand in his, our fingers twining together as we turned to face Preacher.

Clearing his throat, Preacher intoned the opening of the classic wedding ceremony before addressing Ace and I directly.

"Do you, Ace, take Emma to be your lawfully wedded wife, and do you promise to love, honor and be faithful to her so long as you both shall live?"

"I do." Ace squeezed my hand.

Preacher turned to me. "Do you, Emma, take Ace to be your lawfully wedded husband, to love, honor and be faithful to so long as you both shall live?"

My heart melted. "I do."

Preacher grinned at us. "Prez, you may kiss your bride."

Ace lifted the veil, and captured my lips, devouring them with a kiss that was both achingly tender and blazingly passionate. Ignoring the cheers and whistles of his brother bikers, he made sure I knew just how much I meant to him.

The ceremony was beautiful, with the sun shining brilliantly on the outdoor venue. Birds sang in the branches of the surrounding trees, and wildflowers lent their fragrance to the festivities. Food and drink were served under a big white tent, and Ace and I had the first dance on a carpet of newly mowed grass.

The sun was starting to set when I saw Jasmine approaching with my wedding bouquet in her arms. "Are you going to throw the bouquet before Dad banishes Jewel and I to the games room?" she asked.

"Of course!" I took the flowers from her.

"Can you get everyone's attention?" I asked Ace.

"Quiet down, you animals!" Ace had the kind of voice that commanded attention. "Emma is gonna throw the bouquet, so get ready."

I laughed up at him as I turned my back on the crowd of bikers and their dates and tossed the bundle of flowers over my head. Turning to see who'd caught it, I locked eyes with a stranger standing in the shadow of the club's treasurer, Deuce. A petite brunette. I wasn't sure she looked old enough to be at a party like this. Her mouth formed a shocked "oh" as she stared at the flowers in her hand.

"I don't think I've seen her before. Do you know who she is?" I raised my brows and looked up at Ace. Not much got past him.

"Deuce has been chasing her for a few months now. She's not making it easy for him." He grinned. "Name's Sophia. By the way he's looking at her, this might not be the last wedding out back of the clubhouse."

Jasmine and Jewel distracted me from asking any more questions, sweeping Ace and I up into a group hug.

"Congrats, you two. We knew you'd tie the knot the first time we saw you together!" Jasmine tossed her head, showing off the blue streak she'd dyed into her hair.

Jewel nodded. "Yup. Ace never looked at anyone the way he looked at you."

"Bet you get anything you want just by smiling at him." Jasmine giggled.

"Don't you two have to go now?" Ace lifted one brow pointedly.

"Yeah. Dad wants us out of the way before things get wild."

"Things are going to get wild?" I looked up at Ace.

"Yes, but you won't be seeing any of that either."

"I won't?"

He shook his head. "Definitely not."

"How come?"

"Because we have our own wild party to go to." He swept me up in his arms and stalked toward the clubhouse amid the hoots and catcalls of his brothers. I wrapped my arms around his neck and hung on as we headed into our future.

Together.

Forever.

Deuce (Riptide MC 2)
A Riptide MC Romance
Anne Kane

First impressions and all that? Sophia tried to nail me with a tire iron.

Sophia:
My first two dates from the *Premier Dating App* were total duds. Date number three gave me the creeps. Turns out my instincts were spot on. He slipped something in my coffee, threw me in the back of a van, and headed out to sell me! Lucky for me, Dad's a doomsday prepper. Taught me mechanics, hand to hand combat... all the things you teach your little girl if you think the world is going to hell. So I pried the door open with a tire iron and jumped out. And landed at the feet of a 6′ 6″ tatted up biker.

Deuce:
When Rattler and I stopped behind a van at a railroad crossing, a woman came hurtling out the back like an avenging angel and tried to nail me with a tire iron. Turns out she isn't keen on being sold to the highest bidder. She has guts, I'll give her that. After my old lady split, I thought I was done with couples' shit, but Sophia makes me rethink my life. Sophia's mine, and if those assholes want her back, they're going to have to go through me.

Chapter One

Sophia

Current wisdom says dating apps are a step above those blind dates arranged by well-meaning friends. I wasn't so sure about that.

This was the third first date I'd been on this month after signing up for what was supposed to be the top-of-the-line dating app, and unless things improved in the next half hour I'd be looking for first date number four as soon as I managed to extricate myself from this one.

Staying single was starting to look like an attractive option.

Online, George Landry had looked and sounded like a reasonably good guy. We had several things in common, including our love of sitcoms and our lack of sympathy for the whining of vegans. We'd done the first steps, the back-and-forth messages. I'd even Googled his name and nothing had raised any alarm bells.

In person, however, he sent chills down my spine.

Creepy.

That one word described him to a T. From his eyes that shifted restlessly and didn't quite meet mine, to the disturbing way he used that plastic fork to stab his slice of apple pie into tiny pieces. He didn't actually eat any of the pie, just dissected it and pushed the ragged pieces around on his plate.

Like I said, creepy. The guy was a definite no-go for a second date, and I hadn't even tasted the coffee yet.

We'd agreed on a local coffee shop for this first date, and I picked one a fair distance from my house. It was one of those Mom and Pop kind of places. The neighborhood was a little run-down, and the place could use a good coat of paint, but this coffee shop had one stellar thing to recommend it -- this was one place I didn't frequent. That way, if things went south I wouldn't have to worry about an accidental meeting in the future.

Normally I liked to do these meetings during the afternoons, when it was still daylight out and there were lots of people roaming around, but George had mentioned he was on call during the days and he didn't want our first meeting to be interrupted by business. At the time, it had sounded reasonable, even thoughtful. Now I wasn't so sure.

I blew on my steaming cup of coffee. No need to add a burnt mouth to the reasons this date sucked.

Sadly, my dating life up to now hadn't been all that great. I'd learned the hard way to be careful about where I met strange guys. Before I'd left home, I'd texted my BFF to let her know where I was going and who I was meeting. If I didn't check back in with her by midnight, she'd alert the cops. And my dad.

Not sure who'd be scarier.

"So you're a teacher?" George gazed at something over my left shoulder.

"Yes. I teach chemistry to high school kids." A little white lie. Some instinct made me reluctant to let him know where to find me during the working day. "What about you?"

"I'm in the import/export business." He shrugged. "People want something, they let me know and I supply it for them."

His profile had been rather vague on what he did for a living, but I just thought he didn't want to give out too much detail on a public forum. What the heck did import/export mean? Did he sell cheap Christmas decorations made in some factory in China or was he talking hardcore drugs?

Did I mention creepy?

"That sounds interesting. What kinds of things?"

"Stuff they can't get easily at the local Wal-Mart. Like specialized parts for vintage cars."

That made sense, I supposed. "How do you find them if they're not easy to get?"

He smirked down at the mutilated pie. "I've got connections."

That sounded ominous. Like maybe the connections weren't exactly legal. Surely I hadn't managed to date someone with ties to the mob!

"Sounds fascinating." Time to change the subject. "Are you into vintage cars?"

He shook his head. "Nah. Too much work to keep them up and running." He reached for the sugar dispenser, knocking his coffee over in the process.

I jumped up, managing to avoid most of the hot liquid cascading in my direction.

"Shit, I'm sorry!" George grabbed a handful of napkins from the dispenser in the center of the table and started to soak up the spilled liquid. "Can you get a wipe or something from the girl at the counter?"

"Sure." This was definitely in the running for the worst first date ever, and I'd had some doozies.

Heading over to the counter, I saw the server already holding out a fistful of wipe.

"Sorry, I can't leave the till to come help you." She gestured at the empty space beside her with an apologetic grimace. "My coworker is on break so it's just me."

"No worries. We can get it cleaned up." I grabbed the rags and scurried back to the table.

George stood up and took the rags from me, wiping up the rest of the mess with surprising efficiency. Maybe import/export meant janitor in disguise?

"Sit down and enjoy your coffee." He gathered up the wet rags and his empty cup. "I'll get rid of these and get me a fresh coffee."

Good plan. I could make short work of the coffee and then pretend I had gotten a text and had to leave. Watching reruns of some sitcom would definitely be a step up from this.

I took a mouthful of my coffee. Not the best brew I'd ever had, but at least it had cooled off enough to drink. There was a bitter taste to it. Probably the reason George had been going to add more sugar to his cup. I disliked sugar in my coffee though, so I'd just suffer through it. One cup of bad cup of coffee wasn't going to kill me.

George returned with a fresh cup just as a wave of dizziness rolled over me. I must have made a strange face or something because he took one look at me and frowned. "You okay? You look a little pale."

I managed a weak smile. "I'm fine." I took another sip of my coffee. Probably just nerves. I wanted out of here. Away from George who, despite his superior cleaning skills, still sent shivers of unease down my spine.

A fresh wave of dizziness assailed me, and my vision blurred.

"You don't look so good." George sounded concerned, meeting my eyes for the first time since we'd met. "Some fresh air might help. How about we step outside for a minute?"

"Good idea," I mumbled. My tongue felt too big for my mouth. What was happening?

I pushed myself to my feet, and George came around the table. Putting an arm around my waist, he helped steady me as I stumbled toward the exit. Thank goodness we'd picked a table near the door. The dizziness worsened, and I was having trouble seeing.

"Can I help?" It was the girl from the counter. "Should I call someone?"

By now, if George hadn't been holding me up, I would have fallen flat on my face.

"Can you get the door for us?" George sounded confident, like a man who had things under control. "She just needs a little fresh air."

"No problem."

She opened the door and I staggered outside, leaning heavily on George. The fresh night air hit me in the face, but it didn't make me feel any better. My stomach started to churn. Add nausea to the list of symptoms.

Someone wrapped an arm around me from the other side and helped George half carry me across the parking lot. I turned my head, attempting to see who the new person was but a fresh wave of dizziness assailed me.

"Parked the van over there away from the lights."

That would be the new person. A guy. I didn't recognize the voice. Deep. Possibly creepier sounding than George. I tried to pull away, but whatever was happening left me too weak.

We stopped for a moment, and the creaking of metal hinges sounded loud in the night.

"Up you go." George grasped me by the waist. The touch of his hands grossed me out, but I was too weak to protest.

"Careful. Don't want to bruise her up. Hard to

get full price for damaged goods." This comment came from the mystery man as I concentrated on keeping the contents of my stomach where they belonged.

"I know what I'm doing. Not like this is my first time."

I felt myself being lifted and placed down on a pile of material that smelled like used motor oil. George's presence disappeared, and I heard the metallic echo of a door slamming shut.

I rolled over, and the sudden movement increased the nausea. I pushed myself up on all fours, my head hanging down as I took deep breaths and tried to steady myself. The smell from the questionable stuff under me did not help with the nausea.

The floor shifted suddenly, and I lost my balance, falling to the floor. My stomach heaved in protest, and I vomited up the bitter coffee along with the lasagna I'd had for dinner before heading off to meet George.

Having emptied my stomach, I collapsed on my side, breathing heavily. The nausea and dizziness retreated to a manageable level. I opened my eyes cautiously.

I could see better now. It was dark, but as my eyes adjusted to the dim lighting I realized I was in some type of vehicle, and it was moving. I recalled the words of the mysterious second man. A van -- like a delivery truck. There was a wall. I couldn't get up front to where the guys were sitting. And I damn sure I didn't want to go where they were taking me.

I pushed myself upright into a sitting position. Despite the lingering dizziness in my head, one thing was abundantly clear. I needed to get out of here.

I used a handful of whatever I was laying on to wipe my face, gagging at the smell. Standing seemed like a bad idea, with the van lurching back and forth. It needed a decent alignment. Or some new shocks. Whatever. Not my problem.

I crawled to the back of the vehicle. I was still weak, but as my head slowly cleared, I realized I must have been drugged.

The bitter tasting coffee. George must have slipped something in my coffee when I went to get the wipes to clean up his mess. Had the mess been intentional to get me out of the way so he could spike my drink?

These guys knew what they were doing, and that spurred my need to escape. There were two of them and one of me. Even if I managed to throw off the effects of the drug, there was no way I could fight off two full grown men. My imagination went into overdrive. I had to assume wherever they were taking me was not public. They could do whatever they wanted and there would be no one to hear me scream.

Fear-fueled adrenaline overpowered the remaining drug in my system. I scrambled my way to the back of the van and clawed at the doors.

I screamed as loud as I could. Surely someone would hear me and go for help. Or call the cops. People didn't seem to want to get involved these days, but surely a woman screaming from inside a van would get some kind of response.

"Scream all you want. No one else can hear you," George shared with an repulsive chuckle.

Weren't these delivery vans supposed to have a release on the inside so people didn't get trapped in them? I got unsteadily to my feet and reached up as high as I could, sliding my hands down the loading doors. It had to be here somewhere.

Two thirds of the way down, I found it. My heart sank. There was a latch all right, but someone had broken it off. When I tried to push it, the latch swung loosely around in a circle without any effect on the doors.

I screamed in frustration and banged on the doors until my hands felt raw. Sinking down on my haunches, I let out a helpless sob.

Then I pulled myself together. I wasn't going to just sit here and wait for whatever sick plans these guys had for me. I crawled across the floor, feeling frantically for something, anything, that I could use to pry the doors open.

In the front corner, I found it. A tire iron. Gripping it tightly, I made my way to the back of the van just as it lurched to a stop.

I could hear loud engines, other vehicles pulling up behind the van. I screamed again. And again. Surely they could hear me, but I wasn't going to count on it.

Standing was a whole lot easier now that the van was still. I inserted the sharp edge of the tire iron between the two doors and pried. Nothing happened. I screamed in frustration and jerked harder on the tire iron. Nothing.

I could feel time running out. Fear of what George and his buddies had in store for me intensified with each passing moment. I had to get out of here. No knight in shining armor was going to ride in on a white horse and save me.

I moved the tire iron down so that it was in line with the broken release and threw my entire body weight against it. For a second, it held fast. Then the lock gave way with a loud *screech* of bending metal.

The doors burst open.

Off balance, and still gripping the tire iron with both hands, I fell out of the van and landed on the pavement with a painful jolt. I rolled over and staggered to my feet.

Less than a car length away, staring at me from the back of a shiny red and chrome motorcycle, was the most dangerous looking man I'd ever seen.

* * *

Deuce

What the hell?

Rattler and I were headed into town to the bar that Riptide owned on the lower east side of town. It was a nice night for a bike ride, and a cold beer sounded inviting. The sky was clear and there was just a hint of a breeze. The smell of fresh-cut hay permeated the air.

We'd stopped at the railroad crossing on Seventh Ave, behind one of those cargo vans. Kind of scuffed up. Serviceable, but not memorable. What had once been a name on the side was illegible, worn off by years of weather.

I kicked my Harley back down into first, scanning the tracks to gauge how long we'd be stationary. I had just flipped the visor up on my helmet when the back door of the van flew open and a woman half jumped, half tumbled out onto the pavement.

Seriously, what the hell?

She looked stunned. Or stoned. Not sure which. If I'd been any closer, she would have landed on my damn bike. Her eyes were open wide, and she stared up at me like she'd just seen a ghost. Or a monster.

Not that I hadn't had that effect on women before. I didn't look like your typical CPA. I'd ditched the office and three-piece suit a lifetime ago. Six-foot-six, riding a Harley, and sporting a leather cut that proclaimed me to be a patched-in member of the

Riptide MC? I didn't exactly scream *Wall Street.*

The woman's mouth moved, but if any sound came out, I didn't hear it. The train made a shit ton of noise, and Harleys aren't quiet either. There's a saying in the motorcycle world --"Loud pipes save lives." The theory was people could hear us coming so they paid attention or got out of the way. Not sure how true it was, but I had to admit you could hear us coming long before you saw us. Add that to the clank and rattle of the train, and you couldn't hear much else.

I glanced over at Rattler, who was just taking off his own helmet. We'd been in lots of shit together back in our SEALs days. Communication didn't have to be verbal. That nod he gave me meant he'd watch my back while I checked the chick out to see what the fuck was going on.

I killed the engine and set the kickstand before dismounting. Hanging my helmet on the handlebars, I stalked up to the woman.

Might be a little paranoid of me, but I did a visual sweep of the area to make sure it wasn't a trap. The back doors of the van were still open, revealing an empty cargo area with a pile of rags in one corner. What the fuck had she been doing in there?

My internal radar screamed trap. A couple of deployments in Afghanistan made me leery of anything that could be used to sucker a guy into range for an attack. A female in distress was the number one lure.

The woman rolled over and used her hands to push herself upright. Lurching to her feet, she glared at me, brandishing a tire iron in front of her like some kind of magic wand. Not sure where that came from. Must have been under her when she landed.

"Don't touch me!" Her voice broke as if she'd

been drinking, but I didn't detect the smell of alcohol on her.

"I'm not going to hurt you." I reached for the tire iron, dancing out of reach when she took a swipe at me with it.

"Stay away!" She looked about as menacing as a little kitten hissing at me. Just about as cute too.

I glanced over at Rattler and gave a slight shake of my head. He obligingly revved up his bike, and the woman instinctively looked over at him, giving me the chance to dart in and relieve her of that tire iron before someone got hurt. Like me.

"No!" Her face crumpled, and she wobbled on her feet.

I stepped forward, putting an arm around her to steady her. Noting the way she flinched at my touch, I tried to sound non-threatening. "Not sure what's going on, but we aren't the enemy."

I took a quick visual inventory of her condition. She had a slight case of road rash on one arm and her shirt was a write-off, shredded to pieces when she'd hit the ground. Her bra, a lacy confection of pink and white, barely covered her nipples. Despite the circumstances, she had a sensual allure that wasn't lost on me. Dark hair cut in a cute, pixie-type style framed a heart-shaped face. Her eyes were a dark chocolate color and at the moment were wide open. Terrified.

"What's your name?" Basic interrogation skill. Asking a simple question often calmed a person down.

She frowned, not replying right away. When she answered, it was with a question of her own. "Are you with them?"

I frowned. "Them? Who's them?"

She jerked her head toward the van. "Them. George and his buddy. The guys that threw me in the van."

I looked from her to the van, and the pieces of the puzzle fell into place. "They kidnapped you?"

The panicked expression in those dark eyes tore at my heart. She nodded. "First date. Drugged my coffee. I could barely walk, let alone fight back. Heard them call me 'merchandise'."

"Well, shit." Wasn't sure what else to say. The club had heard rumors that a human trafficking ring was operating in the area, but this was the first tangible evidence of it. Ace would want details, once we had this situation under control.

I turned to Rattler. "You up for a little fun?"

Rattler's eyes narrowed. "Always."

I switched my attention back to the woman, pointing at the deep ditch at the side of the road. "Get down in there and hide. Grass is tall enough to cover you. Keep your head low and don't come out until I tell you it's safe."

Her eyes wide, she scooted over to the side of the road and slid into the ditch. I watched as she got down on her belly and squirmed out of sight into the tall grasses. Satisfied she was safely hidden, I pulled my handgun out of the shoulder holster and flicked the safety off.

Rattler stood beside his bike, holding his favorite shotgun in front of him, the muzzle pointed at the passenger side of the van.

I pursed my lips, jerking my chin toward the target. We approached cautiously on either side of the vehicle, guns held at the ready. My trigger finger hovered in place, ready to act at a moment's notice.

The noise of the train must have covered the sound of the woman's escape, or those jackasses would have been jumping out to reacquire her. In the side mirror, I could see the driver lighting a cigarette as if he didn't have a care in the world.

I could no longer see Rattler, but we'd worked as a team in combat situations with multiple hostiles when we were on active duty. I'd trust him with my life. Always had.

The driver glanced in the mirror, his face registering shock when he saw me. He turned and reached for something on the seat beside him before heaving the door open. He threw himself out of the vehicle and I saw the flash of metal in his hand as he turned to face me.

Auto reflexes kicked in. I took the shot. Chest. Hit him in the heart. He was dead before he hit the ground.

Ignoring the corpse, I held my gun at the ready and circled the front of the van just as Rattler's shotgun boomed. Damn.

I expected to see another corpse.

Wrong. Must have been a warning shot.

Rattler and the second perp were in a standoff, yards apart with weapons pointed at each other. A stone rolled from under my foot, alerting the asshole to my presence behind him. He pivoted to target me with the weapon, and his head swung wildly back and forth between me and Rattler. If he knew his buddy was dead, it didn't seem to faze him.

"The bitch belongs to us. Give her back, and you don't get hurt." The idiot spat on the ground and took a step toward me.

Not only ugly, but stupid.

"I don't think so." Rattler stood with his legs planted solidly on the ground, the picture of a Capone era gangster as he pointed his favorite short-barreled shotgun at the asshole's head.

"She's not worth fighting over." The gun wavered just a bit as the asshole switched his attention to Rattler. "You don't want to do that."

Rattler's smile was devoid of humor. "Yeah, I think I do." His aim held steady as he made a point of moving his finger just a hair on the trigger.

"She's not worth it." The idiot repeated his statement as if it might be more persuasive the second time.

"Then maybe you should call it a day and move on."

The asshole narrowed his eyes. "You don't know who you're dealing with." He took a step backward so he could see both of us without constantly swiveling his head.

Rattler shrugged, drawing the motherfucker's attention back to himself. "Don't care. You pulled a gun on me. Can't let that shit go." His eyes shone with a wicked light. "Maybe you don't know who you're dealing with."

With a frustrated grunt, the idiot gave it one last, desperate try. "Just give us the girl, and we all leave happy."

Dead quiet descended as the last of the train's cars cleared the crossing and disappeared around a bend in the tracks.

Rattler didn't take his eyes off the asshole as he raised his voice, not giving away the woman's hiding spot. "You want to go with this guy, lady?"

"No."

The jackass raked the area with his eyes, trying to determine the woman's location.

"You heard the lady," Rattler snarled. "She doesn't want to go with you. Now why don't you just hop back into that piece of shit and disappear into whatever hellhole you came from?"

"I could shoot you right now and take her." The gun wavered between me and Rattler.

"You might want to be real sure of your aim." Rattler grinned menacingly. "Because one shot is all you're going to get with that little peashooter before I blow you into pieces so small they'll need dental records to identify you."

The kidnapper hesitated, as if deciding how serious Rattler was.

"Well?" Rattler dropped the muzzle and sent another round into the ground just in front of the idiot to drive his point home.

"Fine!" The asshole jumped back, glaring furiously at Rattler. He lowered his gun and reached for the van's door handle. Hauling himself back into the van, he hurled one last threat. "You're gonna regret this!"

He slammed the door shut, and moments later the van peeled across the tracks with a squeal of tires. My eyes darted down to the van's license plate, committing the number to memory. Shadow should be able to trace it. He was a magician with a computer. I swear that guy could trace a single ghost hiding in a graveyard.

I relaxed, grinning at Rattler as I holstered my weapon. "You are a crazy son of a bitch."

Rattler stalked back to his bike and settled the shotgun into its sheath. His mouth quirked up in a grin. "Not really. We had him outnumbered two to one, and you were the one he had in his sights. If he planned to smoke me, he should have done it before you joined the party."

"Good point."

But I knew he meant it in jest. Rattler had my

back. Always. Just as I had his.

I nudged the dead thug with the toe of my boot. "I'll call Beast and have him send a crew to clean up the garbage."

"We should probably get him off the road in case anyone comes by before Beast and the team get here. Grab his legs." Rattler spat on the ground. "One less waste of oxygen on the planet."

Together the two of us lugged the body to the far side of the road and rolled it into the weeds. Unless someone looked carefully, it wasn't visible from the road. It would do until the cleanup crew got here.

I turned and addressed the tall grass in the ditch. "You can come out now."

"Are they gone?" The woman's head popped into view from behind a stand of tall grass.

"Yeah."

She clambered out of the ditch, shivering visibly and I realized how cold she must be. There was no way I could put my cut on her; the symbolism would be too much. Putting my cut on a female was tantamount to declaring her my old lady. Did that once and it turned out badly. Not planning on going for round two.

I sighed and took my cut off before shrugging out of my shirt and handing it to her. "Here. Put this on."

She took the shirt, frowning. "What are you going to wear?"

"This." I pulled my cut back on.

"Oh." That single, little word, barely a whisper, sounded so forlorn I almost wished the remaining asshole in the van would circle back so I could teach him some manners. I made a point of turning my back to give her the illusion of privacy as she donned my shirt.

Over to my right, I could see Rattler's shoulders shaking with suppressed mirth. He knew how cold it was going to be riding with just my cut to block the wind.

The shirt would help keep the woman warm, but it wasn't exactly a fleece sweater and would do zilch to cut the wind. We needed to get her somewhere warm. Fast.

I still needed to find out what her name was, and how she ended up in that van.

"There's a coffee shop not far from here. We can talk there. Okay?"

She nodded slowly, eyeing up my Harley. Right. Not everyone thought a bike was a great way to travel.

"You okay to ride behind me?"

She looked from me to the bike and gulped. "I guess so."

Not the most enthusiastic answer I'd ever heard, but it would do. I grabbed the extra helmet from the backrest and helped her fasten it on her head. "What's your name?"

She paused. "Sophia."

At least I had something I could call her now. I wasn't about to push for a last name. Given the circumstances, she'd probably lie anyway. "Nice name."

Satisfied with the fit of the helmet, I slung one leg over the bike and held out my hand to help her on. She climbed aboard behind me and put her hands on my waist, holding on gingerly.

Obviously, she'd never been on a bike before.

I grabbed her hands and dragged her arms around me. "You need to hang on tight or you'll end up splattered on the ground again."

That point certainly hit home. She scooted closer,

plastering herself against my back and tightening her arms.

I flipped the kickstand up and cranked the engine, glancing over at Rattler. "Heading to *Coffee Quest*. You coming?"

Rattler nodded. "I'll cover your back. Just in case."

I wasn't the only one with a paranoid streak.

Chapter Two

Sophia

I sure hoped I hadn't jumped from the frying pan into the fire. I had no idea who the guy was that I was pressed up against, the smell of his leather vest filling my nose as we flew down the highway. I just knew he'd saved me, him and his sidekick.

The cool air, carrying the scent of damp earth and freshly mowed hay, filled my lungs and lifted my spirits. The knot of dread in my stomach unraveled. I'd never been on a motorcycle before, and was surprised at how much I liked it. I'd always pictured motorcycles as a sort of dangerous, borderline illegal method of transportation. Like for people who were too poor or too dumb to buy an actual car.

Now that I was on one, I suddenly understood the attraction. Maybe it was just because I'd been trapped in that van, but riding on the back of a motorcycle, I felt free. Almost giddy. I hung on tight, and every turn, every corner gave me a primeval high.

We swooped around another corner and into the parking lot of a strip mall. At the far end was a sign that read *Coffee Quest*. A vague blip of disappointment tumbled through me. The ride was over.

My savior maneuvered through the parking lot and pulled up in front of the coffee shop. His feet dropped to the ground to balance us as he cut the engine.

I loosened my arms, reluctant to let go quite yet. He might be the most dangerous looking man I'd ever seen, but he was also the sexiest. How come I never saw guys like this on dating apps?

His dark hair was shaved military short, and that day-old scruff of a beard softened his appearance. His chiseled features were tempered by a generous mouth. A faint scar on his face barely missed his eye. Mostly healed, it suggested he'd been in a nasty fight a few months ago. I could feel the solid wall of muscle under my arms as I held onto him, not to mention the intoxicating smell of leather and male that assailed my nose.

He might not be wearing shiny armor or be mounted on a white horse, but he had come to my rescue like the knight in a fairy tale.

The second bike pulled up beside us and the rider looked at me with a crooked grin before addressing my hero. "She looks good on you, Deuce. Who would have thought it." He parked his bike and turned to hold a hand out to me.

I let him help me off the bike, feeling shy. I didn't know either of these guys. I suddenly realized that my phone, my wallet, my purse, everything was gone, and I was standing shivering in front of a strip mall with two complete strangers who didn't exactly look like upright citizens. And yet I felt safer than I had with George. Neither of these guys gave off the creepy vibe I'd felt with him.

My savior slid off his bike. Giving me a quick once over, he nodded. "You don't look too badly scuffed up, other than your hair. We wouldn't want to raise any suspicions in there."

"Suspicions?"

He shrugged. "Bikers with a woman who looks like she's been roughed up?"

"Oh. They might think you hurt me." I reached up self-consciously and finger-combed my hair. "Better?"

He nodded. "Let's get inside and get a warm coffee into you."

I shuddered. I wasn't quite ready for another coffee after how that last one had ended. "Can we make that tea, please? But I don't have any money on me."

Biker number two shrugged. "I think we can afford to buy you a cup of tea after you livened up our evening." He grinned over at his buddy. "I haven't had that much fun in ages."

Biker number one rolled his eyes. "You are trouble, Rattler."

I cocked my head. "Your name is Rattler?"

"My road name, yes. And your arm candy there is Deuce."

"What's a road name?"

The two exchanged a glance over my head. Rattler opened the door to the coffee shop and held it for Deuce and me to scoot inside before answering. "It's sort of like a nickname that the club gives you when you patch in."

Deuce held up his hand to forestall my next question. "Patching in is when you become a full-fledged member of the motorcycle club, in our case Riptide. Before that you're a prospect, as in prospective member."

"Maybe we should get our drinks before we finish playing twenty questions." Rattler exchanged another cryptic look with Deuce. "How about you two go find a table and I'll get Rylie to make the drinks. You want sugar or milk in your tea?"

I shook my head. "No, just black please. Who's Rylie?"

"The owner of *Coffee Quest*. She's Cyclone's old lady, which is how we know this place is safe."

"I take it Cyclone is a road name for another biker?"

Deuce grinned. "Yeah, it is. You catch on fast."

He led the way to a booth in the back of the building, and I noted how he seated himself so he could see the entire shop. It made me think of my dad, who did the same thing whenever he was forced to appear in public. Thoughts of my dad reminded me I needed to call Janet.

I slid in across from him. "Can I borrow your phone for a minute? I need to let a friend know I'm okay or she'll have the cops and my dad out looking for me, and you do *not* want to meet my dad."

Deuce reached into the inside pocket of his jacket and pulled out his cell, unlocking the screen before handing it over. "Why don't I want to meet your dad?"

I took the phone. "He still thinks I'm his little girl, and he's a prepper, so he doesn't tend to play nice." I dialed and held up a hand to stop Deuce from saying anything else until I'd assured Janet that I was fine and the date hadn't been great without going into detail. She wanted to know why I wasn't calling from my own phone and I told her I'd misplaced it and had to borrow one from a friend to call her. Not exactly a lie, but it satisfied her for now and gave me an excuse to keep the call short. I agreed to meet her for a drink the next day so we could dissect yet another failure to find my soul mate. Ending the call, I handed Deuce back his phone and looked up just as Rattler put three cups down on the table and slid in beside Deuce.

"Sophia here was just going to explain why meeting her dad would be a bad idea." Deuce looked at me expectantly. "I'm not sure if you meant he's the kind of guy who's likely to call the cops on me, or an end-of-the-world prepper who'll beat the crap out of me for looking at you."

I sighed. "The second one. He's got enough guns

and ammo to blow up half the town, and enough practice in hiding in the bush to make sure no one ever finds the bodies." I looked from one to the other and realized how that sounded. "Not that he's ever killed anyone, except maybe when he was in the SEALs," I added hastily.

"Sounds like my kind of guy." Rattler grinned and took a big gulp of his coffee.

I shook my head. "You don't get it. If he thinks you two were the ones who hurt me, he'd shoot first and ask questions later. That's assuming he doesn't decide he's got enough time to beat you to death with his bare hands. He loves me, but he's not a gentle, cuddly kind of dad."

"I do get it," Deuce said. "If I had a daughter, I'd probably feel the same way. Sounds like he really cares about you."

"He does." I picked up my tea and took an experimental sip. "He's always been there for me."

"What about your mom?"

I shrugged. "Don't really remember much about her. She took off when I was three. Dad says she just wasn't into being a parent. I was an accident she didn't want to deal with, so she split."

"Ouch." Rattler grimaced.

Why was I telling these guys my life story? "Not really as bad as it sounds. Dad was great and always made sure I knew I was loved. He just finds it a little hard to accept that I'm an adult now and can take care of myself."

Rattler and Deuce exchanged one of those looks.

I rolled my eyes. "Okay, I kind of got in over my head this time, but who the hell expects drugs in a coffee?"

Rattler's phone pinged, and he pulled it out of

his pocket to glance at the screen. "Gotta take this." He slid out of the booth, putting the phone to his ear as he strode away from us.

"You were drugged in a coffee shop?" Deuce frowned, and I realized I hadn't told these guys the whole story. Somehow, we'd skipped over to my family situation.

"Yeah. There's this dating app that's supposed to be super safe and easy." I explained the whole sequence of events to him, stressing how I'd taken every precaution to protect myself even though it hadn't been quite enough. Hindsight being 20/20, the only way I could have possibly avoided the situation was to have a bodyguard nearby for the whole date.

Needless to point out, if I'd felt that was necessary, I never would have gone.

"Does this George guy know where you live? Or where you work?" Deuce looked thoughtful.

I shook my head. "No, but I'm not sure where my purse or phone is. I think they got left behind at the coffee shop, but if those guys have them, they'll know where to find me. My phone is locked to my faceprint, but my driver's license and credit cards are all in my purse."

"I don't think it's a good idea for you to be home alone tonight." Deuce sounded dead serious. "Any chance this prepper dad of yours could come stay with you for a day or two? Just until you're sure this whole thing is over? Sounds like he could scare off just about anyone."

"Hell, no!" I snorted. "If I tell him what happened he'll hunt George down, and then I'd have to spring for bail, and a lawyer."

"I thought you said he knew where to hide the bodies?" Deuce sounded amused.

"Doesn't mean I want him to have to."

"Good point."

"Maybe I should report this to the police." I paused. "You know, in case they try it again with some other woman and there's not a couple of awesome bikers nearby to whisk her away to safety."

"Good idea, but don't expect too much."

"Why not?" I frowned.

"Cops are understaffed and overworked. Since you obviously escaped, they might decide it's not worth pursuing."

"Oh." I wanted to protest, but these guys probably had more of an insight into the local police situation than I did.

Deuce held out his phone to me. "Pull up the guy's profile for me. I'll bet George isn't his real name, and there's nothing on there to lead back to him."

I took the phone and pulled up the app on the web. It didn't take much to log in, but when I did the conversation between me and George had disappeared completely.

In fact, George was nowhere to be found.

I stared at the blank screen in disbelief. "Son of a bitch!"

* * *

Deuce

"What's up?" Rattler slid back into the booth, and I caught him up on what Sophia had told me while he was gone.

"She's checking out the app now, looking for George's details," I said.

Rattler turned his attention to Sophia. "Your plans to meet at the coffee shop not there?"

A look of disbelief on her face, Sophia nodded.

"It's like I made it all up. It's all gone. Every chat we had just poofed. Vanished. His profile has disappeared too." She handed my phone back to me.

I quickly scanned her bio. Her profile pic was adorable, but chaste. Not exactly a Tinder kind of shot. Pretty generic, nothing to ring any alarm bells. I saved her login and the website before closing it. Technically an invasion of privacy but given the circumstances, justified. Maybe Shadow could dig deeper into it when we got back to the clubhouse.

I exchanged looks with Rattler over Sophia's head. Neither of us were surprised George had wiped his profile. He'd just set up a new profile as Sam or Henry or some other common name and continue the scam. Chances were, this was the gang Ace was looking for. They were slick. Professional. It was pure luck we'd been there when Sophia managed to free herself. How many before her hadn't been that lucky?

"Not much point in calling the cops. It's going to look like you made up the whole story."

She repeated her earlier expletive, but softer. "Son of a bitch."

"Exactly. These guys are pro. How much does this George guy know about you?"

Sophia gave me a blank look. "What do you mean?"

"Personal details. Anything that will make it easy for him to find you?"

"No. Unless he has my purse." She shook her head. "You think he's going to come after me?"

"Maybe, maybe not, but it's better to play it safe." I didn't want to scare her, but chances were good this George character would want to reacquire her. She could ID him, and possibly his henchman. Pros didn't like to leave loose ends.

"I didn't have any of that on my profile, and I didn't tell him when we met. I told him I was a teacher, but I didn't say which school or that I'm a sub so I go to whichever school needs me for a day or two. Other than that I do custom sewing, mostly from home. I picked that place to meet because it isn't too close to where I live, and it's not one I normally go to."

Rattler nodded. "Good. He still might be able to find you, but you didn't make it easy for him."

"I just didn't want to run into him again if he turned out to be a jerk." She snorted. "I didn't expect this." She wrapped her hands around the tea mug and lifted it to her lips.

Gorgeous lips. Full and sensual. I could see why she'd been targeted. She had that innocently seductive look about her that aroused both my inner demons and my protective streak. George was lucky I didn't know where to find him.

Rattler cleared his throat, giving me a meaningful look. "That was Ace on the phone. Something came up and he wants me back at the clubhouse. You okay with me leaving?"

"Sure." I wasn't about to ask what was up with Ace. Not in front of a civilian. We didn't share club business with outsiders. "I'll let you know if I need anything."

Rattler gulped down the rest of his coffee and got to his feet. "Nice to meet you, Sophia."

She gave him a warm smile. "Nice to meet you too, Rattler. Thanks for everything."

I tamped down an unexpected surge of jealousy. I wanted her to smile at me like that. Rattler gave me a lopsided salute and strode to the door.

Sophia took another sip of her tea. "Can I get a ride back to my car? It's still at the coffee shop where I met George."

I shook my head. "Bad idea. Chances are George will be watching for you to come back. I can take you home and send one of the prospects to pick up your car and move it to a safe place for the night. Do you have your keys?"

She grimaced. "No, but I have a spare set at home. I can get them for you if you take me home."

I resisted the urge to smile. "That would be good. The prospects could probably hotwire it, but it's easier if we give them the keys. It's a long shot, but they can ask at the coffee shop to see if your purse is still there. Don't get your hopes up, though. I'm guessing George and his buddy made sure to snag it when they grabbed you."

She tilted her head. "Thanks. I need my car. Even if you take me home, I want to be available if I get called to work on Monday."

I could tell the moment reality hit home. "They can't call me. I don't have my phone!"

That hadn't occurred to me, but it posed a problem. I wasn't interested in her going to work on Monday, but she needed to be able to call for help. "I'll have someone drop off a phone for you. There are always a few burners hanging around the club. You'll have to get hold of your service provider and let them know you lost it so they can lock it and switch the service to the new one. They might be able to load your contacts and apps on a new one as well if you have a cloud backup."

She sighed. "I have no idea if I have a backup in the cloud, but I'll ask when I contact them. I want to say you're already doing too much for me, but I really need a phone, so thanks."

"No problem. Not every day someone throws

herself at my feet." I smiled to let her know I was teasing. "We can make sure no one is following the car and get it to you over the weekend. Shadow can sweep it to make sure there's no tracking device on it."

"I'm starting to feel out of my depth. Who is Shadow, and how come it sounds like those prospects are doing a lot of the work?"

"Shadow is our tech guy, and part of being a prospect is getting stuck with all the grunt work."

"Like picking up vehicles that might be watched by dangerous guys?"

"Exactly. I doubt this George character is a match for any of the prospects. My guess is if he sees them retrieve your car, he'll try to follow them in the hopes of finding you. If he does that, they'll know, and they can nab him."

She didn't ask how. Her head was probably reeling from everything that had happened. Did she know I'd smoked the driver of the van? I didn't know if that was George or his sidekick, not that it mattered.

"Oh." She stared down at the table. "I really screwed up, didn't I?"

"Absolutely not. Not your fault. You couldn't have known these guys were lurking on that app. You were just unlucky enough to catch their attention." When she didn't reply, I reached out and covered her hand with mine. "I'm going to see if Rylie's husband happened to leave a shirt here that I can borrow. Be right back."

I slid out of the booth and strode over to the counter. "Hey, Rylie. Any chance Cyclone has a shirt laying around I can borrow?"

"I'll see what I can find." She disappeared into the back room and returned with a sweatshirt which looked like it had seen better days. The edges were tattered, and it had paint splattered all over the front. She knew enough not to question me as to why I only had my cut on, and why the woman with me appeared to be wearing my shirt.

I thanked her and pulled it on, walking back to Sophia. "Ready to go?"

She eyed my new wardrobe doubtfully as I pulled my cut on over it. Getting to her feet, she hesitated a moment before giving me her address.

I totally got it. After the events of the day, giving out personal details like this must seem like a really bad idea.

* * *

The ride to Sophia's house made me want to keep rolling on down the highway. She clung to my back, with her head resting between my shoulder blades. Her arms were around my waist, her touch sending shivers down my spine, and if she had moved her hands a few inches lower, she would have discovered the extent of my attraction to her.

We stopped in front of a modest two-story house in a family friendly section of town, and Sophia sat up straight. I missed the warmth of her body pressed against me.

A cement path dissected the neatly trimmed lawn and led to the front door. Nice setup. I guided my bike into the driveway, then under the carport. Sophia slid off the bike and I dismounted, pulling off my helmet. Hanging it from the handlebars, I helped Sophia off with hers and placed it on the seat.

Sophia ran her fingers through her hair, fluffing it up from the helmet's flattening effects. "I'll disable the security system." She walked over to the side door and entered a code into the electronic door lock. A blipping sound emerged, and she scurried over to the number pad and entered a code to shut off the security system.

I nodded my approval. "Is that motion activated throughout the house, or does it just register entry at the door?"

"Motion activated," she replied. "Why?"

"If it was just attached to entry points, I'd suggest you arm it when you're in the house but that's not going to work with a motion activated system."

She sighed. "No, but I will make sure to lock the doors even if I'm home. This sucks. I wish I'd never agreed to the damn date."

"Yeah, it does suck, but hindsight is never helpful. You have to look at the bright side."

"There's a bright side?"

I grinned. "You met me and got to ride on an awesome motorcycle."

I could tell she was struggling not to smile. "I suppose it is a nice bike."

"You suppose? That bike is my pride and joy!" I followed her into the kitchen and spotted an electric kettle on the counter. Time to change the subject.

"You should have someone stay with you tonight. You sure you don't want to call your dad?" Filling the kettle with water, I plugged it in.

She shook her head. "Absolutely not. I don't want him to know what happened. I'll see if Janet can come over." She sighed. "Right. No phone. Can I borrow yours again, please?"

I would have felt better with an overly protective dad, but a BFF wasn't a bad idea. And I'd have a couple of prospects keep a discreet eye on the place.

I handed her my phone and watched as she punched in her BFF's number and waited for an answer.

The call went to voicemail and she looked up at me. "What's your number? I'll send her a text, and hopefully she'll call when she gets in." She sounded doubtful.

I gave her the number and watched her send the text. I didn't know this Janet person, but it was a Friday night. What were the chances she'd get in before midnight? "I'll stay with you until she does. Where do you keep your tea?"

She blinked. "I don't need tea, and I can't ask you to keep watch over me all night. I'll lock the doors. It'll be fine."

I shook my head. "Nope. Not happening. And maybe the tea was for me. I need something to fortify me if I'm going to have to resist your tempting body all night."

A reluctant smile curved her lips. "My tempting body?"

I raked my gaze over her. "Big tits and curves all over the place? Hell yeah, that's tempting! All I can do to keep my hands to myself."

Sophia laughed nervously. "You're crazy!"

I grinned. "You are not the first to point that out. So, do you want to join me for a warm cup of tea, or are you heading straight for the sack?"

"I'm too keyed up to sleep. I think I'll watch a movie while I wait for Janet to call back."

"I'll be staying until she calls." I made it a statement, not a question.

Sophia looked like she was going to argue but then shrugged her shoulders. Was that a hint of relief I saw in her expression?

"Your choice. A shower is probably a bad idea, but I need to wash up and get into something a little more comfortable. The living room is that way." She waved her hand toward the far doorway.

I turned back to the kettle, which was now whistling cheerfully. Opening the cupboards one at a time, I found an assortment of tea along with a teapot and one of those crocheted covers people used to keep the tea warm. I chose a decaf Earl Grey blend and made a full pot, just in case she changed her mind.

Grabbing two mugs from the carousel on the counter, I took the tea in search of the living room. Just as I set everything down on the coffee table, I heard a shriek from upstairs.

Shit! Now what?

Chapter Three

Sophia

I stripped off my clothes, tossing the remains of my shirt in the trash can. Deuce's shirt went in the laundry hamper. The least I could do was wash it before I returned it to him. The road rash on my arm looked better than I'd anticipated. It had started to scab over, but it needed to be cleaned. The last thing I wanted was to have it get infected.

Stepping into the adjoining bathroom, I picked up a clean facecloth. Wetting it under a stream of warm water, I added some liquid soap. My mind was only half on the task at hand, the other half wondering what that mouthwatering biker was doing downstairs. It had been ages since a man had been in my house, and even longer since one had made my heart flutter like a schoolgirl's.

Still daydreaming about Deuce, I gently wiped the soap-laden cloth across the patch of raw skin on my arm. A searing, white-hot pain shot through my arm, and I let out a high-pitched scream of agony.

Damn, that hurt!

I gritted my teeth. I didn't have a choice. If I didn't want to end up with an infection, I had to clean the road debris out of the wound. I could see grime mixed in with the clotting blood. I raised the cloth once again, steeling myself against the anticipated pain.

The door to the bedroom burst open and Deuce barreled in, pistol in hand. He looked like an avenging angel, sweeping the room with a smooth confidence that made me think he made a habit of this. Gliding across to the closet, he stood to the side while he opened it and checked for... what? Mice?

It was just the last straw after the day from hell. I

started to giggle.

His attention snapped to me.

"You screamed." It sounded more like an accusation than a statement.

I nodded as tears of laughter rolled down my cheeks. I felt dangerously close to hysterics.

"Why?"

I gasped for air, trying to get myself under control. Holding up my arm, I pointed to the road rash with the soap-laden cloth. "It hurt. Soap. Clean."

Not exactly my most lucid speech but I could see the moment realization dawned on the overprotective biker. Sliding the gun back into its holster, he strode toward me.

This bathroom wasn't built for two. Or at least, not if one of them was a huge, muscular biker. Trapped between the counter and his delectable frame, my body started to want things it hadn't had in a very long time. Like sex. Hot, naked, yummy sex. Probably didn't help that all I was wearing was a towel. Admittedly a big, fluffy towel, but if it were to slip off…

I reined in my overactive libido. He was here because he felt some kind of duty toward me. He thought of me as an obligation. Someone he needed to look after because they'd gotten in over their heads.

That sure put a damper on my lust. The one thing I did not want from this big bad biker was pity.

A deadpan expression on his face, Deuce grasped my wrist and tugged gently, stretching my arm out to expose the raw road rash. No longer pinned in place on that side, the towel started to slip.

I gasped and grabbed at it, managing to snag the material before it slid too far.

I looked up, but the biker's attention was on my wounded arm. Picking up the facecloth, he rinsed most of the soap out of it before gently stroking it back and forth across the raw flesh, removing the debris left behind by the brutal contact with the road.

I didn't quite manage to stifle a whimper as he cleansed a particularly painful spot. His eyes snapped to mine. "They won't ever hurt you again."

I recalled the sound of gunfire, but I didn't ask him to elaborate. Maybe he'd killed George. Maybe he'd killed the second guy. Or maybe he'd just scared the hell out of them. Either way, I was okay with it, but I didn't need details.

I dipped my head, peering up at him through my lashes. "Thank you."

Deuce nodded curtly and continued to minister to my arm. When he was satisfied it was clean, he found some salve in the medicine cabinet and applied a liberal amount before covering it with a layer of gauze and taping it in place.

"That should do it." He placed a finger under my chin, tilting it up. "Keep an eye on it. If it starts to get infected, you'll need antibiotics."

I bit my lower lip. The increase in my heart rate had nothing to do with the thought of an infection. "Okay. I can go to a clinic if I need to."

He shook his head. "Call me. We have a medic. He can get antibiotics for you."

"You have a medic? You... who?"

That lopsided grin made my heart skip a beat. It should be illegal for someone so wrong for me to be so damned attractive. "The club. Riptide. Bikers, remember? We have a medic who takes care of us when we need it."

"Oh." I frowned. "You get hurt a lot?" I clutched the towel tighter, aware that I was all but naked with a stranger in my home. The fact that it didn't bother me might be something I needed to consider. Later. When I was alone. Again.

Maybe I should consider getting a cat.

That irresistible grin widened. "Not a lot, but it's handy when we do. Joker was part of our team in the SEALs, and he joined us when we landed stateside." Deuce pivoted and stepped out of the tiny bathroom. "Tea's in the living room. I'll head down there while you get something on. We can play twenty questions in comfort."

"You're not leaving?" I needed him to confirm it. I did not want to be alone. I'd left a message for Janet to come over, but if she'd found someone to amuse her, chances were she wouldn't be home till dawn.

"Not until your friend shows up." He paused and glanced back at me. "Are you okay with that?"

"Sure." I lowered my head to hide the sudden heat that filled my cheeks at the thought of Deuce sleeping over. Not that he meant it that way. Or any way. I needed to get my mind out of the gutter. He probably had attractive women throwing themselves at him all the time. Hell, just because he didn't have a ring on didn't mean there wasn't a wife and a couple of kids waiting for him at home. He just felt responsible for me because I'd practically fallen into his lap.

Maybe a dog would be better than a cat. I'd have to give the idea of a pet some serious thought. I doubted I'd venture back onto dating apps anytime soon.

* * *

Clean and dressed in comfy flannel pajamas, I pulled on my housecoat before I checked Deuce's phone. He'd left it with me so I'd see if Janet texted me back. She had, but it wasn't the news I wanted to hear. She wasn't coming over. She was gone for the night.

Since I hadn't revealed anything in my message suggesting it was urgent, I couldn't blame her. She probably thought I was just bored and wanted some company.

Now that I was safely home, I was starting to feel a little sheepish. I wasn't sure I wanted to talk about the whole thing yet, not even with my BFF.

I headed to the living room. Deuce sat on the sofa with his legs splayed out in front of him. A teapot and two mugs sat on a tray on the coffee table, with a plate of cheese and crackers beside it.

The man appeared to have a domestic streak, which clashed wildly with my mental image of him as a dangerous biker. He stood when he heard me enter the room.

He lifted one brow. "You hear from your friend yet?"

I nodded. "Yeah. She's not coming. She's out for the night."

He lifted one brow. "I thought she was your BFF. As in cover your butt, be there when you need her kind of friend."

I shrugged. "I didn't exactly tell her what happened. I just asked her to come watch an old movie with me."

He gave me a quizzical look but let the subject drop. "I'll stay the night then. You shouldn't be alone."

I frowned, not sure what to say.

He held up one hand. "I'll behave. I promise. I can sleep on the couch."

Although being alone normally didn't bother me, having someone stay sounded like a great idea tonight. Since I didn't want to drag my dad into this mess, Deuce was the next best choice. He'd already demonstrated his ability to make the bad guys turn tail and run.

"I'll get you a pillow and some blankets."

"I can get them. You sure you're okay with leaving the cops out of this?"

Probably picked up from my dad, but I had a distrust of authority figures in general and that included law enforcement. "What if they're in on it? Cops can be bought, right?"

He gave me a quizzical look. "You sound like you've had some dealings with them that didn't turn out so well."

I shook my head. "No. Not really. Just hearsay and listening to my dad talk. He doesn't have much faith in them."

He stared at me for a long moment. "Your choice, but you can sleep on it and decide in the morning. Not like they're going to do much about it tonight anyway."

Relief flooded through me. I really didn't want to deal with anyone right now, and I didn't want to argue about it. "Sounds like a plan. I'll go get you that bedding now."

Deuce shook his head. "Not necessary. Just tell me where and I'll get it myself. You sit and drink your tea. I made decaf Earl Grey. Something warm in your belly will help you sleep."

This guy was almost too nice to be real. How come I never met anyone like him on the damn dating apps? I smiled gratefully and reached for one of the mugs. "There's a linen closet at the top of the stairs to the left."

Deuce turned and left the room, and I heard his footsteps ascending the stairs. The man was not light on his feet. He returned moments later, his arms full of bedding. He tossed it on the overstuffed chair on the far side of the room. Plucking one of the blankets out of the stack, he spread it over me and tucked it in.

Picking up the other mug, he tossed the remote control to me. "So what are we watching?"

I crinkled my nose. "An old favorite of mine. *Darlin' Bride*."

* * *

Deuce

It didn't take long for Sophia to fall asleep. She looked adorable, snuggled up in the corner of the sofa with the blanket pulled up tight to her chin. The gauze bandage on her arm was still dry, which I took to be a good sign. The bleeding had stopped.

I picked up my phone and texted Rattler. I wanted a couple of prospects over here watching the house. Sophia didn't think the kidnappers knew where to find her, but it was better to be safe than sorry. He replied within minutes, which meant whatever business Ace had pulled him for was done. He promised to send a couple of guys over ASAP.

I got up as quietly as possible and carried the tea tray back to the kitchen. Sophia's house was cozy and inviting. I liked it. The kitchen had a small island in the middle, and French doors leading out to a patio. I did a quick security loop of the house, checking to make sure all the doors were locked and the curtains were closed. If anyone was out there, I didn't want them to be able to see the inside layout.

Hopefully the sight of my bike parked under the carport would deter any would-be bad guys from thinking Sophia was alone and an easy target. If not, I'd take care of them, but Sophia didn't need any more drama tonight.

I considered carrying Sophia up to her bedroom,

but I wasn't sure how sound a sleeper she was. She looked comfortable where she was, so I decided to leave her alone.

Loading the dating website she'd accessed earlier on my phone, I browsed for a while, using the login details I'd saved from her earlier. It looked like a legit site. Lots of lonely guys and gals looking to hook up. If George and crew were using it to target women, it was unlikely the admins knew about it. Maybe Shadow could dig a little deeper. I needed to let Ace know what was going on, though. As Prez, it would be his call as to whether or not Riptide got involved. I sent him a quick text. Moments later, my phone rang.

I moved to the kitchen before answering so as not to disturb Sophia.

"You think it's the human trafficking ring our buddies in the bureau have been looking for?" Ace didn't waste any time on small talk.

"Kind of light on details so far, but it looks like a possibility." I leaned against the counter. "Thought maybe Shadow could dig a little deeper into the dating app Sophia was targeted from."

"Sophia is the woman you and Rattler rescued?"

"Yeah. I'm staying with her tonight, just in case. She called a friend but they aren't available tonight, and she doesn't want to involve family."

There was a pause on the other end of the line. "She okay with you being there?"

"Yeah. She seems to trust me. Feisty thing, but this shook her up."

"Understandable. Rattler mentioned she took a fall from the vehicle. She okay, or do you need Joker to come look at her?"

"She's got some road rash on one arm, but she seems to be okay other than that. If it looks worse in the morning we can reevaluate."

"Fair enough. Did she report this to the cops?"

"No. Seems to have some hesitation about trusting them. Told her to sleep on it and see how she felt in the morning."

"Good instincts. Intel from our friends in the FBI is that there might be some kind of payoff going on. Tips aren't being acted on fast enough. Could be one rogue cop, or the whole department. Or maybe just a coincidence. Impossible to tell, but I'd be careful if I were her. Do they know where to find her?"

"She doesn't think so." I paused. "Maybe contacting the cops is a bad idea. If she reports the incident, anyone on the force will know who she is and where to find her."

"Good point. Think you can talk her out of reporting?"

I snorted. "She's not keen on the idea, so yeah. Pretty sure I can do that."

"I'll get Shadow to investigate the dating app. I'll have him do a background check on her as well. Can you send him any info you have?'

"No problem. I'll do that as soon as we're done."

"Good. And, Deuce?"

"Yeah?"

"Be careful. I don't like the looks of this on the heels of that murder Emma witnessed a couple months back. Don't have anything solid, but it feels connected."

"Roger that." I had the same feeling.

I pocketed my phone and wandered back into the living room. Sophia hadn't moved. If I left her sleeping where she was, she was going to wake up stiff and sore. I could either rouse her and tell her to go to bed, or I could just carry her up and tuck her in.

The temptation to hold her in my arms won out. I slipped upstairs and folded the sheets on her bed back so I could place her in it, then went back down.

She let out a soft moan when I picked her up, turning to snuggle in tight against me.

I'm no saint. My cock rose with alacrity, straining against the rough material of my jeans.

Note to self. Don't go commando if Sophia's around.

It was all I could do to just carry her up the stairs and lay her on her bed. My body wanted me to snuggle up with her, but sanity prevailed. I'd promised to behave myself.

Sucks to be a guy who always keeps his promises.

I slid the housecoat off her shoulders and tossed it onto the chair in the corner of the room. She was wearing a set of flannel pajamas with kittens cavorting all over them. First time I'd ever been jealous of a bunch of kittens.

I pulled the bedding up to her chin. Her brow wrinkled, and she let out a little whimper. I wondered if it was because she missed the feel of my arms holding her safe. She tossed and turned restlessly for a few moments before settling back down to sleep.

When had I become such a wuss? After my old lady bailed on me, I'd vowed to be a love 'em and leave 'em kind of guy. I made sure the women I bedded had no expectations beyond a mutually agreeable roll in the hay, but with Sophia I felt something different. I barely knew her, yet she intrigued me. I found myself wanting more than just a casual roll in the hay.

I padded downstairs, making one last sweep of the ground floor for security. Satisfied nothing was amiss, I unbuckled my holster and hung my gun over the edge of the coffee table within easy reach of the sofa. I tossed a pillow and a blanket on the sofa and stretched out. My feet hung over the edge, but I'd certainly slept in much worse places. The movie had ended long ago, and I turned the television off.

Setting my phone on vibrate, I tucked it under the corner of the pillow so it would wake me without disturbing Sophia if anyone called before morning. Tiny and Thor were on perimeter guard and they'd alert me if anything needed my attention.

I closed my eyes and slowed my breathing. One thing I'd learned in the SEALs was to snatch whatever small pockets of sleep I could in the midst of battle.

This felt like the start of a battle, and I intended to be victorious.

Chapter Four

Sophia

I woke up in my own bed, and that confused me. The last thing I remembered was watching *Darlin' Bride* with the hot biker who'd rescued me yesterday. It really was one of my favorite movies, but mostly I'd chosen it to see the look on his face. Turns out he was a pretty good sport, hadn't even flinched at the title.

The cell phone sitting on the bedside table chimed, lighting up with an incoming text, and I reached for it. It wasn't Deuce's phone and it definitely wasn't mine, but Janet's name and number were on the display.

I swung my legs over the edge of the bed, wincing as bruises from yesterday's escapade made themselves known. Hesitantly, I picked the phone up and hit the call button, setting it on speaker mode.

"Hello?" Definitely Janet, but she sounded much too perky for first thing in the morning. I glanced at the clock on my dresser. Okay, maybe not so early.

"What's up? I'm betting George didn't turn out to be Prince Charming or you wouldn't have texted me to come over so early last night."

"Prince Charming he was not. I don't want to do this over the phone. Come on over and I'll fill you in. But give me an hour or so. I need to get rid of some company."

"Interesting." Janet sounded intrigued. "Not Prince Charming but you kept him for a night of rousing sex?"

"Hardly." I snorted. "It's not George, but it's a long story. You coming over?"

"Absolutely! I have to now, just to find out who you spent the night with."

A floorboard creaked, and I looked up to see Deuce leaning against the doorjamb again, the ghost of a smile curving his lips. He'd obviously overheard that last remark.

I met his gaze and felt a flutter of heat in my belly. If anything, he looked more scrumptious this morning with his hair slightly mussed from a night on my sofa.

I picked up the phone and turned off speaker mode. "Thanks. See you soon."

"Put the coffee on!" Janet laughed as she disconnected the call.

Deuce straightened up and entered the room, placing a steaming cup on the bedside table. "Heard you moving around and figured you could use a coffee. That was your BFF returning your call?"

I nodded. "She'll be here in an hour, so if you're still here you can expect the third degree. She'll be nice about it, but she's like a terrier with a bone. I'd give you ten minutes before she knows everything about you including your shoe size and where you went to kindergarten." I wrapped my hands around the coffee mug and took a deep gulp.

He cocked his head. "If I'm still here? You giving me the option of avoiding her?"

I picked up the coffee and inhaled, dragging the awesome aroma deep into my lungs. "Your choice. I love her to pieces, but she's not subtle."

"I'll be okay. I like it when people are upfront."

I wrinkled my nose and took a mouthful of coffee. "Upfront. I suppose that's one way to put it. Most people call it rude and nosy. And on that note, where did the phone magically appear from? It wasn't here last night, and I'm pretty sure you haven't had time to go shopping."

"Prospects brought it over earlier this morning. Ace thought it best you have a new number, so I programmed your friend's info into it from my phone and texted the number to her. The rest of the setup is up to you. It should do until you have time to go buy one you like. You can always have your provider forward calls from your old number to this one for now."

I shrugged. "A phone is a phone. I don't really have a favorite brand or anything like that. Thank you, though. I can't believe how lost I felt without one."

A ghost of a smile curved his lips. "You're welcome. I need to get a few things done today, but I'll hang around until your friend shows up. How's the arm this morning?"

I held it up so he could see the bandage. "It's good, but I really want to have a shower, and I probably shouldn't get it wet again. That hurt like hell."

"No problem. I can wrap it for you. You have any plastic wrap in the kitchen? Maybe some duct tape?"

I suppressed a laugh, picturing an old TV show where the redneck host fixed just about everything with duct tape and a can of WD40. "Plastic wrap is in the pantry cupboard and there should be a roll of duct tape in the tool caddy by the back door."

"Be right back." He pivoted and disappeared down the hallway.

I sipped coffee and contemplated the drastic change in my life. Less than twenty-four hours ago I'd been deciding what to wear on yet another blind date, wondering if there were any good single men left out there. Now I was sitting on my bed in my jammies, while the sexy biker who'd spent the night on my sofa went looking for supplies so I could have a shower.

The reason he'd spent the night on the sofa came rushing back, ruining my cheerful mood. I'd been kidnapped and nearly sold like a piece of merchandise, or a pet dog. I might still be in danger.

One part of me wanted to call my dad and let him handle things his way. The other part acknowledged this wasn't his fight, and if he got involved things could turn ugly. He wouldn't hesitate to do whatever he felt necessary to protect me, and I didn't have enough cash in the bank to post bail.

Deuce strode back into the room, plastic wrap and duct tape in hand. "Let's see that arm."

I obediently held out my arm.

Deuce studied it intently before wrapping it in plastic and securing the ends with the duct tape. Between that and my flannel jammies, I presented the least sexy picture possible.

"Thanks." Yup. Crazy cat lady was definitely a possibility in my near future.

"You okay to shower alone?"

My gaze flew to his face. "You offering to join me?"

"You considering letting me?"

I licked my lips, and his gaze dropped to my mouth. The temperature in the room rose dramatically.

He reached out and took my hand, pulling me to my feet and into his embrace.

"We shouldn't do this." I melted against him.

"Why not?" He dipped his head, and his lips brushed across mine.

"Janet will be here in less than an hour." I flicked my tongue out to taste him.

"Then we're wasting time, aren't we?" He muttered the question against my lips.

"I don't have sex on a first date."

"We're not dating. Are we?" He nibbled on my ear.

"No." I was losing this argument fast. "I need to have a shower."

"I can scrub your back for you. Multitasking is good."

I sighed, conceding defeat to my overactive libido. "Yes, it is."

A grin lit his face from one side to the other and he scooped me up like I weighed nothing. Striding into the bathroom, he set me down beside the shower stall and reached in to turn on the water.

Pivoting to face me, he pulled a foil-wrapped package out of his pocket and tossed it onto the counter before he quickly shucked his shirt. Pinning me with his gaze, he unzipped his jeans.

His eyes never wavered from my face. "Are you sure you want to do this?"

I loved that he paused to ask. A gentleman biker. Who would have thought it?

I nodded silently.

He wasn't wearing anything under those jeans, and when he let go of the waistband, his cock sprang free.

I gulped. He was big. Impressively big. I was no virgin, but I'd never seen a cock that large before.

Shimmying the jeans down to his feet, he kicked them aside and stood before me in all his naked splendor. His eyes blazed with lust. "Your turn."

I reached up and slowly undid the buttons on my shirt. I loved the way his gaze tracked the progress of my hands as I flicked each button. Mindful of my plastic-wrapped arm, I wiggled my shoulders and let the top slide off in slow motion to land in a flannel puddle at my feet.

Deuce wrapped one hand around his cock and gave it a long stroke from tip to base. "Can't wait to taste those gorgeous tits."

I lowered my head and peeked out at him from under my eyelashes. Hooking my thumbs in the waistband of the pants, I lowered them inch by slow inch. I'd never done a striptease before, and flannel pjs seemed like the least sexy outfit for it, but the look on Deuce's face sent my pulse racing.

I paused with the pants barely covering my mound.

Deuce gave his cock another stroke.

I turned and wiggled my butt, letting the pants fall to the floor.

Deuce let out a deep breath. "Gorgeous." He reached out and turned me to face him. Placing one finger under my chin, he tilted it up and blazed a sizzling hot kiss on my mouth.

I opened my lips, reaching up to wrap my arms around his neck. My breasts pressed against the solid muscle of his chest as his tongue invaded my mouth, claiming it.

I strained to get closer, craving the heat of his male body. Yearning for the feeling of power it gave me to know I was the one he wanted. I was the reason his cock was rock hard.

He held me with one hand on my hip and the other cradling my head. He was gentle and passionate at the same time, the perfect mix of gentleman and lustful lover.

Excitement ripped through me as I felt his hard length pressed against my belly. I needed this, needed to feel alive. Needed to feel in control after the horror of being drugged and thrown in that van.

"I wanted to be gentle with you," he whispered in my ear. "But I'm not sure I can. I want you so bad."

I reached down with one hand to circle his hard length. "I don't need gentle. I want to feel alive."

"Oh, fuck. You have no clue how badly I want you."

I tightened my fingers around his shaft. "I'm getting the idea."

He wrapped one arm around me and reached in to test the water temperature. Satisfied, he lifted me and placed me under the warm spray.

The wave of water washing over me felt deeply sensual. The temperature and the pressure sent darts of liquid heat down every nerve. Add to that the sight of Deuce, all tatted muscle and rock-hard cock, and I could barely contain myself.

Picking up the bar of soap, he slowly rubbed it across my chest and down between my breasts. I closed my eyes, letting the feelings wash over me. It had been way too long since I'd felt a man's hands on me.

"Like that, do you?" He turned me around and I braced my hands against the shower wall.

I tried to answer, but all that came out was a little moan of pleasure.

He soaped up my loofah and proceeded to work on my back, circling lower and lower. When his hand slipped between my thighs, I gasped and spread my legs wider. Discarding the loofah, he teased his fingers through my folds and rubbed the tight little bundle of nerves at my entrance.

I whimpered his name.

"Tell me you like that," he growled.

"Like that." Apparently whole sentences were no longer a thing for me.

Deuce chuckled and inserted one finger, then two, pumping them skillfully in and out until I was on the verge of a climax.

Withdrawing his fingers, he turned me around and dropped to his knees, his hands on the cheeks of my ass. He pulled me to him and fastened his mouth over my pussy, stabbing his tongue deep.

I let out an incoherent scream, grabbing him by the hair and holding him tight to me as a monstrous orgasm swept over me. I arched my back, pressing myself as close to him as I could. Wave after wave of intense pleasure blazed along every nerve ending.

As my orgasm died down, I loosened my hold on him, and he tilted his head to look up at me. Water dripped off his face in rivers as he licked his lips, his eyes alight with an unholy lust.

"That was the sweetest fucking thing I've tasted in a long time." He rose to his feet, towering over me.

This close, I studied the tattoos that covered a good portion of his body. A couple I recognized. One matched the picture on the back of his cut. I'd have to ask him about them.

Later. When we weren't naked. When I wasn't about to feel him inside me.

I reached out and grasped his cock, running my hand down the length.

Deuce let out a strangled groan.

"That feel good?" I asked.

"Fuck, yeah." He squinted through the dripping water. "Keep it up and you're not going to get what you want."

That put an end to my explorations. I so needed to feel that gorgeous cock inside me.

Deuce reached out of the shower and snagged the condom he'd left on the counter. Ripping it open with his teeth, he quickly rolled it over his massive hard-on.

Yup. I was about to get exactly what I wanted.

Deuce lowered his head to sear my lips with a kiss. I raised my arms and held onto his shoulders as he grasped his cock and guided it through the soft folds guarding my entrance.

I had a brief moment of panic as I realized just how big he was.

As if he could read my mind, Deuce whispered in my ear. "It's okay, you can handle me." Lifting me, he wrapped my leg around his hips, cradling me against his hard body. He worked his way into me one agonizingly slow inch at a time until I felt his balls slapping up against me.

I felt full. Tight. Stretched to the limit. But he was right. I could handle him. Barely.

He paused for a moment, let me adjust to his size. Then he rocked his hips. Exquisite pleasure lanced through me. He rocked them again.

I let out a low moan. I wanted more. I wanted faster.

He stopped moving. "You okay? Did I hurt you?"

What guy asks that when he's buried balls deep?

"No. More." I wasn't nearly as lucid.

He must have understood me. Pulling back a tad, he thrust deep.

I was on fire, heat building in my belly and blazing outward.

I locked my arms behind his neck, afraid I'd fall if I let go.

The warm water cascaded over me, adding to the intense sensations.

A second orgasm blasted through me and I

sagged, barely able to hold myself upright. I let out an incoherent cry as pleasure so sharp it almost hurt racked through me. Moments later, Deuce let out a triumphant yell as his own orgasm consumed him.

We stayed there, locked together, his cock still buried in me. Time ceased to matter as we gasped for air, cocooned in the wet warmth of the shower.

A voice from downstairs penetrated my blissful haze.

"Hello? Sophia? Where are you, and what's with the motorcycle in your carport and who are those guys outside?"

* * *

Deuce

Sophia stiffened against me. Must be her friend Janet, or the prospects wouldn't have let her in the house.

Fuck. No way we'd been that long.

I frowned down at Sophia. "I assume that's your BFF. How did she get in the house? I had it locked down tight."

Sophia looked confused. "She knows where the spare key is hidden."

Seriously? She left a key outside? "Under the doormat?"

"No." She frowned, taking a step back from me. "I'm not an idiot."

I shook my head. "I didn't say you were. I'm just saying it's not a great idea to leave a key anywhere outside until we get this thing under control."

I could see the emotions chasing each other across her face before she let out a heavy sigh. "You're right. I didn't even think about it. It's in one of those magnetic things. I stuck it on the steel supports of the carport. I painted it black so it's practically invisible even if you're looking directly at it." She paused, and a ghost of a smile crossed her lips. "Dad came up with that when he found out I had it under a rock by the front door."

I was starting to think I needed to meet this dad of hers. Sounded like my kind of guy.

"Sophia? Where are you?" The woman sounded impatient.

Sophia jumped out of the shower and slammed the ensuite door shut. Grabbing a towel from the rack, she wrapped it around herself and pivoted to stare wild-eyed at me. "We need to get dressed!"

I bet that was how she looked when she was a toddler and she got caught doing something naughty. Her eyes were wide, and her wet hair stuck out at odd angles. No makeup, and that fluffy bath towel clenched tight to her as if it could somehow ward off the incoming problem.

She locked her gaze on me, one finger pressed to her lips to keep me silent. Lifting her head, she hollered, "You're early, Janet. I'm in the shower. Give me five minutes. I'll be right down. Grab yourself a coffee."

"Sure." Janet's voice was laced with laughter. "Then you can tell me all about the guy that fits in these size fourteen boots. Is he scrubbing your back for you?"

Sophia shook her head, giving me an apologetic look. "Too late to quietly sneak out the back door now."

I grinned. This was way more fun than I'd had in ages. "I didn't plan on it, darlin'."

She rolled her eyes. "I warned you about her. I should have known she'd show up early just to catch us."

"I'm a big boy." I turned the water off and slicked my hair back with my hands. "I'm fine with her asking questions. Whether or not anything happened is none of her business unless you want to tell her."

I stepped out of the shower stall. The closed ensuite door emphasized just how small the room was. I caged Sophia against the counter, one arm on each side, and proceeded to ravish her mouth. She wound one arm around my neck and opened her mouth, participating enthusiastically. When we finally came up for air, she had the stunned look of a woman who had been well and truly kissed. I liked that look on her.

I grabbed a towel from the overhead rack and secured it around my waist. Opening the door with a flourish, I gestured. "After you, darlin'."

Ducking under my outstretched arm, Sophia strode into the bedroom, towel wrapped firmly around her. "Can't say I didn't warn you."

"I think I can handle one nosy woman." I toweled myself off and reached for my jeans.

Sophia turned to me and chuckled. "I'll remind you of that after Janet gets her claws into you."

I found my borrowed shirt and pulled it on before strapping my shoulder holster in place. Sophia eyed the gun doubtfully. "Do you really need to wear that?"

"I do. Don't worry. I have a concealed carry permit." I donned my cut which mostly hid the weapon. "You did know I was a biker, right?"

She didn't bother to answer, turning to grab a pair of yoga pants and a sweatshirt out of the closet. I sat down on the bed, leaning back on my hands as she rummaged through a drawer and snagged some fluffy bits of lace.

Dangling the lace from one hand, she pivoted to face me, arching her brows. "Are you just going to sit there and watch me get dressed?"

"Planned on it." I eyed up the bits of lace. "Not as much fun as watching you take it all off, but I'm good for now."

"Really." She let go of the towel and it floated down to her feet in slow motion. Kicking it aside, she held my gaze as she grasped one bit of lace between her teeth and stepped into the other, pulling the black thong up to her hips. Pivoting, she wiggled her ass seductively and adjusted the thin straps over her hips before twirling around to give me an eyeful of generous breasts bouncing unconfined, just begging me to pay attention to them.

I took a deep breath and ran my tongue around my suddenly dry lips.

Sophia smiled knowingly, dropping the remaining scrap of lace into her hands and wrapping it around her chest. The bra fastened in the front and barely managed to contain her ample breasts. "Like it?"

I nodded dumbly, wondering how long we had before her friend came looking for her. My cock had recovered from its shower activity and was eager for another round.

Sophia moved over to the bed and picked up the pants. She made putting them on the most fascinating show I'd seen in over a decade. The woman had a flair for performing, even without the usual musical accompaniment. The stretchy material of the pants hugged her figure as if it had been painted on, and my imagination pictured that tiny scrap of lace on her mound, now hidden from view.

Fuck, I needed to start wearing boxer shorts

under these jeans!

Pulling the sweatshirt over her head, she tilted her neck. "Ready?"

I slid off the bed and grabbed her hand. "I was born ready, darlin'."

She paused, her expression suddenly turned serious. "Just because we, you know, it doesn't mean we're a thing. It was just..." She paused and took a deep breath. "It was just sex. I don't expect anything from you. It was awesome of you to stay last night, but I'm good now. I can handle this."

I shook my head. "Nope. This isn't over."

"Yeah, it is."

The woman had a stubborn streak, but so did I. We headed downstairs, still holding hands. Before I could continue, her friend came out of the kitchen, and at the same time, my cell phone pinged. I pulled it out of my pocket and glanced at the screen. Ace.

"I have to take this." I nodded at the woman assessing me from the kitchen doorway and dropped a swift kiss on Sophia's forehead before striding back upstairs. I had a feeling whatever Ace had to say wasn't meant for everyone to hear. I could fill Sophia in on whatever I needed to later.

I waited until I heard Sophia and Janet retreat to the kitchen before I hit the call back button. Ace picked up on the first ring. He didn't waste any time. "You still with the woman?"

"Yeah. Her friend just got here."

"Good. Shadow ran a check on that dating site. Mostly it's aboveboard, but in the last two months three women registered on it have gone missing right after setting up dates. The men involved mysteriously disappeared from the database at the same time. Not deactivated or account cancelled. They wiped all traces of their profiles and any chats, likes, and activities. Gone like fucking ghosts."

I frowned. "That doesn't sound good. How do they manage that?"

"Shadow found a back door, but he hasn't managed to trace it back to the source. Which means this isn't a local scam run by a couple of con men. You need big guns to pull that off. Shadow put out a few feelers on the dark web. Rumor has it you can pick a woman on that site, and for the right price she can be delivered to you. Not as in a date. As in, you're buying her, and they guarantee no consequences."

"Fuck."

"Exactly." He paused. "Someone picked that woman you're with and paid for her. They're not just going to let her go. It appears she used a fake address when she set up her account, so that's in her favor, but she needs to keep a low profile for now."

"What do our friends at the bureau have to say about this?"

"They're extremely interested. It appears this isn't the only dating app that's been compromised. They promise full cooperation and whatever backup we need if we pursue this."

I glanced toward the stairs. From up here I could just hear the low murmur of voices. Sophia and her friend. Sophia's laughter rang out at something her friend said, and I felt a surge of protectiveness.

"Yeah, we're going to pursue this. That woman pried open a locked door and jumped out of a moving vehicle to escape. That takes guts. A lot of guts. How many others didn't make it?"

"Figured that would be your answer. First off, you need to warn that woman… Sophia, is it?"

"Yeah. I'll warn her. I've got a couple of

prospects running perimeter guard now. I'll keep them in place."

"Good. If she goes out, one of them needs to shadow her at all times. The other can keep watch on the house. I'll leave it up to you to coordinate that."

"Roger that." I ran my hand over the scruff on my chin. I'd need to fetch some supplies if I was going to stay for a while. Those cute pink razors in Sophia's bathroom weren't up to the job.

Chapter Five

Sophia

That kiss on my forehead nixed any chance I had of convincing Janet there was nothing going on.

"Well, that's handy." Janet handed me a steaming mug of coffee as I slid onto the seat at the island.

"What's handy?"

"Bring the guy home with you so you don't have to worry about who sees you all disheveled and happy the next morning. But if that's not George, who is he and where did you find him?"

I sighed. "Long story."

Janet grinned. "I was counting on it. Spill."

I related the events of the previous night but went light on the details. Talking about it in the light of day made it seem worse, and hindsight didn't help. We both giggled when I described falling asleep and waking up in my own bed.

"Alone in your own bed, or..." Janet smirked.

Just then, Deuce popped his head into the kitchen. He nodded at Janet. "Nice to meet you. I'd love to stay and chat, but something's come up." He turned his attention to me. "I'll be back later. Walk me out?"

I got to my feet. The shower had helped, but I could still feel the aftereffects of my tumble from the van. "Sure."

I tried to ignore the knowing look on Janet's face as my traitorous heart jumped at the thought that he would be back later.

He held out his hand, and I put mine in it. "She giving you the third degree?"

I nodded, not meeting his gaze. We reached the

door, and he turned to face me. Placing one finger under my chin he tilted my head up and stared down at me. "Just remember to tell her I'm hung like a stallion and can kill a grizzly bear with my bare hands to protect you. If she's really a good friend, that should satisfy her."

I burst out laughing. "A stallion? Really?"

He grinned. "I thought you'd question the grizzly bear."

I shook my head. "You're coming back later?"

He grunted, one hand on the door handle. "Yes. I'll bring dinner. And I'm leaving Tiny and Thor here while I'm gone. One of them is going to be with you at all times for the foreseeable future. At least until we figure this thing out. If you go out, one of them goes with you. Got it?"

I nodded. "Deuce?"

"Yeah?"

"Thank you. Just… thank you."

He looked uncomfortable. I got the feeling he wasn't used to being thanked. "Just stay safe till I get back."

I watched as he went over to talk to one of the guys on guard duty who was lounging on the far side of the carport. The two of them turned to look at me, so I waved and closed the door.

"Hung like a horse, huh?"

I turned to see Janet watching me from the kitchen doorway. "You were eavesdropping!"

"Only way to find out what people don't want you to know. So, hung like a horse?"

I giggled. "I don't kiss and tell!"

"Not interested in the kissing, although that would be interesting too. Is he good with his mouth?" She wiggled her brows.

"I am not discussing this with you!" I tried to keep my face straight as I walked back to retrieve my coffee. "But I have no complaints."

"So, hung like a horse and good with his mouth. Does he have a twin by any chance? I could use a good roll in the hay!"

"No, but he had a friend with him when I met him, plus those two guys hanging around outside. He mentioned a clubhouse, so there could be dozens of them."

Janet sobered and shook her head. "Not interested. I'm betting they're worse than your dad for being controlling. You know I like to love them and leave them with a grin on their face the next morning."

I could see her point. Right now, Deuce seemed to like bossing me around, but given the circumstances it was coming off more as caring than controlling. And he certainly made a point of making sure I was satisfied in the sex department.

"So. The date. George was a bust, so how did you end up with a hot biker guy in your bed this morning? Oh right, it wasn't your bed, it was the shower. Did he show up to fix the plumbing?"

I laughed. "No, he's not a plumber. And there is nothing wrong with the plumbing. Mine or the shower stall's." I took a sip of my coffee, wondering just how much to tell her.

Everything. I needed to tell her everything. Almost everything. We'd been friends since grade school, and I trusted her to keep it to herself. I proceeded to recount the activities of the previous night, including the fact that Deuce had slept on the sofa.

Janet stared at me, her expression turning to horror as I described being drugged, then shoved in the van and my subsequent escape.

"You were drugged? And kidnapped?" Her voice escalated to a squeak.

I nodded. "Yeah, I was. By the way, get off that damn dating app."

"Doing it now! Crap. That's unbelievable. Did you report it?"

"No. You know how I feel about cops, and they always blame the woman."

I watched silently as she picked up her phone, her hands shaking as she pulled up the app and deleted her profile.

Putting the phone back down, she frowned. "So, two guys on motorcycles, with gang symbols on their vests, just happened to be behind the van that you were kidnapped in. And now you have one of them in your house. And another couple outside making sure no one finds you. Don't you find that a bit suspicious? How do you know they aren't part of George's crew?"

I hesitated. Janet was my best friend, but Deuce had possibly killed someone to save me. "He's not. I'm sure."

Janet looked skeptical. "How? Just because he screwed your brains out this morning doesn't make him a good guy."

"Janet! You can't think I'm that naive."

"I hope not. I took one look at the pair of you and knew what was going on. So how can you be so sure he's a good guy?"

I sighed. Did I mention she was like a dog with a bone? "Fine. We had sex. But I know he's not part of the bunch that tried to kidnap me because he and his buddy got into a gunfight with the guys in the van, and he might have killed one of them."

Her brows shot up. "Might have?"

She wasn't going to let this drop. "I don't know. I didn't see what happened. I heard gunshots, but I was too scared to look."

This was probably the first time I'd seen Janet speechless. I had no idea if the guy was dead or not. When I'd come up out of the ditch he'd been gone, so maybe not. He could have got into the van. There was blood on the road, but he could have just been wounded. Bodies don't evaporate like on some kind of sci-fi show on TV, and it was hard to imagine the other guy dragging a dead body into the van with him if he was trying to get away.

"Maybe you should call your dad." Janet dropped the happy party-girl persona. "Or go up to his homestead for a while. This sounds deadly scary. What if those guys come looking for you?"

"Deuce has a couple of his buddies watching the house, and he's going to be back later. I don't want Dad involved in this. You know how he is. He'd probably kill George in broad daylight on Main Street if he thought the guy was going to hurt me. I don't want him to land in jail just because he cares about me."

Janet let out a long sigh. "You're right. He's the definition of an overprotective parent."

"Besides, I have a taser and a can of bear spray. I'm not totally helpless."

"Maybe you should reconsider keeping a gun in the house." Janet held up a hand to forestall my objections. "Can't hurt. You don't actually have to shoot anyone."

"Not a chance." We'd had this argument before. My dad had taught me to shoot when I was a kid, and I was good. I could hit a moving target at a hundred feet, more if I had a rifle with a scope instead of a handgun. But there was a huge difference between shooting a piece of paper and shooting a person. I wasn't sure I could do it, so it seemed safer not to take the chance of having someone reverse the tables and take the gun from me. Taser and bear spray, though, I was good with. They were nasty but not deadly.

"Your new boy toy has a gun."

"And he has a concealed carry permit for it."

"Interesting." She looked intrigued.

"How so?"

"If this club of his was a one-percenter, I doubt he'd bother to get a license."

I frowned. "What's a one-percenter?"

"A motorcycle club that operates outside the law. Most clubs don't although there's a lot of gray area."

I grimaced. "And exactly how do you know so much about motorcycle clubs?"

"Remember Jarred? That guy I dated for a while last summer?"

I nodded.

"Turns out his father was in a one-percenter club, and he got caught running drugs over the Mexican border. Jarred asked if I wanted to go with him to visit, and that was the end of that relationship."

I remembered Jarred, only because at almost two months it was the longest relationship Janet had been in for years. She'd never told me what went wrong, putting it down to lack of interest on her part. "That's tough, but Jarred wasn't part of it, was he?"

She shook her head. "No, he didn't even own a bike, but it scared the heck out of me anyway. Those guys are ruthless. What if they came after Jarred to get to his dad? Or used Jarred's girlfriend to send a lesson? No thanks."

"Oh." I didn't know what else to say.

"Hey. Cheer up! Sounds like your new boy toy isn't one of the bad guys."

"Right." I made a mental note to see that concealed carry permit. Not that I doubted Deuce, but anyone can claim they have something without it being true.

"So about having a gun in the house..."

"No!" I glared at Janet. "And don't you dare tell my dad what happened."

"Wouldn't dream of it. So, tell me more about this guy who's hung like a horse."

I shook my head. "Not sure he's quite up to horse standards, but he's big, and he knows how to use it."

"Do tell!" Janet put her coffee mug down and leaned forward, chin resting on her hands.

I blushed, just as the doorbell rang. I took the opportunity to dodge answering the question. I checked the doorbell app and saw Deuce standing on the front deck with a grocery bag in his hands. I unlocked the door, confused.

"I didn't expect you back until tonight."

He held the bag out to me. "I looked in your fridge last night. There's barely enough food in there to keep a mouse happy so I picked a few things up to tide you over."

I automatically took the bag, almost dropping it. "This weighs a ton. What did you get?"

He grinned. "Food. If I'm going to be spending time here you need real food, not just snacks."

I stared wordlessly as he headed to his bike. He paused and turned back to me. "I'll be back around 5:30. Do you have a barbecue?"

"Yes. Why?"

He gestured at the bag in my hand. "Steaks.

We're having steak for dinner. I can grill them."

"We are?" I felt like I was floundering out of my depth.

"You're not a vegetarian, are you?"

I shook my head.

"Good. Steak and baked potato with all the fixings. I'll see you tonight." Fastening his helmet on, he slung a leg over the bike and took off down the street.

I watched as he disappeared around the corner.

"Not quite hung like a horse, and he cooks." Janet peered over my shoulder. "If you don't want him, you can send him my way."

I turned to my BFF, looking her straight in the eye. "Not a chance."

Janet laughed. "Thought so. You're smitten with that biker dude."

"I've barely known the guy for twenty-four hours!"

"Doesn't matter. I've seen that look before. You're hooked."

"I've never looked like this before."

"Didn't say I'd seen it on you."

"I need to put these away." I walked into the kitchen and opened the fridge. Deuce was right. I had lots of snacking type things but no real food. Being single, I often ate out or grabbed something at the local drive-through.

"Those are premium steaks. You should marinate them."

I shrugged. "I don't have anything to marinate them in. I wasn't exactly expecting steak to push its way into my dinner plans."

"Listen to you. Talking like you make dinner plans." Janet grabbed the package of steak. "We can go to the store."

"Deuce told me to stay home."

"No, he told you that you had to take one of those brawny biker boys with you if you went anywhere."

I looked at her with one brow arched. "Exactly how long were you eavesdropping?"

She grinned. "Long enough. Now get this stuff put away and we can grab some lunch while we're out."

I rolled my eyes. It did sound like a good idea, though. Apparently early morning sex gave me an appetite. "Fine, but you get to pay for lunch."

She grinned. "Can I choose which biker to bring?"

* * *

Deuce

I pulled my phone out and glanced down at it. A text from Thor let me know Sophia and Janet were going out for lunch and he was tagging along. Tiny was staying behind to guard the house. I slipped my phone back in my pocket.

"Everything okay?" Ace asked.

"Just an update. She's going out with a friend, but Thor is with them. Tiny's on guard duty at her house."

He nodded. "Good. She's our only solid lead so far. Our contact at the bureau is excited. Up to this point, they knew an active human trafficking ring was operating in the area, but they had no idea how the victims were targeted. This dating app scam is a new twist. Prior to this they were going on the assumption that the victims were random, chosen by opportunity."

He continued, bringing the brothers up to date

on missing women from the area and theories on how the victims were being transported. This wasn't just a local problem. They had credible intel that the women were being shipped overseas to buyers in Asia and Europe.

My mind wandered as he went over the details I already knew. The idea that someone had deliberately targeted Sophia, had chosen to buy her like a piece of meat or a pet dog infuriated me, but anger wasn't going to help us find and take down this ring.

We were a team. We might not belong to the SEALs anymore, but the training and years of experience were hammered into our brains. We needed to be clinical, look at the data from all angles. I needed to put aside personal feelings if I was going to make sure Sophia was safe. That was going to be tough.

"Do we need to upgrade the security on her house?" Beast was the enforcer for the club.

"I think she's good. Her father's some kind of doomsday prepper and he's got it rigged up tight. Might be a good idea to hack into the feed though, so we can keep a watch on her from here." Ace glanced over at me. "Think she'll be okay with that?"

"Can't see why not. There's nothing inside so not like it's an invasion of privacy. We probably want to be careful not to trip any hidden hooks in it though. She doesn't want her father to know what went down."

"Why?" Ace frowned.

"Seems to think he might go hunt the guys down and land himself in jail. Sounds like the kind of guy who's not into polite debates when it comes to his daughter's wellbeing."

Beast snorted. "Understand that. Someone touches one of my kids, they might as well just put a bullet in their own brain and save me the trouble."

Ace shot Beast a quelling look before turning his attention back to me.

"Then we need to be careful around the father. You can ask her about tapping into the camera feeds if there are any. We need to know exactly what kind of security system the house has. Anything else we need to know?"

I cleared my throat. "I like her."

That got everyone's attention. Eight pairs of eyes zeroed in on me.

"Figured that out right fast." Rattler had been silent up to this point.

"Explain." Ace crossed his arms.

"Pretty simple. She's cute, she's feisty as hell, and she doesn't take shit from anyone, including me. But she's also smart. She knows she's in a bind, and she knows when to accept help. Plus, she feels protective of her gun toting, 'knows where to hide the bodies' father. I've only known her since she landed herself at my feet yesterday, but I can see a future for us if I don't fuck it up." I glanced around the room. "So hands off."

"You told her yet, or is it a secret?" Shadow had a smirk on his face.

"'Knows where to hide the bodies'?" Blast, our munitions master, picked up on that one pretty quick.

"Her description, not mine." I shrugged. "Think she was just trying to make a point."

"You being a biker isn't an issue for her?" Ace narrowed his eyes. "How much have you told her about our club?"

"Not much. Told her I used to be a SEAL and left the rest out."

He nodded just as my phone vibrated. Pulling it out, I gave it a casual glance, expecting an update on the lunch. I did a double take as a picture of a strange man opening the door to Sophia's house filled the screen. What the hell? The text was from Tiny.

House is empty. What do you want me to do?

Detain the fucker. On my way. Warn Thor to keep the girls out.

I clenched my fists, choking down a rush of anger. "Gotta go. Some guy just broke into Sophia's place. Tiny's going to hold him till I get there."

Ace nodded. "Rattler and Beast can back you up."

I didn't bother to answer, heading for the door double time. Might be getting some answers sooner than we thought.

I pushed my bike to the max, ran a few stop signs, and pulled into Sophia's place in half the time it had taken me to leave it. I parked my bike and ripped the helmet off my head, tossing it onto the seat.

The place was quiet, the back door not quite closed. I'd talk to Tiny about that later. "Tiny!"

He didn't answer right away, which given my current mood pissed me off even more.

I stepped through the open doorway and opened my mouth to holler again when I caught a blur of movement out of the corner of my eye.

Years of instinct and training kicked in. I dropped to the floor and rolled. The baseball bat whistled through the air and made a sizeable dent in the wall where I'd been standing seconds before.

Son of a bitch. Asshole must have taken Tiny out. Hopefully not permanently.

I twisted sideways, sweeping a leg out to take the asshole down, but he danced out of the way. I leapt to my feet and got a good look at my assailant.

Guy probably had twenty-five, thirty years on me. Grizzled beard that looked like he'd used a dull knife to hack it off short. Lots of muscle though, and he still had the fucking bat.

I'd committed the one cardinal sin of urban warfare. I'd let my emotions dictate my actions. I'd outpaced my backup, and I'd walked through that door without considering whether there might be an enemy behind it.

Rookie mistakes.

A quick glance around told me there wasn't anything close at hand I could use as a weapon.

My opponent gripped the bat in both hands and took a step toward me, his eyes blazing with murderous intent.

I took a step backward. Now that he'd lost the element of surprise, it was a standoff. I didn't want to kill the guy. Dead guys don't answer questions, and I had a lot of them.

I pulled my gun and held it by the barrel, safety on. I didn't want to kill him, but you don't have to shoot a pistol for it to hurt.

"Fucking pervert." He took another swing at me with the bat.

Okay, now I was pissed. "You want to die, old man?"

"Could ask you the same question, pervert."

"You brought a bat to a gunfight, old man."

"Looks like you don't know which end of the gun the bullet comes out, pervert."

I sneered at him. "Thought I'd take it easy on you given your advanced age."

The guy snorted like he thought that was funny. "Still young enough to lay you out alongside your buddy."

I'd worry about Tiny once I'd taken care of this guy.

"Don't think so." I hefted the gun, estimating how long it would take if I needed to reverse my grip and shoot the guy. Didn't have to be a kill shot but I didn't want to get blood on Sophia's flooring.

The faint sound of motorcycles approaching filled the hallway. Rattler and Beast. The old man's eyes flickered toward the sound right before he rushed me. I turned, letting my left shoulder bear the brunt of the first strike. He outweighed me, and his attack took me to the ground. He landed on top of me and sat up, straddling my chest.

I took a swipe with the pistol, and the blow glanced off his chest. He dropped the bat and started to pound me with his fists. I twisted, trying to free myself, and hit him again. He grunted, but didn't stop pummeling me.

The door slammed open so hard it bounced off the wall. Rattler stood in the doorway, his shotgun pointed at the old guy. "Hands up or I shoot."

The old guy didn't even bother to look up. "You shoot, we're both dead."

"Guess we'll do it the hard way then." Striding into the hallway, Rattler clocked the guy on the side of the head with the stock of the shotgun. The old guy collapsed on top of me, out cold.

Beast entered, shaking his head at the sight. "The old guy got the drop on you, Deuce? That's sad. And where the hell is Tiny?"

I squirmed out from under the old man, feeling the side of his neck for a pulse. It was strong. He'd live to answer a few questions. "Don't know. Guessing this guy took him out. And yeah, he jumped me when I came in."

"Tsk, tsk." Rattler looked amused. "Didn't think I'd live to see the day you'd get taken by a grandpa."

"Funny. He's a tough old geezer. Go find Tiny. Hopefully he's still breathing."

"Found him." Beast's voice came from the kitchen. "All trussed up like a pig ready for roasting."

I got to my feet and dusted myself off before holstering my weapon. Rattler followed me into the kitchen. Beast was busy cutting freezer twine off Tiny, who looked as angry as a hornet.

"Old guy did this?"

He nodded. "I asked how he got in the house, and he made like he was confused or something. Stumbled over his own feet, and when I went to help him, he clocked me. Bastard!"

It was my turn to chuckle. "Wily old bastard. He jumped me from behind the door when I came in. Had a bat aimed at my head."

Beast raised his brows. "So that geriatric old buzzard out there managed to get both of you?"

"He looked old. I didn't want to hurt the guy." Tiny looked sheepish. "Didn't expect human traffickers to be guys in their sixties."

He did have a point. The guys in the van had been younger. Much younger.

Something here didn't make sense.

Chapter Six

Sophia

"Dad!"

The sight of my dad lying motionless on my hallway floor sent a punch straight to my gut. He was annoying, grumpy, hard-headed, and stubborn, but he was my dad, and I loved him.

When Thor had shown me the picture of the guy breaking into my house, I'd realized things could go real bad real fast. It was my dad, and he had the code but probably forgot it. He was never really good with that kind of thing. He didn't know what was going on, and none of the Riptide guys would recognize him so they'd assumed he was one of the bad guys.

I had Thor text both Deuce and Tiny, but neither of them answered. Thor was adamant that we not go back to the house until Deuce okayed it.

I don't take orders well.

Janet and I had smiled nicely and told him to go to hell. We tossed some bills on the table for our lunch and headed back to the house. Thor trailed behind on his bike. I didn't think anyone would die in the time it took us to get there.

I knelt down beside Dad and slipped a hand under his head. He made a grunting noise, and his eyelids fluttered. He was alive!

Janet put a comforting hand on my shoulder. "I'll get some ice. He's got a nasty bump on the side of his head."

"Thanks, sweetie." Dad gave her an innocent smile.

I rolled my eyes. Faking it, at least somewhat. He was hurt, but not as badly as I thought.

"I'm going back on perimeter guard." Thor beat

a hasty retreat out the front door as Deuce came out of the kitchen, followed by Rattler.

I jumped to my feet and stomped over to him, hands on my hips. "That's my dad! What did you do to him?"

Deuce caught me by the shoulders, holding me at arm's length. "I didn't know it was your dad, and he jumped me from behind the door when I got here. I just defended myself. What the hell is he doing here, anyway? I thought you said you weren't going to involve him."

"Involve me in what?" Dad sat up, one hand going to the lump on the side of his head.

Deuce let go of me and I dropped to my knees beside my dad. "Are you okay?"

He grunted. "Takes more than an uppity biker or two to kill me."

Yup. That was my dad. Grumpy to the core. Janet returned with a bag of frozen peas and handed them to him.

I winced as he placed them against the lump on his head. "What happened?"

"He took out Tiny and jumped me with a baseball bat." Deuce sounded grudgingly impressed.

I glared at him. "I asked Dad, not you."

"What he said." Dad jerked his chin at Deuce. "I would have took him out too, but that other guy come in. Two young fellas against one old guy. Not fair odds."

Amazing how he could play the age card when it suited him. He couldn't be that badly hurt. "I wasn't expecting you, and they were just trying to protect me. They didn't know who you were."

Dad gave me a shrewd look. "And why do you need a bunch of bikers to protect you?"

Damn. I looked up at Deuce.

He raised his brows but kept silent.

Rattler stirred. "I'll put on a pot of coffee. It's a long story."

"I'll help you." Janet winked at me as she skirted the two men and followed Rattler into the kitchen.

Dad looked up at Deuce. "You plan to stand there all day?"

"Don't have anything else to do at the moment."

"Lazy bugger." He turned his attention back to me. "So what am I not getting involved in?"

I sighed. "You know those dating apps you thought were a bad idea?"

He narrowed his eyes. "Yeah?"

"Well," I said. "Turns out you were right."

"Coffee's ready!" Janet's voice sounded from the kitchen.

I stood, holding a hand out to help my dad get up. "We might as well go sit in the kitchen while I explain."

Beast was busy stuffing loops of rope into the garbage can, and a sheepish looking Tiny was standing by the stove rubbing the angry red welts on his wrists.

I didn't ask, but I noticed the smirk on my dad's face when Tiny glared at him. Someone could fill me in on that later.

When we were all seated, coffee in hand, I took a deep breath and explained the whole situation to my dad. I left out the part where I suspected Deuce or Rattler had shot one of the guys. As I recounted the prior day's events, I realized the story sounded bad enough without adding dead bodies.

"So, Deuce offered the services of Riptide to watch over me until it's safe," I concluded.

"Why leave me out of it?" Dad sounded hurt.

"These guys are pros, Dad. I've only got one of you, and I don't want you to get hurt."

"I'll stay until they find the guys who hurt you and deal with them. I was in the SEALs for over a decade. I'm not exactly helpless." Dad slapped one palm down on the table for emphasis.

Janet choked on a mouthful of coffee. "Well, that could be awkward."

I glared at her.

Dad looked from one biker to another, his attention lingering on Deuce. "Why? Which one you sleeping with?"

"I'm not sure there was much sleeping involved." Rattler snickered.

"Careful, son." Dad glared at the biker. "That's my little girl you're talking about."

Deuce cleared his throat.

Afraid he was about to confess; I held up a hand. "I'm not a little girl anymore, Dad, and my sex life is none of your business."

He reached across the table and took my hand in his big callused one. "You'll always be my little girl."

I tried to hide the wince as he gave my hand a gentle shake, causing the road rash to bump onto the table.

"You're hurt."

I nodded. "Just a little. Road rash. From jumping out of the van."

He pursed his lips and turned to the group of bikers. "I'd like a few moments with the assholes when you catch up with them."

"No." It was my turn to glare. "You are not going to land yourself back in jail on my account."

"*Back* in jail?" Rattler spoke up.

"It was nothing. Bar brawl that got out of hand.

Some idiot college kid got his face messed up. His rich-assed parents pressed charges, and they gave me a couple of days in the clink to keep everyone happy. Just because I served in the SEALs, they thought I had an unfair advantage."

"It left you with a criminal record," I pointed out.

He shrugged, the ghost of a smile on his face. "Keeps the nosy neighbors out of my hair."

I rolled my eyes, trying to make my point. "I don't need you here. Deuce and his buddies will make sure nothing happens to me."

Dad turned to give Deuce a careful once-over. "So you're the one she's got the hots for. Be careful. If you hurt her in any way, you'll have to deal with me." He grinned. "Next time you won't be so lucky."

I heaved a big sigh. "And now you all know why I wanted to keep my dad out of it. Speaking of which," -- I tried to sound firm -- "I do not want you staying in my house while this is going on."

"No problem." He sounded much too calm.

"So you'll go back to the homestead?"

He shook his head. "Camper is on the back of the truck. I'll just park in front of the house."

"Not to interfere in a family matter, but that's a bad idea." Rattler put his coffee mug down. "The perps will see you out there, and they could target you. If they take you while you sleep, they'd have a hostage to use against your daughter here. You wouldn't want that, would you?"

Dad shrugged. "Huh. Biker with brains. Guess I'll be staying in the house then. Spare room still made up?"

"No. You are not staying here." I looked to Deuce for help. "There's a campground just outside town. You could stay there."

Deuce looked thoughtful. "You're an ex-SEAL?"

Dad nodded. "I am, and proud of it. Why?"

"Thank you for your service. Give me a minute to check on something." He pulled out his phone and strode out of the room.

I frowned. "What was that about?"

"I think I know, but let's wait until he comes back." Rattler stared at the empty doorway, a thoughtful look on his face.

Janet bounced out of her seat. "Well, this was fun, but I need to go home and get ready for work. Got bills to pay and all that."

I stood up and went to give her a big hug. "Thanks for coming over. I'll let you know how things turn out."

She leaned forward and stage-whispered in my ear. "I'll be back tomorrow. You don't get to keep all these gorgeous hunks to yourself!"

Thor let out a muffled snort, his eyes dancing with laughter.

Janet grinned and blew him a kiss. "Later, gentlemen." She sashayed her way out the door, with Thor trailing close behind.

Rattler shrugged. "He'll make sure she makes it to her car safely."

I rolled my eyes. "Right. That's what's going on." I got up and went to refill my coffee cup, only to find the pot empty. If these guys planned to stick around, I was going to need a bigger coffee machine. I busied myself putting on another pot.

Deuce came back in. "You can stay at the clubhouse. Ace okayed it, pending Shadow doing a background check on you."

Dad frowned. "Why would I want to bunk down with a bunch of bikers?"

"We're all ex-SEALs. Seems like you'd fit right in."

Dad looked intrigued. I opened my mouth to object, but realized he was probably just as safe there as hiding up on his acreage waiting for the end of the world. At least he'd be out of immediate danger. Might even do him some good to be surrounded by guys who understood him.

"Can I bring my dog?"

I stared at him. "You brought Willow with you?"

"Didn't know how long I'd be gone. I couldn't very well leave her to fend for herself."

"I'm not sure." Deuce frowned. "Never had a dog at the club before. Have to check if everyone's okay with it."

"She can stay with me." I realized I hadn't seen his truck when I got home. "Where did you park?"

"Around the corner at that playground. Wasn't sure your neighbors would appreciate my old bush buggy in their neighborhood."

That explained why Tiny hadn't seen him coming. "Go get it. After all the bikes in the past day or two, your truck might look like an improvement."

Dad lumbered to his feet, dropping a paternal pat on my head before heading out.

"So, Willow?" Deuce strode over to the coffee maker to help himself to a fresh cup. "Doberman? Shepherd? Pitbull?"

I shook my head. "No, she's a mutt. Hard to tell what kind of breeds she might have in her. Someone dumped her on the side of the road a few years back and Dad brought her home. She's very sweet."

Dad's truck wasn't much quieter than the bikes. I heard it turn the corner and got to my feet. I hadn't seen Willow since my trip home last Christmas and I missed the furry little brat. I'd considered getting a dog of my own, but somehow it never seemed like the right time.

On top of my substitute teaching, I did freelance work as a seamstress, specializing in weddings and formal occasions. I was occasionally away on location if the event was out of the country, and I wouldn't be able to take a dog with me. That wouldn't be fair to the critter.

The front door opened, and an overexcited bundle of fur streaked into the kitchen. Willow threw herself into my lap, squirming in every direction as she tried to get her twelve-pound body high enough to lick my face.

"Probably safe to say she'd be okay at the compound. Mom would just love her to pieces," Beast noted wryly.

Deuce met my gaze over the top of the excited dog and shook his head.

* * *

Deuce

I felt surprisingly nervous getting ready for my first official date with Sophia. Silly really. Fuck, she'd been through hell the night we met, and we'd already slept together, but we'd never gone out somewhere socially. I'd asked her if she was okay with going on my bike and she'd replied *yes* with real enthusiasm.

That made me happy. The bike was a huge part of my life, and it was important that the woman I planned to claim as my own understood that and shared in the joy of riding. After the drama with her dad showing up, the steak dinner had been postponed for now in favor of a meal out.

I put on a new pair of black jeans I'd bought just

for the occasion, and a button-down shirt over my usual tee. Checking my image in the mirror, I shook my head ruefully. A lifetime ago, when I worked for one of the top accounting firms, this outfit would have been considered slumming. Amazing how a person's perspective could change.

I slipped my leather cut on and hesitated. I never went anywhere without my gun and it seemed like a bad idea to leave it behind. Striding to the closet, I grabbed my shoulder holster. Strapping it on, I checked the safety and slipped the gun in place. The cut mostly hid it. Pocketing my phone, I grabbed my keys and the pics Shadow had printed out for me, and headed out the door.

The ride to Sophia's place helped to clear my head. I'd polished my bike to a high shine, and it sparkled in the evening sun. I left my helmet on the seat and ran my fingers through my hair to make sure it wasn't sticking up in all directions. I straightened my shirt. A button-down wasn't something I was used to anymore, and I wanted to look my best. Striding up to the back door, I knocked.

No one answered.

I swallowed a lump in my throat. Surely, she hadn't forgotten our date? Or worse yet, changed her mind and was now pretending she wasn't home despite her car in the driveway?

I knocked again. A ferocious barking startled me, and I jumped back a step.

"Quiet, you little heathen!" Exasperation laced Sophia's voice. "He'll think you don't like him!"

The door opened and Sophia rolled her eyes. "Just ignore her. She thinks she's a guard dog."

"She did make me jump," I said, leaning down to offer my hand to the little pooch.

Willow sniffed my fingers, gave them a tentative lick. Apparently satisfied I was harmless, she danced up on her hind legs and tried to reach my face. I scooped her up, rubbing her little belly.

"Now you've done it. You're going to have dog hair all over that nice shirt."

"Angel dust."

"What?"

I grinned as Willow let out a happy little yip. "My mom used to say it wasn't dog hair, it was angel dust."

Sophia tilted her head.

"Our dog's name was Angel," I explained, "and whenever my dad complained about all the dog hair in the house, my mom would just laugh and say it was angel dust."

"That is adorable." Sophia grabbed a coat and tugged it on. Shiny black leather with a heavy-duty zipper, it looked suspiciously new. "I guess by that logic, I have Willow dust in the house."

"Yup. Is Willow okay being left alone?"

"Yeah, doesn't seem to bother her. My dad made a run back up to his homestead to pick up some supplies or he'd stay with her. She'll just jump up on my bed and make sure there's Willow dust on my pillow when I go to bed tonight."

I pretended to wince. "Yikes. A passive aggressive pint-sized attack dog."

Sophia shook her head. "Yeah, but I cheated. I pulled my pillows off the bed and put out a couple of spare ones. She might be cute, but I don't relish waking up with dog hair in my mouth."

I put Willow down and she ignored us both, trotting back to her water dish. She made impressively loud slurping sounds as she took a drink.

I glanced at Sophia. With the leather jacket and a pair of biker boots, she looked good enough to eat. I felt my cock twitch at the idea. I hastily shifted my position to hide the sudden bulge at my crotch.

I took a deep breath. I didn't want to put a damper on the date, but I needed to do this and I figured I might as well get it out of the way. It could help us find the trafficking ring.

I pulled the papers out of my pocket. "Before we go, I have a couple of pictures to show you. Shadow managed to track down the guys who deleted their profiles from that dating app the day you got abducted. Want to take a look and see if any of them look familiar?"

She frowned. "Sure. Shadow is the computer whiz, right?"

"Right."

She reached out and I handed over the pictures. She studied them carefully, shaking her head at the first two. When she got to the third one, her eyes widened. "That's him," she snarled. "That's George. The son of a bitch. Can you track him from here?"

I took the picture. Not the guy I'd shot, so he was still out there somewhere. Not for long though. I had a new goal in life. Find George and kill him. Slowly. Painfully.

"Shadow will be able to. That kid is a wizard with a computer." I filed the picture back in my pocket and sent Shadow a quick text to let him know we had a positive ID. I put the phone back in my pocket.

"Ready to go?"

Sophia nodded. "Where are we going?"

"I thought I'd take you to the bar the club owns. Should be safe enough with all the bikers around and as a bonus, there's karaoke tonight."

She looked intrigued. "You sing?"

"Very little, and surprisingly far off-key. How about you?"

She wrinkled her nose. "A little less than very little, but I love to listen and tap my feet."

"Sound like a plan then. All those wannabe singers need an audience, right?"

"Absolutely." She locked the door behind us and tucked the key into her purse. Slinging it over her head and shoulder, she twisted it around behind her. Smart. It was firmly attached but wouldn't get between us on the bike.

I handed her the helmet I'd picked up for her earlier before fastening my own. The one I'd bought her was pink and girly as fuck. I wanted her to have her own, not the spare I kept for anyone who happened to need a ride.

Sophia was special, and she deserved to be treated as such.

A questioning look crossed her face as her gaze slid from the shiny new helmet to me, but she didn't comment as she fastened it on her head. She slid the visor up and down a couple of times as if testing how well it worked.

I slung my leg over the bike and kicked the starter. Newer bikes all had key starts but I liked the feel of a kick-start. My ride was my pride and joy, a burgundy-red 1985 FXSB lowrider that I'd spent many an hour tweaking and working on. I could tell if she needed a little TLC just by the sound of her engine.

Sophia clambered on behind me and snuggled up close, wrapping her arms tight around my waist. I closed my eyes and enjoyed the feel of her against my back.

After my old lady ran out on me, I figured I was

done with that couples shit, but now I realized I just hadn't met the right woman. Sophia was that woman. My woman.

I savored that thought as I dropped the bike into first and puttered down the street at a stately pace. No point in giving the neighbors reason to think poorly of me, or of Sophia by association.

I'd told her we were going to the bar Riptide owned, but I planned to take the long way getting there. Instead of heading downtown, I took a right at the end of the street.

It was a beautiful night for a ride. The sun was just starting to set, throwing a pink and gold glow across the landscape. The smell of pine and damp earth hung in the air as I headed for the road that curved around the lake. Mature trees overhung the pavement, and the generous shoulders on the road made for an exhilarating ride. Once clear of town, I sped up, sweeping through the curves at speeds probably not approved of by the local police. But they weren't here. They were out on the main highway, handing out tickets to the tourists passing through on their way to all the attractions in the bigger cities.

Sophia stroked her hands up and down my shirt, coming dangerously close to that bulge in my pants. The woman was playing with fire. Now my concentration was divided. Part of me still wanted the thrill of racing around the lake with my woman hugging my back, but the other part of me was already plotting where I could pull over and enjoy what she was offering. Because that hand wasn't shying away from my cock.

The little tease knew exactly what she was doing.

There was a roadside park up ahead, and a little path led from it to a secluded clearing where a spring-fed brook flowed down and into the lake. Perfect spot to pull off and teach my handsy passenger a thing or two.

Chapter Seven

Sophia

I knew I was playing with fire, but I just couldn't resist. Riding behind Deuce with my arms wrapped tight around him meant I could feel his muscles rippling every time he moved, and the smell of leather and musky male was a heady sensation.

I let my hands drift low enough to feel the bulge in the front of his pants.

I was starting to rethink the whole cat lady thing.

When he slowed and turned into a parking area on the side of the road I expected him to stop, but he just geared down and followed a narrow trail that wound beneath tall trees before opening up to a small meadow. He guided the bike to the far side before killing the engine and flipping the kickstand down.

Pulling his helmet off, he twisted his neck to look at me. His eyes smoldered with the promise of retribution. "Get off."

I felt a flicker of uncertainty. Was he mad, or horny?

Dismounting, I undid my helmet and turned my back on the big, bad biker, running a hand through my hair to fluff it up. Helmets might save lives, but they did nothing for my hair.

Deuce came up behind me. I could feel his hot breath on my neck as he wrapped his arms around me. He slid one hand under my shirt and splayed his fingers across my belly.

I felt heat blaze through me in anticipation. Not mad. Horny. His hips were firmly against me, the unmistakable hardness of his arousal pressing against me.

"Think you were going to get away with teasing

me like that?" He muttered the words against my tangled hair while his hand wandered up toward the skimpy lace of my bra, the one I'd bought especially for tonight.

"Maybe. You going to punish me?" The thought sent a flood of wet warmth to my pussy.

"I'm afraid I'll have to. Can't have you thinking you can do whatever you want without consequences." He slipped his hand under my bra and stroked a fingernail across my nipple.

"Mmm. True." I reached behind me and cupped his crotch, feeling his cock grow even harder. "What do you think would be a fitting punishment?"

He pulled his hand out from under my clothing and grasped me by the shoulders. Turning me to face him, he lowered his head. I placed a hand on his chest and met his lips halfway.

The world ceased to exist. He worshipped me with his mouth, gentle and persuasive at the same time. I opened my mouth and slid my tongue across the crease of his lips, and suddenly he wasn't quite as gentle.

His hands went to my hips as he opened his mouth and consumed me. He pulled me in against him, and I could feel how hard and ready he was.

I gasped. "Deuce."

"Yeah?" He answered without letting go of my lips.

"I want you."

"That's good, because I plan on taking you. Maybe more than once. Maybe I won't stop until you beg me."

My heart raced as he took his hands off me and shrugged out of his cut. He removed his shoulder holster and set the gun aside before unbuttoning his shirt and taking it off. He pulled his tee shirt over his head and spread it out on the grass, then held out a hand to me.

Damn, he looks good without a shirt on! I dropped to my knees next to him and he reached for me again. We kissed. Forever. It wasn't enough.

"I need to feel you. Naked. Inside me." Where had this wanton side of me come from? I'd always been the one who held back, who worried about decorum and what people might think. But with Deuce, I couldn't get enough and if anyone had an issue with it, screw them. My inner slut was coming out to play.

I slipped my jacket off and sent up a prayer of thanks that I'd had the foresight to wear a sweater that slipped over my head. Taking the time to undo reams of buttons would have been sheer torture.

Deuce reached for the bottom of the sweater and pulled it up over my head before tossing it carelessly aside. I leaned back on my hands, leaving my breasts to thrust forward in a blatant invitation.

"Beautiful." His eyes gleamed with lust.

Arching over me, he teased one nipple through the sheer red lace before ripping the bra off me with his teeth. I gasped, my nipples pebbling into hard peaks.

Deuce leaned forward and nipped my neck right below my left ear, kissing the hurt away as soon as he did it. He pushed me gently until I was laying on my back with him towering over me in all his shirtless glory.

He nibbled and kissed his way from my neck to my breasts, and I tangled my fingers in his hair, mewling softly as he suckled on first one breast and then the other.

Without stopping, he reached down and undid

the button at my waistband and slid the zipper down. Slipping his hand into my pants, he traced the outline of the thong covering my mound.

I arched up and reached down to push the jeans down over my hips.

Deuce chuckled. "I don't think you're taking your punishment seriously."

I tried to give him a snarky answer, but my wit had abandoned me along with the capacity for coherent speech.

He renewed his assault on my breasts and slid one finger under the thong that matched the destroyed bra.

I was wet and ready. More than ready.

He explored between the soft folds at my entrance and slipped a finger inside me. I gasped, arching my hips against his palm. He ripped the thong off and tossed it aside. Slipping a second finger inside along with the first, he thrust the pair in and out in a slow and gentle rhythm.

I growled in frustration, and he picked up the pace sliding his fingers in and out, faster and faster as heat blazed along every nerve and pooled low in my belly.

As his thumb caressed my clit, a powerful orgasm surged through my body. I clenched my fingers in his hair, holding tight as it crested in a blazing rush of pleasure.

When it receded, I let him go, watching as he rested on his side, propped up on one elbow. He caught my gaze and held it as he pulled his fingers out of me and licked my juices from them.

I'd never seen anything so sexy in my life.

When I managed to get some breath back in my body, I sat up. "My turn."

Deuce's nostrils flared as he considered me through slitted eyes. "What did you have in mind?"

"Get your pants off, for starters."

He grinned and obliged. At least this time he had boxer shorts on. Not for long, though. Freed from the confining material, his cock sprang to attention, rock hard and just as big as I remembered. I licked my lips.

"Roll over. On your back." I gave him a push to emphasize my point.

He obliged, his arms folded under his head so every part of him was on glorious display. He grinned. "Now what?"

"Now I get to play." I climbed on top of him, my knees on either side of his hips. Bending forward I traced the bird tattooed on his shoulder with my tongue. He tasted like sex and sweat, a heady flavor I could easily become addicted to.

I worked my way lower, flicking my tongue over his flat nipples.

He hissed in a deep breath, causing his pecs to flex beneath my hands.

I squirmed a bit, moving lower as I licked my way down his chest to his taut belly, pausing to nip playfully at his belly button. That earned me a soft growl.

I continued my explorations, tasting his hips, and the faint V of hair pointing to my ultimate goal. I wrapped my hand around his shaft, giving it a gentle squeeze as I ran my fingers from the base to the tip.

A sticky wet drop coated the broad head, and I wiped it with my finger. Lifting my head, I caught his gaze and opened my mouth to delicately lick it off with my tongue.

He groaned. "You're going to be the death of me, woman."

I smiled. "Then you'll die happy."

Without giving him any warning, I lowered my head and took his cock in my mouth. I cupped his balls in one hand, massaging them gently as I swirled my tongue along the side of his shaft. I sucked and teased. Used my tongue and my lips. Played with his balls.

I felt so in control, in command. I was on top of him, in a position of dominance, and he let me do whatever I wanted. His body responded, jerking and arching, his cock growing even larger until with a groan, he laced his fingers through my hair and urged me to look at him.

"I want to be inside you when I come, and that's not going to happen if you keep this up."

"Do you have a condom?"

He nodded. "In my wallet. Jeans." He gestured to his discarded pants.

I rolled off him and reached over to drag his pants closer, pulled the wallet out of the back pocket, and tossed it to him.

He took it and pulled out a foil-wrapped package. Ripping it open, he reached down to sheath himself.

"Ready?"

He nodded. "Fuck, yeah."

I climbed back on top and took his shaft in one hand, positioning it with the tip just grazing my entrance. Taking a deep breath, I slowly lowered myself onto his rock-hard cock. I was wet and ready, and he slid inside me like we were made for each other.

I closed my eyes and threw my head back, moving slowly at first as I adjusted to his size. My biker was not small. I rode him like a horse. My body, already sensitive from the orgasm he'd wrung from me with his fingers, felt like it was on fire. Flames of lust danced down my spine and along every nerve ending. Within minutes, another orgasm washed over me with the strength of a tsunami.

I screamed out my pleasure to the trees and birds and grasses.

He wrapped his brawny arms around me, his hands splayed across my ass and rolled us over, reversing our positions so that he was on top. I wrapped my legs around him as he started to move, thrusting fast and deep. It wasn't long before he let out a primal yell of triumph as he came, collapsing beside me.

"Damn," he murmured, his chin resting on top of my head. "Just, damn!"

I snuggled in closer. "Yeah. Damn."

* * *

Deuce

We pulled into the parking lot at *The Riptide Rest*, and I parked my bike alongside those of the other Riptide brothers. Looked like a full house tonight, which was good. I wanted to show off Sophia, and at the same time I wanted her to be safe. It was unlikely anyone would be insane enough to try to get to her on Riptide turf.

I held out my hand, and we walked to the entrance with our fingers entwined like a pair of giddy school kids. It felt good.

I held the door open for her like a Goddamn fucking gentleman, which drew the attention of Beast. Looked like he'd drawn bouncer duty tonight, although "duty" might be pushing it a bit. He had a bar bunny sitting on his lap, hand feeding him French fries dipped in a puddle of ketchup.

"Look who came out to play!" Beast shooed the woman off his lap and stood up. "And you brought this poor creature you've tricked into thinking she wants to spend time with you."

"Nice to see you too, Beast. I believe you met Sophia back at the house when her dad tried to kill me."

"Yes, I did." Beast gave me a sideways smirk, bowing his head to Sophia. "If you get tired of this guy, let me know. I'm available."

I gave him a good-natured cuff across the side of the head. "She adores me, so keep your hands to yourself."

"You adore him?" Beast shook his head, pretending to be shocked. "No accounting for taste." He turned his attention to me. "Get it? No accounting?"

I rolled my eyes. "Funny. Now go back to playing with your friend while we get some adult type beverages." I led Sophia to an empty booth at the side of the dance floor. "What would you like to drink?"

"Beer, please." She looked a little unnerved as she surveyed the patrons. "Are these guys all bikers?"

The place was hopping. A couple were up on the karaoke stage, crooning a duet, and over in the far corner, a crowd was cheering a guy on the mechanical bull. Just then the bull dumped him on the ground and the crowd groaned in unison.

"Nah. Some are bikers. The rest are just regular guys looking to blow off steam at the end of the work week." I held up my hand and motioned the server to bring us over a couple of beers.

"That looks like fun." Sophia nodded at the mechanical bull.

"It is when you're twenty. Now it's more fun to

watch the youngsters get dumped off."

She raised her brows, a smile curving her luscious lips. "Look at you being all mature and careful."

The server maneuvered her way between the dancers and placed two bottles of beer on the table. "You want glasses for those?"

I looked at Sophia, who shook her head.

"Bottles are fine," I said. "Run us a tab, would you, Sherry?"

"No problem, Deuce. Enjoy." She was halfway back to the bar by the time she answered. I twisted the caps off the beer and handed one to Sophia.

"She seems nice." Sophia took a long pull on her beer.

"You're not jealous, are you?"

Sophia snorted. "Not a chance."

That kind of stung. "Not even a little?

She shook her head. "Nope."

"How come?"

She grinned. "She has a ring on her finger and someone else's name tattooed on her arm."

"Oh." I knew Sherry and the mechanic next door were an item, but I didn't realize it was that serious.

"So what was that quip about at the door?" She tilted her head.

I frowned, not sure what she meant.

"What Beast said. No accounting for taste."

"Oh that. I'm a CPA, and the guys like to kid me about it."

She looked surprised. "As in Certified Public Accountant?"

I nodded and took a swig of my beer.

She frowned. "How do you go from CPA to bad boy biker?"

"In my case, by way of the Navy SEALs. I got bored pushing papers in a cubicle and joined up. Thought I'd get to see the world and be a hero. I did a few tours with Ace, Rattler, and some of the other guys. Found out being a hero isn't all it's cracked up to be. It's ninety percent boredom with about ten percent terrifying action. Living like that for years does something to you. When I mustered out, I found I couldn't go back to the office routine. Maybe PTSD, or maybe just life." I shrugged. "Didn't go the therapy route, but something in me changed. I can't do the suit and tie, sit behind a desk, and punch numbers thing anymore. Just can't. I'm good with looking after Riptide's investments and things. They don't expect to see me in a tie, and they're fine with me sitting outside with my laptop and a beer while I work on it. Officially, I'm the club treasurer. I keep my designation up to date, but that's it. Can't see me ever going back to four walls and a clock."

I watched her face, wondering how she would take that. Most people thought I was crazy. CPAs made a shitload of money.

Sophia nodded slowly. "My dad's kind of the same way. He's got a bachelor's degree in business administration, but I don't remember him ever using it. He's always just been Dad. He raised me himself as best he could. Set up the homestead and kind of withdrew from the world." She narrowed her eyes, as if searching for words. "He has trust issues, hence the prepper lifestyle. He doesn't want to have to rely on anyone, ever."

"Except you."

She nodded. "Except me. The fact he approves of you is huge. I can't believe he agreed to stay at your clubhouse."

"I'm not so sure he approves of me, but him and Jake seem to be getting along pretty good. They seem to be good for each other. Mom likes him too, which is telling. She has a second sense about people."

"I haven't met either of them, have I?"

I shook my head. "No. They live at the clubhouse and don't go out much."

Sophia grinned. "Do I get to see this clubhouse sometime, or is it off-limits to females?"

"Not necessarily off-limits, but some of the parties get rowdy. The young guys don't have a lot of inhibitions. Not sure you'd be comfortable with it."

"You mean there's naked people running around having sex on the kitchen table?"

"Like I said, parties can get pretty wild."

Sophia just looked at me. "And you have a mom who's okay with that?"

"She's not *my* mom. We just call her that. And she and Jake usually make themselves scarce when the parties get out of hand."

"Oh." She lifted the beer to her mouth and took a long swig.

I watched her lips as they formed a circle around the top of the bottle. Fuck, I envied that bottle.

She cocked her head. "You want to dance?"

"Sure." I'd never pass up an opportunity to hold her in my arms. I put my beer down and stood, extending a hand to her.

She grasped it and bounced to her feet.

I led her onto the dance floor and turned to face her.

Wrapping her arms around my neck, she clasped her hands together and melted against me. Someone was crooning a slow song, and I couldn't quite make the words out over the noise in the bar, but I didn't care. My world was complete.

We swayed in time to the music, and I closed my eyes, resting my chin on her head. She fit me perfectly, and the subtle smell of our earlier activities teased my nostrils. If I had any persuasive skills at all, there would be a repeat performance when I took her home.

The song ended, and someone started a lively jazz tune. That was the risk of karaoke. No continuity. One song jazz, the next one pop, and then you find yourself trying to dance to a country ballad.

Sophia was up to the challenge, her face flushed as she sashayed her way around the floor. I grinned as the other dancers cleared the way for Sophia and me to show off our moves. Considering this was the first time we'd danced together, we put on a stellar show. When the song ended, the spectators gave us a rousing round of applause.

I pulled Sophia into my arms and blazed a sensuous kiss across her lips. Raising herself on her toes, she kissed me right back, earning raucous hoots and cheers from my Riptide brothers. She was going to fit into our self-made family just fine.

I led her back to the booth, both of us out of breath from our exertions. Waving my hand in the air, I signaled Sherry for another round of beers.

We both slid into the same side, and I laid my hand on her thigh, needing to feel the physical connection. Yeah, I was that far gone. "Where did you learn to dance?"

A slight smile ghosted across her face. "Dad has some old movies we'd watch on a VHS player at night. Fred Astaire. Ginger Rogers. Elvis Presley. He loved musicals and I'd watch them and imitate the dancers."

"You had a good childhood, didn't you?"

She nodded. "I did. Even though my mother

deserted us, I always felt loved and wanted. Dad made sure of that." She paused. "I think that might be why I've never had much luck with dating. Subconsciously, I compare the guy to my dad, and they always come up short."

"Do I come up short?" I wasn't sure I wanted to hear the answer.

She shook her head. "A knight on a shining motorcycle who rides up to rescue me from kidnappers in the nick of time? I think you managed to wow my subconscious into silence."

I puffed out my chest in a pretense of victory. "I applaud your subconscious. Very observant."

Sophia laughed, her eyes sparkling. "So, when do I get to see you ride the mechanical bull?"

I snorted. "Not gonna happen."

Chapter Eight

Sophia

I woke up feeling sleepy and deliciously sore between my legs. When we got home from the bar, we'd made love.

Then we'd done it again. And again. We'd fallen asleep in each other's arms, and when we woke up, we did it again.

The sun was starting to come up, soft rays peeking over the horizon.

"You awake?" Deuce sounded about as groggy as I felt.

"No. I'm still sleeping."

"Good. I don't want to get up yet." He spooned me from behind, one arm resting lightly on my belly. We were both naked. Why bother with clothes if you're just going to rip them off?

"If you cared about me, you'd go make coffee," I said.

"Not my house. I'm a guest. You should make coffee."

"I would, but I need a shower first. I smell like sweat and sex."

"It smells good on you, but if you want a shower, I'll help."

I giggled. "Oh, you will, will you? How thoughtful of you."

"I do what I can."

Willow let out a soft *woof* from her perch at the bottom of the bed, as if to tell us to shut up and let her sleep. We looked at each other and smiled, sliding quietly out of the bed so as not to disturb the furry dictator any further.

It was a long time later when we finally made it

to the kitchen for coffee. I looked at the clock. "Crap. I need to get moving. I'm supposed to be at a client's in an hour to do measurements for her wedding dress."

Deuce looked up from the coffee he was pouring. "I have club shit this morning. Take Thor with you."

"Can't you get Thor to do the club shit?"

He shook his head. "He's a prospect. This is patched member kind of shit. You want me to go, you need to wait until tomorrow."

I sighed. "Fine. I'll take Thor."

Deuce glanced at his watch. "Speaking of which, I should probably get going. Text me when you leave and when you get there."

I wrinkled my nose. "Yes, sir."

He reached over and swatted my ass. "I'm worried, and until we figure this shit out I need to know you're safe. Otherwise, I spend all my time worrying about you and I'm no good to anyone."

"Oh, you were very good to me. Very good." I giggled and skipped back out of reach. "I'll keep you updated on my every move."

"I appreciate it." He put his coffee cup in the dishwasher and grabbed his cut off the chair he'd dropped it on when we came in last night. Slipping it on over his shoulder holster, he stalked over to me and took me in his arms to give me a quick kiss. "Be careful."

"I will." I walked to the door with him and watched as he mounted his bike and rode off.

Willow gave a little bark and turned to trot back into the living room. Jumping up on the sofa, she circled three times before lying down and closing her eyes. Apparently, our boisterous activities had interrupted her beauty sleep.

My gaze softened as I looked at the little critter

fondly. "Spoiled brat."

I returned to the kitchen and gulped down the rest of my coffee. Texting Thor that I'd be going out and needed an escort, I gathered my supplies and loaded them into the back seat of the car. One last trip inside, I made myself another coffee in the biggest travel mug I had and checked myself in the mirror.

All good. I texted Deuce to let him know I was leaving.

I made sure to set the alarm and lock the door behind me as I left. If I hadn't already been security cautious due to my dad's paranoia, the events of the past few days would have hammered the message home.

Thor was sitting on his bike when I backed out of the driveway. I wasn't used to having someone follow me everywhere, but I was thankful for the added presence. A couple of weeks ago I wouldn't have dreamed a person could be abducted from a busy coffee shop without anyone noticing, and yet it had happened.

Seems the world was out to prove my dad right. The world was a dangerous place.

I arrived at the client's house in plenty of time and sent off another text to Deuce. It felt good to have someone other than my dad worry about me.

Katherine, my current client, was easy to work with and willing to listen to my advice on the best styles to suit her figure. Some brides had their hearts set on dresses that didn't suit them, and it took a great deal to convince them to change their minds. Since the advent of computer modeling, that task had become easier. I could take a photo of the bride-to-be and show them a computer simulation of how they would appear in different styles and materials.

I loved my work. I loved being a teacher on call, and I loved being self-employed, setting my own hours and deciding who I wanted to work for. I adored the creativity, the sense of accomplishment and the joy on a bride's face when she looked in the mirror and saw her dream become a reality.

Katherine and I managed to nail down her preferred style and materials within the first hour. I spent some time taking measurements and agreed on a time for the first fitting. Usually, it took at least two fittings, and with the wedding still eight months out there was lots of time for alterations especially if she lost the weight she was hoping for.

I packed my supplies back in the car and waved to Thor, who had remained discreetly down the street from the client's house while I conducted business. I didn't want to have to explain his presence.

I glanced at my watch as I slid into the driver's seat. Almost noon. A nap sounded like the perfect way to spend the afternoon. Maybe if Deuce was finished with his club business, he could join me. I fired off a quick text to him and headed home.

I was still daydreaming about Deuce when a motion in the rearview mirror caught my attention. Thor was trailing me by a couple of car lengths, hugging the center line as bikers tended to. A black sedan came barreling up behind him and pulled into the oncoming lanes. As I watched in horror, the driver pulled up beside Thor and yanked the wheel to the right sending the car careening toward the biker.

Thor braked sharply, falling back.

The car missed hitting him by a fraction of an inch, fishtailing for a moment before the driver regained control. With the bike behind him, the sedan pulled out again and gunned it.

I gulped. Was he going to try to ram me instead?

I stomped my foot down on the accelerator, praying my car had enough guts to outrun the threat.

The needle on my speedometer leapt up, and I hung onto the steering wheel with both hands as the car surged forward. I'd never driven this fast, and I prayed to whatever god was out there that I didn't lose control.

A loud honking sounded ahead of me. To my horror, I saw an eighteen-wheeler barreling toward us. If it hit the sedan head on, I'd become collateral damage.

I tried to coax a bit more speed from my valiant old car, but it was going as fast as it could. I was afraid to brake hard at this speed, afraid I wouldn't be able to maintain control. I could see no chance for escape. A rock cliff rose sharply on one side of me, and a guardrail blocked a steep downhill slope on the other. The sedan remained stubbornly in the opposite lane.

At the last possible second, the driver slowed and dropped back in behind me. The transport truck flashed past in the opposite direction, horn blaring angrily.

I let out a deep breath I hadn't known I was holding.

But it wasn't over yet.

The black sedan was inches from my back bumper, so close I could see the angry set of the driver's face.

I heard approaching motorcycles minutes before they swept round the curve and joined Thor behind the black sedan.

Before the driver could react to the reinforcements, Thor zipped around the sedan and pulled in front of me. Turning his head, he motioned me to follow him. I had to trust him.

Up ahead, the road forked in two directions. The main highway continued on while the secondary road led to a rest area with an outhouse and some picnic tables. Thor pulled into the rest area with me right on his tail. Beside us, the sedan flashed past on the main road, with the remainder of the bikers chasing close behind.

I brought the car to a stop and dropped my head to rest on the steering wheel. I started to shake. Tears rolled down my face.

When the tap sounded on my window I lifted my head. Thor motioned me to roll down my window. I fumbled for the control before managing to lower the glass.

Thor ran his hands through his hair, pulling it away from his face. "Deuce is on his way."

I looked at the empty highway. I couldn't stop shaking.

Thor followed my line of sight and shook his head. "You're okay. That asshole won't be back. The guys will take care of it."

"Thank you. Thank all of you." I didn't ask what that meant. Part of me hoped it was a permanent solution, but that didn't solve my main problem. Someone wanted me, and it was starting to look like alive was optional. I shuddered to think where I'd be if Deuce and Rattler hadn't been behind that van when this all started.

The rumble of a motorcycle sounded in the distance, growing louder as it approached. It came into view, and I fixated on the way the sun glinted off the chrome.

Deuce. It had to be Deuce. I *needed* it to be Deuce.

* * *

I barely managed to get off the bike before Sophia threw herself at me, sobbing. I wrapped my arms around her and looked over at Thor. He nodded in answer to my silent question. One less asshole left in this world.

In a short time, Sophia had become my whole world. I needed to feel her warm body against me to convince myself she was okay. She'd escaped their clutches. Again.

We needed to find out who "they" were, and we needed to do it fast. My heart couldn't take many more messages like that one.

The current threat had been eliminated, but he was just a hired gun. Until we found out who the head honcho behind the trafficking ring was, Sophia wouldn't be safe. No woman in the area would.

"It was deliberate." Sophia looked up at me, swiping at the tears on her face with one hand.

"Yeah. It was." I held her a little tighter.

"He tried to run Thor off the road."

I glanced at Thor. "Looks like he missed."

She nodded. "Thor outsmarted him."

"Good to know." I made a mental note to talk to Ace about patching Thor in. We could use a few more good brothers.

"I saw his face. When he was behind me. He was mad."

"Doesn't matter now." I brushed my lips across her forehead. "He won't bother you again."

She didn't say anything, but I felt her relax just a little bit.

When Thor had messaged me that they were in trouble, my heart dropped. I should have been there. I should have protected her. If anything had happened to her, I would never have been able to live with myself.

I'd underestimated the enemy. I wouldn't make that mistake again.

Thor cleared his throat. "We need to get out of here."

"Yeah." Chances were the faceless enemy would know they'd failed and might send out a backup team.

I loosened my grip on Sophia. "You want to ride on my bike, or should we take your car?"

"Bike." She shivered. "I want to hold onto you."

Good choice. The bike was more maneuverable than her car. I looked over Sophia's head to Thor. "You're coming with us. Lock the car up. We can send someone back for it."

He nodded and strode over to the vehicle.

Sophia grabbed her helmet from its perch on the back seat of my bike and strapped it on. I buckled mine as well, and we mounted up. I started the bike and let it idle, waiting for Thor to finish with the car before setting out.

* * *

The invisible assholes were escalating, and that meant it would be safer for Sophia at the clubhouse. It had been built with defense in mind and had the advantage of sheer numbers. Most of the brothers were there at one time or another. Hard to have a discussion on a bike at highway speeds. I'd explain it to Sophia when we got there. I was done taking chances with her safety.

We pulled into the driveway, and the prospects on gate duty waved us through. I stopped next to a row of bikes and killed the engine. I took my helmet off and hung it on the handlebars.

Sophia slid off the bike and unbuckled her helmet. She looked like the ride had helped her settle down. Placing the helmet on the seat, she ran her fingers through her hair and gazed up at the renovated mansion. Her eyebrows rose in disbelief. "This is what a biker clubhouse looks like?"

I smiled. "Not sure about other clubs, but this is what Riptide's looks like."

"I'm speechless. Somehow, I expected a rickety shack, with maybe a satellite dish and a broken down sofa in the front yard."

I shook my head. "Nah. We're too spoiled for that. Ace likes his comfort, and he's rubbed off on the rest of us." I reached for her hand and led her up to the front door. I was starting to like this handholding thing.

"Your dad should be around here somewhere."

"He knows we were coming?"

I shook my head. "No, but he was here when I took off. He's going to have questions."

Sophia rolled her eyes. "He always has questions."

"Yeah, he does. But he cares about you so I'm going to let him ask all he wants."

She stopped and I pivoted to face her. "You're not trying to recruit him into your biker gang, are you?"

"It's not a gang," I said. "It's a club. A group of ex-SEALs who understand each other better than anybody else could. Your dad seems to fit right in."

"He doesn't own a motorcycle," she pointed out.

"Neither does Jake," I countered.

She frowned. "Who's Jake?"

"I'm Jake." An older guy detached himself from the shadows at the end of the palatial porch and held out his hand. "You must be Sophia."

She took his hand. "Must I?"

"Well, from everything your father has told me about you, yes."

"Then I guess I'm Sophia." She studied him curiously. "Why don't you have a motorcycle?"

"Long story, or short version?"

"Short will do for now."

"I was in an accident."

"And?"

He shrugged. "And now I don't ride. Used to. Gave it up. Miss it sometimes but it is what it is. I'll give you the long version someday but right now I have the feeling Deuce has plans for you."

She looked over at me, and I nodded. "Ace is expecting us."

"Ace is the head honcho, right?"

I suppressed a smile. "He's the president of Riptide, yes."

"So why would he want to see me? I don't own a motorcycle."

"Give it a minute, and he can tell you himself."

Jake stood aside and we entered the house. Sophia paused and looked around. "This is a lot nicer than I expected. Cleaner, too."

"That would be thanks to Mom. She keeps us all in line and makes sure the mess gets cleaned up after a party. You'll meet her later."

"I will?"

"Yes. Right now, we need to see Ace though."

A door opened down the hallway and Ace stepped out. "Yes, you do. Come on in."

We entered his office, and Ace shut the door behind us before striding to his desk. He gestured at two very comfortable-looking chairs. "Have a seat."

Sophia gave me a wry smile. "I feel like I'm back in grade school and I just got sent to the principal's office."

I had to make an effort not to grin at the picture of a young Sophia and what she might have gotten into that would send her to the principal's office.

"I'll get right to it." Ace steepled his hands on the desk in front of him. "I'm not sure how much of this you already know, so I'll just start at the beginning. A cartel headquartered in South America is using dating apps in the US to target women. They have their guys put up a profile, then they pull the pictures and data of women and put them up on a site they've created on the dark web. A price is established. Rich perverts browse the pictures and decide who they want to purchase. They pay a deposit, and a profile is created on the app for a guy guaranteed to spark that woman's interest. A first meet is arranged, and bingo. The woman is snatched. In your case, they used drugs. In others they simply wait for the woman to show up and seize her before she gets into the meeting place. Our guess is that something interfered with you being grabbed right away, maybe witnesses in the parking lot, and the drugs were plan B."

Sophia perched on the edge of her seat. "So now what?"

"I'll be blunt. We assume they've promised you to a certain buyer and have taken money from that individual, so they're going to make another attempt to abduct you, especially since you escaped and can potentially identify one or more of their operatives. Failing that, they're going to want you dead."

She reached over and gripped my hand. "So some creep took my picture from the dating app, sold me like a piece of meat, and then sent George to con me into meeting with him so they could abduct me?"

Ace nodded. "That's about it. I'm guessing they've been cruising in ever widening circles around your meeting place since then to try and find you. You were smart enough not to tell him where you worked or lived. By what happened today though, I'm guessing they've found you. Which brings me to my next point." He looked at Deuce expectantly.

"You can't go back home." I laid it out for her. "Chances are good they have your place staked out. If you go back, they will make a play for you. They'll either take out the perimeter guards or sneak in while they're out of sight to get to you. Or, worst case, send a sniper to take you out from a distance. These are serious bad guys. Given the circumstances, your place isn't a viable option."

Sophia took it better than I expected. "What are my choices?"

"You can stay here. Just until we get this settled." Ace toyed with a pen. "Your dad's here, so it won't be that strange."

"Willow is at the house." She looked at me in sudden panic. "Can I go get Willow?"

I exchanged looks with Ace. "We can send one of the prospects to get her."

Sophia frowned. "She won't go with a stranger."

"Your dad could get her."

"Would they hurt him?"

"Not likely," I said. "They'll figure he's just an old guy coming to get a dog. If he shows up in that truck of his they won't even connect him to us."

"And your dad isn't exactly the helpless type," Ace added. "If one guy jumps him, it ain't going to be your dad who needs the paramedic."

She almost smiled at that. "True. But what about

clothes? Toothbrush? All that kind of stuff? I can't go get anything?"

Ace sighed. "I'm afraid not. We can get you a toothbrush and things. Clothes, I can talk to Mom and have her scrounge some stuff up. Normally I'd ask Emma, but she's got exams coming up this week and she's buried in textbooks. What size do you wear?"

He picked up his phone off the desk and fired off a text message. His phone pinged immediately and he glanced down at the screen. "Mom's out shopping. Said she'd stop at the thrift store and see what she could pick up. You shouldn't need too much. Hopefully this will be over quickly and you can go home."

The door bashed open, and Sophia's dad stomped into the room with Willow on his heels.

Ace stood up, scowling. "This is my office. You knock, or you stay out."

"The hell with you. Where's my daughter?"

Chapter Nine

Sophia

"I'm right here." I scooped Willow up and dropped her in Deuce's lap before facing my dad. "What's up?

He looked confused. "I went to your place to say hi to Willow, and the young guy there said you'd had some trouble with a guy trying to run you off the road. That's all he knew. I was worried."

"That's sweet." I gave him a big hug. "But you knew Deuce was looking after me. He just didn't update the prospects yet." I looked at Willow who was now snuggled down contentedly in Deuce's lap. "That takes care of one concern. Ace and the others want me to stay here but I was worried about Willow. Deuce suggested we ask if you could go get her."

"Well, I beat them to the punch on that one." He looked around. I could tell the minute he realized this was a private conversation. "You *are* going to stay here, aren't you? It will be safer."

I nodded. "Yes. Not overly enthusiastic about the idea, but it makes sense."

"Good girl." He frowned. "You're going to be bunking with Deuce?"

I lifted my brows. "I'm not having this conversation with you, Dad. I'm an adult." Out of the corner of my eye I could see Deuce trying not to laugh. He wouldn't think it so funny if he knew how Dad used to sit on the front step sharpening his hunting knife when I was a teenager and a boy came to call. Not really a surprise that I was still single. Hell, if I hadn't moved a couple of hours away, I'd probably still be a virgin as well.

"No problem." He looked from Ace to Deuce,

giving them a crisp salute. "I'll go see how Jake's making out with that carburetor he's rebuilding."

"You do that." Ace sat down slowly and watched the old guy back out, closing the door behind him.

"He's a little overprotective sometimes." I gave Ace an apologetic look.

He shook his head. "Can't imagine I'll be much better when I have a daughter."

I tried not to laugh. "Poor thing. Nothing like having an armed and dangerous dad."

He smiled. "I'm sure you know all about that."

I nodded. "Yeah. Just to change the subject, any chance Mom could pick up some dog food for Willow while she's out? She'll eat just about anything as long as it doesn't have rabbit in it. For some reason she won't touch rabbit."

"No problem." He picked up his phone and paused to look at me. "Does she need any special dishes or anything?"

I shook my head, looking down at the little scamp. "Considering she's just as happy drinking out of a puddle as drinking out of fine crystal, I think we can find something here. We were using an ice cream bucket for a water dish over at my place."

"That's settled then." Ace fired off another text to Mom. "It was nice to meet you. Wish it had happened under better circumstances, but things are what they are."

I felt like we'd been politely dismissed, so I headed for the door. Willow jumped off Deuce's lap and followed me, with Deuce right behind.

Ace chuckled. "I can see where you fit in the pecking order, Deuce."

I looked back and saw Deuce raise one brow. "You do know I control the finances, right?" His phone pinged and he pulled it out and glanced down. "Gotta take this." He kicked the office door closed and leaned on the wall. "Details?"

I wasn't sure what to do. It seemed rude to eavesdrop, so I wandered to the kitchen with Willow in tow. A woman I'd never met stood at the stove, stirring something in a big pot. She looked up when she heard me come in.

"You must be Sophia!" She smiled and kept stirring. "And that would be Willow."

"I suppose I must." I sighed. "I take it everyone has heard about me?"

"No secrets in the clubhouse. Everyone wants to meet the girl Deuce is drooling over."

I felt my cheeks go red. "Drooling over?"

"That's the gossip, and let me tell you, your dad is not happy about that part. I'm Rylie, by the way."

"Hi, Rylie. I don't think Deuce has mentioned you." I snapped my fingers. "Wait. Do you own the coffee shop we were at the night this whole mess started?"

She nodded. "I'm impressed you remembered. You looked pretty shell-shocked when you came in there. I'm Cyclone's other half and we usually stay at his condo, not the clubhouse, but Cyclone is worried that whoever is behind the trafficking ring might decide to grab someone else. Either as a hostage, or just because. He's a little overprotective."

I rolled my eyes. "I'm getting the impression all these biker guys are."

"They mean well. It just comes across as a little smothering at times." She lifted the spoon to her lips and took a taste. Wrinkling her nose, she added more salt. "It sounds like you'll be staying with us for a bit."

"Yeah. I guess so."

"Oh, don't sound so upset. I'm here for the duration as well." She adjusted the heat and put a lid on the pot. "And I like to cook, so you won't go hungry." She turned and grinned at me. "And then there's the other thing."

I tilted my head, not understanding. "What other thing?"

"You get to sleep with Deuce every night!"

"With my dad in the same house? That should be fun."

"Ah, forget your dad. He'll get over it." She patted her stomach suggestively. "Especially if you give him some grandbabies."

"We're not having babies! We've been on like one date!"

Rylie nodded her head. "It only takes once, you know."

"I can't believe I'm having this conversation," I muttered.

"What conversation?" An older woman, her gray hair trapped in a long braid down her back, strode in and dropped two grocery bags on the table. "Damn, those things are heavier than they look!"

"We were discussing Deuce and Sophia having kids."

"Really? I thought you guys just met." She held out a hand. "I'm Mom, by the way, and you must be Sophia." She looked down. "And this charming little bundle of fur must be Willow. Joe told us all about you."

I felt a little overwhelmed. "Yes, I'm Sophia, yes, that's Willow. I take it by Joe you mean my dad and no, Deuce and I haven't even talked about kids. We've been on one date."

"Aw, that's sweet. Love at first sight."

Seriously? These people only heard what they wanted to, and apparently, they wanted a fairy tale romance. Between a prepper's daughter and a biker accountant?

"I brought you some clothes. The thrift store stuff doesn't always have labels still attached so hopefully most of it fits. Sweaters are easy. I just went for big and loose." She dug into one bag and produced a pink hoodie with a big pawprint on the front. "I thought you'd like this. Wasn't so sure about the jeans though, so I grabbed a couple pairs of yoga pants as well. Those things stretch like rubber so you should be fine." She paused and looked up. "Darn. I totally forgot shoes. What size are you?"

"An eight, but I can get by with the ones I have on. Luckily, they're runners, so they'll be comfortable."

"I take size eight, so you can borrow some of mine if you need to." Two teenagers wandered into the kitchen, one pausing to lift the lid on the pot and sniff. "Oh, chili! Nice!"

The other came over and squatted down to pet Willow. Like the suck up she was, Willow rolled over to get her belly rubbed. "We're the twins, in case you haven't figured that out. Beast is our dad, and we live here with him."

"Jasmine and Jewel." The one petting Willow pointed to herself and her sister.

Deuce entered the room and came over to wrap an arm around me. "Looks like you've met some of the club."

I nodded. "Yes. And Mom brought me some clothes."

Deuce inclined his head. "Thanks, Mom."

She shrugged. "No problem."

He nuzzled my neck. "Let's go get you settled in

our room."

I raised a brow. Things were moving at light speed here. "Our room?"

Both teenagers giggled, and I realized we had an audience that wasn't even pretending not to listen. I blushed and grabbed one of the bags off the table. "Let's go." I looked at Mom. "Thanks again, I really appreciate it."

She held up a hand. "You might want to let me wash those first. No telling how many people pawed that stuff when it was in the thrift store."

"Oh. Right." I put the bag down.

Mom nodded. "It won't take long. I'll run them up when they're ready. I can leave them outside the door in case you two want to grab a nap. Should be done before supper."

"Thank you. I mean it. You have all been amazing to me."

Deuce grabbed my hand mumbling something about women and gossip. He led the way out of the kitchen, with me and Willow trailing behind. His room was on the second floor and had an ensuite bathroom, for which I was grateful. I hadn't considered what bathroom schedules might look like in a house full of bikers.

I took the plastic yogurt container I'd snagged in the kitchen and filled it with water for Willow, placing it beside the counter in the bathroom where it was less likely to get accidentally knocked over.

Deuce sat down on the bed and regarded me with a serious expression. "Come sit down for a minute. Catch your breath. You haven't stopped since that guy tried to run you off the road."

I walked to the bed and sat down straddling his lap so that I was staring straight into his eyes. I kept my expression serious. "Things have been pretty crazy since about two hours before we met. Do you think it has something to do with me and you?"

He cupped his hands on my ass and pulled me a little further onto his lap. "How do you mean?"

"I have this theory that there's a bunch of creatures up there somewhere." I gestured at the ceiling. "And they got bored so they're playing around with us."

"Interesting." He raised one hand to tangle in the hair on the back of my head. "They're probably making things difficult because they're jealous."

"Jealous?"

"Yeah. Because they don't get to do this." He urged my head forward so he could devour my lips.

An hour later, I was in need of another shower.

* * *

Deuce

Waking up with Sophia naked in my arms felt good. We'd made it through our first club dinner without too much drama. Of course everyone was curious, but they mostly managed to tone it down enough that she felt comfortable. Not sure if having her dad there helped or hindered.

I slipped out of bed and pulled on a pair of sweatpants before heading to the kitchen to grab us a couple of cups of coffee. I made a mental note to pick up a compact coffee maker for our room, and maybe one of those pint-sized bar fridges.

Somebody had beaten me to the kitchen. A pot of coffee was sitting on the warmer, all ready to go. I filled two cups and turned to head back upstairs.

Willow whined, placing herself between me and the door.

I looked down at the little mutt. "You hungry?"

She wagged her tail, regarding me with those sad brown eyes of hers.

I put the coffee down and opened the pantry. Mom had picked up dry dog food as well as a few cans. I had a feeling Willow was going to be one spoiled little mutt if we stayed here for long. I found a bowl and poured some kibble in it, topping it off with a couple of spoonfuls of the canned food. I placed it on the floor in front of the dog. "There. That should keep you happy for a while."

Willow wagged her tail as she lowered her head to eat.

Sophia was still lounging in bed when I got back to the room. She smiled as I placed the mug of coffee on the bedside table for her.

"You not coming back to bed?" She took a sip of the dark brew.

I shook my head. "Need to go down to the bar and grab some paperwork to do the IRS filings. Got to keep the government happy."

She wrinkled her nose. "Should I come with you?"

"No, you're probably safer here and I won't be long. An hour, tops."

She yawned. "I should be up and dressed by the time you get back, but no promises."

"You sound like you're going to enjoy the next few days being a lady of leisure."

"I could get used to it." She looked around the room. "Where'd Willow go?"

"She looked hungry, so I fed her some of the chow Mom picked up. She seems to like it." I glanced down at my cup. "I'll pick up a coffee maker while I'm out so we don't have to get dressed before coffee in the morning."

She eyed up my sweatpants. "That's dressed?"

I shrugged. "It's not naked."

"True."

I gulped down the last of my coffee and headed for the shower. Having Sophia around sure upped the number of showers I needed on any given day.

Chapter Ten

Sophia

After Deuce left for *The Riptide Rest*, I got out of bed. Willow had returned after polishing off the food she'd conned Deuce out of. With her belly full, she hopped back up on the bed and lay down, only opening one eye when I started rummaging through the bags of clothing Mom had left outside the room after washing them.

I pulled out a pair of gray yoga pants and the pink sweatshirt with the paw print on it. She was right about the yoga pants. They had enough stretch in them, I could gain twenty pounds and still get them on. They also had the bonus of a cell phone pocket on the side. These could easily become my go-to outfit for lounging around the house.

I gave Willow a little snuggle and left the door to the room open slightly when I headed downstairs. If she woke up and wanted out, she'd be able to nudge it open.

The kitchen was deserted. I poured myself another cup of coffee. I could hear the murmur of voices from down the hallway, and I recalled seeing a games room yesterday when Deuce had given me a whirlwind tour of the clubhouse. I followed the noise and found myself looking at a poker game. The twin girls were there. I couldn't remember their names, but they grinned and motioned me to come join them.

I wandered in and took a seat behind the players. Poker wasn't a game I'd spent much time playing. I knew the basics, but I was a little hazy on which hands were the best and what beat what.

"Want us to deal you in?" Rattler asked.

I shook my head. "No, thanks. I think I'll just

watch for a bit and see if I can remember how it goes."

The twins exchanged glances.

"What?"

"We're trying to decide if you're really don't know or if you're trying to hustle us."

"Hustle you?"

"Yeah. Like you're actually really good but you pretend not to be, so we take it easy and then you skunk us."

I held a hand over my heart. "You're safe. I promise. I can't remember if it's better to have all one suit, all one kind like kings, or a run of numbers like one two three four five."

"In that case, care to join us and make a small wager?" Jake asked.

"No, thanks. I'll just watch while I drink my coffee."

"Too worn out from gymnastics with Deuce last night?" Rattler smirked.

"The walls around here are pretty thin," the one twin explained.

I felt my face getting flushed. "I'll keep that in mind. And no, I'm not too worn out."

"So, Deuce didn't satisfy you? Because my room's right next to his and you were both pretty noisy. Multiple times." The medic, Joker, pretended to study his hand.

"Deuce did just fine. Can we change the subject now?" I looked over at the twins. "I hate to admit it, but I'm not good with names. I remember you two are twins, and your father is Beast, but I can't remember your names."

"I'm Jasmine." The taller of the two, a lithe brunette, spoke up. "My sister here is Jewel."

"Thanks. I'll try to remember but I make no

promises."

"Fair enough. There's a lot of us, and it can get confusing." Jewel put two cards face down on the table in front of her.

I gave her a grateful smile and settled back to watch the game. Money did change hands, but the amounts were small and the game seemed friendly.

My phone chirped, and I pulled it out, hoping to hear from Deuce. He had said he'd be about an hour so he should be done soon. Amazing how I could be missing him already.

I didn't recognize the number, so I sent it to voicemail. Probably a request for me to sub in for a sick teacher, and that wasn't likely happening until we got this abduction thing sorted out.

A few minutes later, it chirped again. Same number. The bookings clerks could be annoying at times, trying to find someone willing to sub in if the class was known to be difficult. I wasn't up to dealing with a class full of hooligans right now, so I hit the decline button again.

I drank the last mouthful of my coffee and stood up. "I'm going to get a refill and let Willow out for a bit of a run."

Rattler looked up from his cards. "Have fun, but keep in sight of the clubhouse."

"No problem. Her legs are only six inches long, so a run isn't exactly miles and miles."

I headed to the kitchen, pulling out my phone to check and see if whoever phoned had left a message.

I hated the steps you had to go through to access voicemail. By the time I finished pulling up the program and hitting all the appropriate buttons, I'd refilled my coffee and was heading to the fridge to get the coffee creamer.

I hit "one" to play the most recent message. My mouth dropped open when I heard Janet's panicked voice.

"I was so dumb to fall for this. Ignore them. Save yourself."

Her voice cut off abruptly, to be replaced by a man's rough tone demanding I surrender myself to them. If I did, they'd let Janet go. If not, they would send her to me piece by piece starting with her fingers.

The phone slipped out of my hands, landing face up on the floor.

I gagged, my stomach rebelling at the thought of my BFF being slowly butchered piece by piece because of me.

Deuce would never let me go trade myself for Janet.

As if conjured by my thoughts, he strode in the door. One look at my face, and he knew something terrible had happened. "What is it? What's wrong?"

I stared at him, unable to speak. What could I say? I couldn't let him stop me.

His eyes dropped to the phone on the floor, and we both made a grab for it at the same time.

He was faster than me, and stronger. He grabbed it, holding it over his head just out of my reach.

"No!" I pummeled his chest with my fists, screaming like a banshee. "Give it back!"

My dad appeared in the doorway, taking the scene in with a glance. Striding over to Deuce, he plucked the phone out of his hands.

Deuce wrapped his arms around me, holding me squirming and straining against him. "Play the message."

My dad looked me straight in the eye and hit replay on the message. Janet's voice hit me like a punch in the gut and I sagged against Deuce. Tears rolled down my face as I listened to the kidnapper list a time and place for a meeting. "I have to go." I whispered. "She's my best friend."

My dad shook his head, his face a mixture of misery and sadness. "You know they won't let her go. They'll keep both of you."

"But it's my fault." I turned and buried my face in Deuces' chest. "It's all my fault."

"No, it's the fault of a bunch of soulless assholes who need be taken down." Deuce hugged me tight. "We need to come up with a plan, and you need to promise me you aren't going to do anything stupid. If you go to them, they'll just keep both of you or maybe kill Janet in front of you just for fun. These people are the worst of the worst. Promise me."

He didn't understand. I hated lying to him, but there was no other way. "I promise."

"She's lying." My dad spoke up. "I can always tell."

Deuce tilted my head up to meet his gaze. "Are you lying?"

"No." He asked me to promise not to do anything stupid. I didn't consider saving my best friend to be a stupid thing to do.

"Are you going to stay on the sidelines and let Riptide deal with this?"

I sighed. "That's not what you asked."

"I don't want to have to lock you in our room to keep you from getting yourself killed."

I narrowed my eyes. "You wouldn't dare."

A look of incredible sadness crossed his face. "I would, if it kept you alive."

"I'll deal with her. If she hates me for the rest of her life, so be it. You go tell the rest of your buddies what's up and see if you can come up with a viable plan to rescue Janet."

My dad grabbed my good arm and led me out of the room. "Let's go find Willow. When you've had time to calm down, you'll realize we're right. We will get Janet back, but we'll do it without throwing you to the wolves."

At that moment, I was so angry I didn't know what to do. Sitting calmly by, not knowing what they were putting Janet through, was sheer torture. Was she even still alive? Had my stupidity in using that dating app cost my best friend her life?

I heard Deuce holler something to Ace about church and I tried to wrench my arm away from my dad. "You have got to be kidding me! They're going to go to church and pray for her?"

"Shhh." He held me to him like he had when I was a little kid and crying about some stupid issue I'd thought was important. "They call it church when they call a meeting of all the members. They're going to brainstorm a solution, and then they're going to go get Janet back. I trust them. That should tell you a lot. You know how many people I trust."

I frowned at him. "You barely know these guys."

He shook his head. "But I do know them. They're SEALs. They may not wear the uniform anymore but deep down, where it really counts, they're still SEALs. Courage, honor, and commitment aren't just fancy buzz words. They're ideals that every one of these guys live by every day of their life. If it's possible to save Janet, they will. And if Janet is hurt, they will rain retribution down on the assholes who dared to lay a hand on her. You could not have stumbled into a better group of guys. You can count on them."

I had to hope he was right.

* * *

Deuce

I was heartbroken to have to forcibly put Sophia on lockdown, but at least she wouldn't get herself killed. I knew her dad understood, which was a bonus. I wasn't sure I had the energy to lock horns with him right now. I quickly updated Ace and played the message for him.

He called church. Immediately. And put everyone on high alert. That meant serious shit was about to go down.

The guys at the bar turned operations over to the prospects. The guys out enjoying the day turned around and made a beeline for the clubhouse. The guys already here dropped whatever they were doing and headed to church.

The prospects doubled up guard duty on the gates and at strategic points around the perimeter. The women and kids all stayed indoors, away from windows and any points of entry. Emma was still away cramming for exams, and Ace called and warned her he was sending a couple of prospects to guard her for a few days. She'd been with him long enough not to ask questions.

Yeah, it was that serious.

It took less than twenty minutes for the fully patched members to gather in church. Ace locked the doors and explained the situation. Then he opened the floor for ideas. They flew fast and thick. These guys weren't politicians, and no one suggested we try to talk the assholes down.

Plans were suggested, considered, and dismissed.

Finally, Ace held up his hand for quiet. "We have

agreement on some key points." He picked up a marker and stood at the board at the front of the room, laying things out point by point. "One, they have one hostage -- female -- no military training and probably scared shitless."

An angry murmur went around the room, and he held his hand up again to silence them. "Two, they're proposing the old stable area at the fairgrounds for the exchange. It's deserted this time of year and it's outside of town so any noise that's made won't draw attention. This seems to indicate they might be expecting us or them to be firing weapons. For argument's sake I'm going to assume they plan on using firepower at some point."

Most of the men in the room nodded in agreement.

"Three, and most concerning, is that they want Deuce's woman as a trade. In her favor, she's smart, she can shoot well and accurately, and she has some hand-to-hand combat training if things do go south. Understandably, Deuce doesn't want to risk her." He looked around the room. "Anything anyone wants to add?"

Beast stood, looking thoughtful. "I have an idea that might work."

* * *

I checked my gun and spare ammunition for the tenth time. I wasn't happy with the plan, and neither was Joe. No one managed to come up with anything better, though, and the calculated odds of success were high.

And Sophia was on board. She still figured this was her fault. We tried to convince her otherwise. If it hadn't been her, they would have snatched another woman and that one might not have been able to escape. She did, and now we had a chance to take the whole shitshow down.

But we were using her as bait, which made me twitchy as fuck. Even Ace admitted there was a risk factor, but he insisted it was low. We geared Sophia up with a flak jacket and reinforced gear. Under her hoodie, it was invisible. We tucked knives into her boots, and a revolver into the back of her Kevlar pants. We used every safety precaution we could think of, but something could still go wrong. Something could always go wrong.

"You sure you want to do this?"

Sophia nodded her head. "I have to try. I know things could go bad, but they could also go well. If things were reversed, she would do it for me."

I took a deep breath. "I just found you. I don't want to lose you."

She looked at me. "Same."

"Stations all a go?" Ace's voice crackled over the intercom in the range rover.

Answers came in from all the teams, spread out around the trade area. I held Sophia's gaze as I answered. "Locked and loaded."

A few moments later the order came down. "Move out."

We were using her dad's Range Rover. Not the prettiest vehicle I'd ever seen but it was in top shape mechanically, and he'd reinforced all the vulnerable parts with heavy gauge steel. We drove to the designated exchange site in silence.

The tension in the Range Rover was so thick you could have cut it with a knife. We parked on the south side of the stables in a wide-open area. I didn't like it one bit. I could see a vehicle at the far end of the compound, but I would be willing to bet it was a decoy. No one stupid enough to park there would have managed to set up an international human trafficking ring.

I checked my watch. Two minutes to go-time.

"I love you." Sophia looked at her father.

"Love you too, baby girl." Joe reached over to give her a big hug. "Remember everything I taught you."

She nodded, then turned to me.

Wordlessly, I grabbed her and crushed her to me. She would come out of this safely. I wouldn't consider any other outcome.

My watch ticked over to noon, and I opened the door. I got out first, motioning Sophia to wait behind me.

"Where's the woman?"

I couldn't see where the voice was coming from.

"In the vehicle," I hollered. "Where's Janet?" Giving her a name was a basic tactic. Make them see her as a person and not a piece of merchandise to be bartered, although I wasn't sure it would work with these assholes.

Janet staggered into view. A man wearing camouflage gear held the end of a rope tied around her waist. Her hands were tied to her sides. She was gagged and looked terrified but otherwise unharmed.

"Send the woman over."

I shook my head. "Not how this works. Janet walks here. Sophia walks to you."

He shrugged. "Dumb Americans watch too many movies." He dropped the rope and gave Janet a shove. "You heard. Walk."

This was the most dangerous part. Sophia met my gaze and mouthed *I can do this*, before she turned and paced toward her friend.

I held my breath.

The two closed the gap between them step by step.

Finally, they were abreast of each other. Out of the corner of my eye, I saw her captor reach for something behind him.

At the same time, Sophia turned and wrapped her arms around Janet, taking her to the ground and covering them both with the Kevlar sheet she'd concealed behind her.

Then all hell broke loose.

When the dust settled, I rushed to the women, Sophia's dad close behind me. I tossed the Kevlar sheeting aside and dragged Sophia to her feet. Holding her at arm's length, I scanned for any sign of injury.

"I'm fine. It worked." She wiped the dust from her face and reached out a hand to her friend. "Are you okay?"

Janet took her hand and clambered slowly to her feet. "I think I twisted my ankle when I went down, but other than that, I'm okay."

I wrapped my arms around Sophia, burying my face in her hair. "I have never been so terrified in my life. You are not doing anything like that ever again. Not ever."

"I love you too."

I lifted my head. "What did you just say?"

She grinned, including her dad and her BFF in the declaration. "I love you, you stupid biker. Now kiss me!"

And I did. In the middle of the scene of carnage, I kissed her until we were both breathless.

Epilogue

Sophia

I grabbed two bottles of beer and headed over to the barbecue area. Deuce was grilling steaks and there were a stack of potatoes baking in a firepit. Mom had put on a spread of salads, fruits, and veggies, along with plates filled with every conceivable item you could possibly put on a baked potato.

I handed one of the beers to Deuce and took a long drink of the other one. Batting my eyelashes, I grinned at him. "Who knew hooking up with a biker would get me so well fed?"

"I'm just full of surprises." He put down the tongs he'd been using to turn the steaks. He twisted the cap off and tossed it in the garbage bin before grabbing my hand. Turning my arm, he examined the remains of the road rash. It was healing nicely and probably wouldn't leave much of a scar, or so I hoped.

"Things turned out pretty good, didn't they?" I draped one arm around his waist.

He nodded. "They did. Seems the whole trafficking ring were caught with their pants down. They planned to take you and send you abroad immediately, so they had all kinds of incriminating information with them at that exchange. Someone tipped off the FBI about the trade, and just after we left they showed up and busted the group while they were trying to mop up their injured. Didn't take much in the way of persuasion to get those guys to turn on the head honchos."

"No honor amongst thieves, or something like that?"

Deuce took a swig of his beer. "None whatsoever." He gestured at Janet who was busy playing horseshoes with Tiny. "Think anything's going to happen there?"

I watched as Janet blew a kiss at Thor behind Tiny's back. "Tonight maybe, but Janet isn't much for long term. I'm not entirely sure she understands the concept."

Deuce leaned down to sear a kiss across my lips. "I thought I was done with it too, until a certain someone threw herself at my feet."

I laughed. "You have to admit it was one hell of a way to catch your attention."

"That it was." His expression sobered. "I do love you, with all my heart."

I leaned into him. "I know it's way too soon, but I think I fell in love with you when I was lying on the pavement, and I looked up to see you. You are my knight on shining armor."

Putting his beer down, he proceeded to kiss me breathless.

"Hey, you two. Get a room!"

Deuce scooped me up in his arms. "Excellent idea, Rattler. You might want to take care of the steaks. We're going to be a while!"

A raucous round of applause and catcalls followed us as Deuce made his way to the clubhouse with me held firmly against his chest.

Author's Note

If you enjoyed this book, I would really appreciate you leaving a review on whatever platforms you participate in such as Goodreads, Barnes and Noble, Amazon etc. Reviews help readers find my stories.

And, if you're not already subscribed to my newsletter, follow the link on my website and you can get a copy of Cyclone and Rylie's story just for signing up!

Anne Kane

Anne Kane lives in the beautiful Okanagan Valley with a bouncy little rescue dog whose breed defies description and an Aussie Shepherd who's too smart for her own good. Anne likes to write spicy stories with sassy heroines and protective, sexy male heroes who love those women. Her stories all have one thing in common: a happily ever after ending.

Her hobbies, when she's not playing with the characters in her head, include kayaking, hiking, swimming, playing guitar, and spoiling the grandkids.

Anne at Changeling: changelingpress.com/anne-kane-a-116

www.ingramcontent.com/pod-product-compliance
Lightning Source LLC
Chambersburg PA
CBHW051241260626
47162CB00002B/551